Chapter 1

The farthest south Dodge Montgomery had ever been before was Fort Jackson, South Carolina, a place he was satisfied to never see again. The nine weeks he had spent there hiking in combat boots with hot, heavy gear sticking to sweat-soaked skin had taught him that the South was no place for him. He did not long for a smoldering Southern sky or the damp ripeness of warm air pushed and pulled on a breeze so slight it barely lifted a hair. A place where the sky teased with its icy blue stillness only to turn against those below it with a rumble of thunder that called winds to move houses and rain to break boulders.

So even he was surprised when he packed up the belongings in his apartment so quickly after the envelope had arrived and found himself departing for Alabama the very next day. As he drove, the contents of his life once again stuffed into two large, black duffel bags seated in the back seat of his truck, he wondered to himself once more if he had, or had not, been waiting for the message the letter contained:

"Based on the analysis performed in our lab from DNA obtained from Mr. Dodge James Montgomery of New York, New York, we have concluded that the probability is greater than 99.99% for paternity originating from the DNA of the deceased, Mr. Dodge William Montgomery."

He had read the first sentence of the letter several times, and as he drove he recalled the phone call he had placed to the law firm of Wallace, Mayfield, and Young, his fingers shaking lightly against the phone while the firm's receptionist put him immediately through to the very Henry Wallace himself.

"Mistuh Mun-gum-ry." Henry's deep voice drawled deliberately over each syllable. "I have been waiting for your phone call as I just today received the letter of confirmation myself from the laboratory." He spoke slowly but not haltingly, and articulated the last word with five syllables. Dodge wasn't sure if he was trying to convey a lawyerly air or if this was his normal cadence of speech. "We couldn't be more pleased that things have worked out in your favor".

Dodge had smiled into the phone. He knew that had the results not come through in his *favor*, that Mr. Wallace's firm stood to make much more from his family's estate, easily dragging out the legal disarray and confusion of an ownerless piece of land long enough to make it well worth their while. His prior communications with the firm had been brief, as clearly they had no intention of spending too much time, nor giving out too much information, before receiving the results of the DNA from the man in New York.

"Yes, Mr. Wallace, it appears I am the person your firm was looking for after all." Dodge hoped to remind Mr. Wallace that it was they who had reached out to him initially. "But please, call me Dodge."

"Of course, of course. We felt sure of these positive results all along, of course," laughed Mr. Wallace. "What are the chances of two Dodge Montgomery's walking around God's green earth?" he chuckled into the phone. He lowered the volume of his voice and began even more slowly, as if speaking to a very small child. "I am so sorry about your granddaddy's passing, as are all of us here, and we of course want to extend our condolences yet again on your loss." While his words were

2

sincere, he also sounded somewhat distracted, and Dodge could hear the subtle shifting of papers as Mr. Wallace moved about to find the file that contained the information on everything Dodge now owned in the world, courtesy of a dead Southern grandfather he had never met.

"Yes, thank you, that is appreciated," Dodge said out of courtesy. "I am – "

Mr. Wallace began speaking again immediately. "We are just so pleased to have all of that nonsense behind us with this D-N-A and what-not and the ability to, uh…" His voice trailed off again over the rustling sounds in the background. "The ability to move forward with your granddaddy's estate and having you come down here of course to go through the paperwork and get the necessary signings."

Dodge had peered out the dirty window of his apartment as he listened to the soothing southern staccato of Mr. Wallace's voice. His direct view from the only window of the fifth-floor walkup was a row of grimy windows identical to those of his own building. The apartment and its meager contents were rented on a month-to-month basis; his poor credit history and unwillingness to commit to an annual lease reflected in the exorbitant monthly fee for a studio in this neglected neighborhood. It was hot already for early June, and a window air conditioning unit hummed loudly beneath him, unable to drown out the clamor of the salsa music that perpetually rose from the apartment below.

"I believe I can make it down there very shortly," Dodge had said off-handedly, moving away from the window. In fact he could do so immediately since his last rent check had not cleared and he knew that he had just a few days to get out before the landlord sent the super to his apartment to change the locks. His was not a building where squatter's rights were protected by the laws of the great state of New York, but instead one where the superintendent's crow bar and lead-filled softball bat decided when one stayed and when one would go.

"Excellent, excellent," Mr. Wallace said, sounding genuinely pleased. "We do intend to assist you as best we can, even after all the necessary papers are signed." He added quickly, "Your granddaddy has been a

3

trusted client of our firm for many years, and even though we were not aware of his having any, um, living descendants, we are more than able, and willing, to accommodate all of your needs. And those of your family as well."

Dodge smiled again. He supposed that Mr. Wallace was now eager to learn more about him, as he too had given out no more information than he felt was necessary to this point. Details of his life were not something he shared willingly. His secrecy and silence on personal matters had more than once been blamed in part for failed relationships and faded friendships. Mr. Wallace and his firm would learn soon enough that as far as he knew there were no family members left, just himself.

"Again, I appreciate that, and I look forward to meeting you and the members of your firm who have assisted my family for so long." He immediately felt awkward at the word *family*, but tried to convey a polite tone. "I'm actually getting ready to head down there in the morning, and should arrive by tomorrow evening. You did say my grandfather's house was available, correct?"

He looked around at the worn furniture in the dilapidated apartment before him. Throughout his life places were always temporary and just 'available' – to crash, or to rent, or to stay for a few nights before moving on somewhere else. Now, in a small, rural town somewhere in Alabama, there stood a house that he owned, a house that had been in his father's family for generations. It had remained in the same spot while he had not, waiting for him without him knowing it. The thought struck him as peculiar, and without seeing it for himself he did not yet completely believe it to be true.

"Available, yes," Mr. Wallace repeated awkwardly. "You just come by here as soon as you get into town and I will have the keys ready for you. We can handle all of the paperwork for the estate from there. You just take your time and we will see you when you get here. Safe travels, uh, Dodge," he added awkwardly before hanging up the phone.

Dodge smiled now as he drove. He had decided that he had nothing to lose, quite literally, by taking the sixteen-hour drive to a small southern

4

town and spending a day or so there. Even if it turned out his grandfather owed someone something and they were just trying to get their debt paid from him he had nothing for them. Rented apartments, used cars, short term relationships - he had made certain throughout his life that he never had anything that anyone could take from him that could not be easily replaced or forgotten once gone.

He turned up the volume on the CD and the jazz tenor saxophone and swift piano notes of the Eddie Lockjaw Davis Quartet filled the cab of the truck. He draped his hands over the worn steering wheel and stared out at the long black highway before him. Just a few weeks ago he wasn't sure what he was going to do with his life, having no current job, very little money left in the bank, and no one and nothing to make him stay where he was. Things appeared to be changing considerably since the first phone call from Mr. Wallace's firm.

He had initially supposed it was just a coincidence that he shared the same name as an old man in the South. He had recalled, however, that while he had never been given the good fortune to meet his own biological father, and his mother spoke little of him, she had vaguely told him once he had been from "somewhere down South". This then, the news that a before unknown paternal grandfather had recently died of a sudden heart attack, and that he was the sole heir to his family's estate did not overwhelm or particularly excite him. There had been no one to call to share the news with; no siblings, parents, or even a long-out of touch aunt or uncle to confirm the details with. A swab of saliva from the cheek of his mouth had told a laboratory of his relation, relayed to him with no more fanfare than a templated letter sent via UPS.

And so with the letter in his pocket Dodge had packed all of his belongings into his truck well before the sun came up. Departing locations in the wee hours of the night under the cover of darkness was certainly not unknown to him. He began the slow drive out of New York City, continuing on the long, lackluster highways, the scenery changing little from state to state and gas station to gas station.

The sun, which had crept its way into the sky some states back, was beginning its descent toward the horizon. The strip malls, grocery stores, and gas stations began to fade while the stretches of lush green landscape between them grew longer. The lanes of the highways shifted from six, to four, and then to two as the cars slowly began to disappear around him, turning off into hidden little towns tucked within the low valleys of the steep hills.

He did not let his mind speculate on what he would find once he arrived at his destination. To him, this was just a stop to sign a bit of paperwork and collect whatever it was that had been unknowingly left to him from a family who never bothered to find him. Even as he spotted the shiny, bright green metal sign on the side of the road welcoming him to Alabama he did not feel even the slightest tinge of excitement to incite him to wonder about this place or these people. One didn't need to worry about forgetting someone or some place that they never cared about to begin with.

"Turn right at the next light," the robotic voice of the GPS broke into his train of thought. He was just ten miles from his destination and the truck's gas gauge was again pointing to empty. He turned onto a narrow two lane road, this one sloping and winding gently between a landscape of alternating swaths of green grass and dense trees. To his left was a small farm with a brightly painted red barn set back behind a large white house. A peeling, white 'No Trespassing' sign was tacked onto the large oak tree fanning out over the drive where a group of horses grazed lazily next to the long wooden fence. The sharp emerald leaves and bright yellow petals of short stocky daffodils erupted from the ground along the road's edge while a dark, leafy ivy greened its way up and over the tall, thick trees, turning them into sinister, misshapen monsters lurking on the side of the road.

His balding truck tires rumbled over a set of train tracks with no warning, just beyond which he found a small gas station, with four rusting pumps sitting idly out front. Taped to the tiny square windows of the old wooden building were the obligatory cigarette and gallon milk prices, hand scrawled in black marker on yellowing pieces of paper. A sturdy, however slightly uneven, wooden roof covered the long front porch, above which a worn *Pepsi-Cola* sign hung precariously. The station was empty of cars, save one worn down pick-up truck that looked almost as tattered as his own. Dodge pulled up to a pump, stepping out and stretching his long legs. He was not far from his destination, whatever that was exactly. He inserted his credit card, started the pump and made his way inside.

A string of tiny metal chimes danced against the door announcing his entrance. His eyes slowly adjusted to the dark interior that lacked the fluorescent overhead lights of the shiny modern gas stations he had been in earlier that day. The wooden floors creaked underfoot and a worn path from the entrance to the register showed the steps of the travelers who had entered before him. The air was filled with the smell of freshly brewed coffee and an almost spicy scent that his nose couldn't place. Three short aisles before him housed the basic necessities of the road - snack foods, candy bars, potato chips, and toiletries – while a long-glass doored cooler filled with drinks hummed against the back wall. These seemed out of place in the dark paneled wood interior of the old building, as if someone had forgotten to change part of a background set in a play before adding the items for the next scene.

Two men stood in front of the long wooden counter before the station attendant behind the register. Dodge's entrance had obviously interrupted their conversation and all three looked at him in silence as he made his way in.

"Afternoon," said the man behind the counter as he squinted at Dodge. He appeared to be in his mid-to-late fifties, with a receding hairline and a tall, thin frame. His weathered face did not suggest unpleasantness, but he did not smile in greeting, and Dodge got the feeling it wasn't often the man was unfamiliar with the people who entered his store.

"Hello." Dodge politely nodded his head as the other two men did the same. He made his way to the back shelves and pulled a bottle of water from the cooler. They did not continue their conversation as he made his way back to the front of the store and set it down on the counter.

The two men stepped aside slightly as he approached. The younger of the two appeared to be in his early forties, leaning comfortably against the counter in his mud-caked blue jeans and a camouflage t-shirt. Short tufts of brown hair stuck out from the edges of a green and yellow John Deere hat perched on his head. The older man was similarly attired, his thin flannel shirt tucked into faded jeans over a pair of well-worn leather boots. He nodded his head toward Dodge as he bit down on the bright green pickle that poked out of the top of a crisp white wax paper bag he held in his hand.

"You heading into town," the tall man behind the counter asked casually as he peered at the screen over his glasses and punched in the price of the water on the register's cracked and yellowed keys.

"I am," Dodge replied, pulling his wallet from his back pocket. The two men casually leaned against the counter and looked him over as they continued crunching the pickles from the crinkling bags.

The older man in the flannel shirt began nodding his head slowly as a large grin came over his face. "Well, I will be." He aimed the top of the half eaten pickle at Dodge as he squinted his eyes. "You're James Montgomery's son," he breathed, leaning farther back on the counter as if to get a better look at him.

Dodge's hand, still gripping the five-dollar bill he had pulled from his wallet, stopped in mid-clutch. He could feel the air leave his body and for a brief moment his lungs forgot how to pull it back in. His stomach leapt upward as if to take the place of the missing oxygen, the muscles tightening around a spot in his chest that until this moment he had not known was there. Never before had someone said to him that he was some man's son, and he had never heard his father's name cross anyone's lips.

"I, uh," he stammered as he quickly handed the crumpled bill to the attendant. "I'm here to sign for my grandfather's estate. I'm heading to the lawyers' office and then to the house." He was immediately unsure why he was offering so much information to this stranger. "Did you know my father?" he asked, trying to sound casual while his heart raced within his chest. *My father*, he repeated the words to himself silently.

"A-yup," said the man, putting his bag down on the counter and wiping his hand on his jeans. He extended it to Dodge. "I'm Earl, your granddaddy's neighbor on the south side," he said shaking Dodge's hand. "This is John Phillips," he said pointing to the store owner as he also extended his hand in greeting. "And this here's Butler," he said pointing a thumb at the man across from him. "Butler helps out on your granddaddy's farm." Butler nodded his head but did not extend a hand in greeting, instead taking a sharp bite of his pickle.

John peered over the register. "Dodge Montgomery?" He looked at Dodge carefully. "We have heard all about your coming into town but weren't sure if it was true or not." Dodge shook the hand he had extended over the register. "You know you can't believe any word that comes out of a lawyer's mouth any more'n you can believe a snake that tells you he ain't gonna bite you."

All three men snickered and Earl murmured, "Ain't that the truth."

John made his way out from behind the register. "We sure are glad to have you here," he said, looking Dodge up and down. His demeanor had changed as suddenly as Dodge's entrance. "Where you coming in from?" As he spoke he reached into a large, dark barrel with a pair of rusty tongs chained to the side. He pulled out a plump, green pickle and dropped it into a small white bag and handed it to Dodge.

Dodge accepted the bag, not quite sure which was odder; to be handed a free pickle by a stranger in an old gas station, or that the stranger knew he was arriving in town at all. "New York City," he said. "Most recently," he added quickly.

The man nodded his head. "Yup, I've been to New York City. Don't care for it much. Too many people and those taxi cabs flying around all over the place," he said waving his hand in the air. "One of 'em darn near killed me once. Was up there for a sightseeing trip that my wife dragged me on. I tell you what, the sights you see in that train station y'all got up there were enough for me and I just about turned around just as soon as I stepped off the train. People scramblin' around about as fast as they can, bumpin' into one another. No sir, not for me," John said. "Why there was

9

this one man, sittin' on a box on the subway platform. He had one of those, what do you call them?" He paused and stroked his chin as he tried to recall his visit.

Dodge assumed he was referring to one of the varied buskers soliciting tips on the subway platforms. "A guitar?"

"A ferret. A huge one too, sittin' right there on his lap. He had put a leash and a little coat on it. I'll tell you what, if not for that coat I would've knocked that thing sideways onto the rail. And people thought it was the cutest thing. They were paying money to feed it treats." He shook his head. "I told him, 'Sir, where I come from you get one of them and a .22 and you've got yourself a nice pot of stew. He didn't take too kindly to that."

Earl shook his head at John. "Aw hush, the man just got here. He doesn't need to hear one of your old stories." Earl looked at Dodge. "Once you're settled in you need to drop by our place and meet my wife, Miss May. She'll fix you up something good. And don't worry, it won't be ferret," he said throwing a sideways glance at John. "We're the drive on the right just next to your grandaddy's, south side of the property. One of us is most always home, 'cept Sunday mornings for church, of course. Always good to get to know a neighbor."

"Thank you, that would be nice," Dodge said politely, taking a bite of the pickle. He hadn't eaten since he'd left the city, and his stomach rumbled as the sweet sugar and bitter vinegar mingled together in his mouth. "So you know my father, then?" He turned to Earl, slowly chewing but suddenly unable to swallow.

The words had just left his mouth when the sound of squealing tires broke through the silence of the store. All four men looked out through the dusty window as the sound of a thumping bass throbbed loudly from the parking lot. They watched as a bright yellow sports car came to a halt just outside the door, the passenger door opening to a teen hitching up his pants as he stepped out.

He made his way into the store and to the back, ignoring Dodge and the other three men as he made his way to the cooler filled with beer. The men silently watched as he pulled out two six-packs and walked casually to the front counter.

"Pack of Marlboro lights," the teen mumbled, dropping the six-packs of beer on the counter and fishing around in his back pocket. One half of his blue cotton shirt poked casually out of the band of a pair of jeans that appeared to be a size too big, like the pristine white baseball hat that sat askew on top of his head.

John slowly made his way back behind the counter. "You got some ID there?" he asked the young man as he reached behind him for the cigarettes.

"Uh," the boy stammered. "I think I forgot it." He continued pulling crumpled bills from his pockets, not looking directly at John or the others.

"Sorry, son." John pulled the six-packs across the counter closer to him. "No ID, no alcohol or cigarettes."

The boy glanced at Earl, Butler, and Dodge nervously. "C'mon man, it's not that big a deal." He pointed to the money on the counter. "I'll have it next time, I swear."

"You come around here swearing and there won't be a next time," Earl spoke up. He made his way to the door and opened it swiftly. "Y'all need to get back to where you came in from." He peered over the idling car, holding open the door for a moment before stepping out onto the porch.

Dodge watched through the window as Earl strode past the car and disappeared from sight. The teens inside the car were now craning their heads to see into the store. John looked at the boy again. "I can't sell you kids beer or cigarettes without identification, and you know that." He placed the cigarettes back into their slot and moved the six-packs under the counter. Dodge noticed that he kept his hand there, his body slightly bent as he looked up at the boy.

"Yeah, whatever," the boy said as he gathered up his crumpled bills and turned to the door.

"You need to mind your manners," Butler said suddenly, pushing his large frame up off the counter. He stood almost a half a foot shorter than the teen, but his wide shoulders and the sizeable muscles in his arms made up for what he lacked in height. It was the first time Dodge had heard him speak, and his voice was tinged with an anger unfitting the situation.

"What're you gonna do about it, redneck?" the boy said over his shoulder as he exited the store. Butler moved forward and John put an arm out to hold him back.

"Ain't no use bothering with the likes of them." He held on to Butler's shirt sleeve tightly. "You don't need any more trouble anyway, Butler." Butler looked at John and tugged his shirt sleeve from his hand. He glanced at Dodge before hooking his thumbs through his belt loops and leaning back into the counter again.

Dodge watched through the window as the young man in the white cap ambled back into the car, slamming the door angrily behind him. John peered out at the car as well, wiping his hand across the dust stricken panes of the window. "Those are just city kids," he said as he continued to eye the car. "They drive out here thinkin' they're gonna trick someone out here in the sticks into letting them buy booze." He craned his head as he continued watching through the window. "City brats is what they are. No manners, no work ethic. Just their daddy's money and cars."

The driver revved the engine and the back tires rotated rapidly, sending up a thick cloud of gray dust and bits of gravel. The tires squealed as it raced across the tiny station lot past the pumps. Dodge watched as the car quickly neared the exit and then jerked suddenly, striking the station's small metal mailbox as it exited onto the road.

Dodge winced at the sound of the exploding mailbox, followed immediately by a loud crack. He instantly recognized the second sound, and watched as the car careened suddenly off to the right, its flattened rear tire wobbling against the road.

He followed John and Butler as they rushed outside. To his right, Dodge could see Earl standing next to the station building, a long black rifle sitting on his shoulder still aimed at the car that now sat idly on the side of the road. The driver exited the vehicle, his hands pressed against his head in disbelief.

"What did you do?" He screamed toward the store at Earl. Earl walked closer, the rifle still propped on his right shoulder. "That's my car, man," the boy shouted as the other three watched Earl carefully from inside the car. The driver was jumping up and down, slamming his hands against the car's hood.

"See," Earl said slowly, "your first problem is you watch too many movies. You think you can destroy another man's property and just drive off without any consequences." Earl was advancing toward the car, the gun still on his shoulder. "Your second problem is, you seriously underestimated my accuracy with a firearm."

As he neared the car the teen backed up slowly toward the front. "And your third problem is," Earl lifted the rifle and shot again, hitting the car's left back tire. Dodge watched as the car leaned slowly down into the road. "You aren't goin' nowhere until the sheriff gets here."

John turned to Dodge, who was gripping the pickle in its bag so tightly the juice had begun to run down his hand. "You should be making your way into town." Dodge nodded, stepping toward his truck but not taking his eyes off of Earl.

Dodge hastily pulled the gas nozzle out of the tank and placed it back into the pump. As he climbed into his truck he heard Earl yell out to him. "You make sure to come by and meet Miss May, you hear?"

He found Main Street lined with aging two story buildings, one four way stop light dividing North Main from South. The road ended in a roundabout, in the center of which stood the old courthouse, its polished and graceful façade setting it apart from the worn storefronts leading up to it. He peered out from his truck's window looking for the law office, oblivious to the sleepy stores and empty sidewalks around him. It was just past six o'clock, and the only signs of life were a smattering of unoccupied cars parked alongside the worn curbs. He made his way to the address that had been sent to him, parking in front of the squat brick building that housed the law offices of Wallace, Mayfield, and Young.

Inside he found Henry "The Wall" Wallace waiting for him. He was a large man, his frame and the nickname he had earned with it while playing football at the University of Alabama sticking with him for nearly forty years. Dodge thought he looked exactly as he had imagined him when they spoke on the phone; his hulking frame squeezed into a well pressed pinstripe suit, his dark hair combed back stylishly from his round, crimson face.

"Here you are, Mistuh Mun-gom-ry," Mr. Wallace started, walking through the small but comfortably furnished lobby toward Dodge with a large hand extended in greeting.

"Please, call me Dodge," Dodge said as he shook his hand.

Mr. Wallace laughed. "That's going to be a bit odd, isn't it?" He quickly added, "The only Dodge I knew was your granddaddy. And please, call me Henry. You know your granddaddy and I used to go duck hunting together from time to time." He turned to the small hallway leading back to his office, motioning for Dodge to follow.

"Your granddaddy was a terrific shot. And he had quite an eagle eye. He could spot a duck in the brush from a hundred yards." Dodge followed him into a comfortably attired office. Two red leather chairs sat in front of a large mahogany desk, and he motioned for Dodge to sit.

"He was old school, you know," Henry continued as he sat down. "Why, your granddaddy probably learned how to shoot a gun before he learned how to walk. You ever shoot duck?" Henry leaned back in his chair and eyed Dodge as if he already knew the answer. Dodge understood that Henry wasn't just asking him if he was a hunter. The question was rather, *Was he able to live up to being his grandfather's kin?*

"Ducks?" Dodge asked, settling back into the thick leather armchair. "The only shooting I've done is in my army training and in Afghanistan," he said, smiling at Henry. "And there aren't any ducks there."

Henry's grin widened. "Well, we'll have to get you out in the woods soon then." He leaned forward and began shuffling through the papers covering his desk. He picked up a small yellow envelope and held it in his hands.

14

"I really shouldn't be giving you these keys until everything is signed, you understand. But since your family has been with our firm for so many years we of course want to extend every effort to make things as, uh, uncomplicated for you as possible." Henry handed the small bulky envelope to Dodge over the desk.

"And I do appreciate that," Dodge said as he took the envelope from him, although his appreciation for Henry and his firm was tenuous at best. "Mr. Wallace, I mean, Henry, I do have to ask, did you look for my father as well? I mean, obviously he would have been in line before me for any inheritance from his father, correct?" His voice trailed off, and he could feel that same small bit of nothing there in his chest begin to squeeze over and into itself.

The words hung in the room for a moment. Henry stopped shuffling and looked up at Dodge. His face softened and his eyes fell to the desk in front of him. "I'm sorry, I thought you were aware," he stammered slightly as he looked up at Dodge, then to the desk and back to Dodge again. He sat back with a sigh. "Your father passed away years ago. Nineteen eighty-four."

Dodge stared at Henry, and for a brief moment no longer saw the man sitting before him. His shoulders pressed into the soft leather behind him as he looked down at the envelope in his hands. A thousand made-up childhood memories of a father who had not even existed filled his mind. Gone was a small boy's certainty, however faint certainty could be, that his father was alive and it had all been a big mistake; that he had loved and wanted him all along.

Dodge collected himself. "That doesn't make any sense. I was born in nineteen eighty-five," he said to Henry, holding on for one brief moment of hope.

"Your father died in August of nineteen eighty-four, six months before you were born. We have his death certificate here somewhere." He opened a thick manila folder on his desk and began looking through its contents hurriedly.

Dodge continued to stare straight ahead, his brain hearing the sounds of words it could not fully put together the meaning of. *Death certificate. Passed away years ago. Before you were born.* His father had been dead, even before Dodge was born. His father had not left his mother, as she had thought all of those years, clinging to her hatred of him for abandoning her and their unborn child. He had been dead.

"Yes, here it is." Henry handed Dodge a piece of paper. Dodge glanced over it and stared at the words at the bottom, the same way he had stared at the letter stating his own DNA matched one Dodge William Montgomery. His father, born in December of nineteen sixty-three, had died in August of nineteen eighty-four, six months before Dodge was born.

He looked up at Henry suddenly. "He died here?" His father had returned and died here, a hometown his mother had said that he had fled from all of those years ago. He had left her pregnant and alone in New York City to come here, a place he had told her he would never again return to.

"Why, yes." Henry shifted uneasily in his chair. "I really thought you knew, or I would have mentioned it sooner." He seemed to be caught off-guard himself at the delicate but weighty subject matter.

Dodge stared at the death certificate in his hand trying to focus on the rest of the words. He looked up at Henry again. "It says here his death was accidental." He pushed the paper forward on the desk toward Henry.

"Yes, a fall I believe."

"A fall from what?"

"I, uh, I don't know exactly, we just received a copy of the death certificate for our files when your grandfather died. Somewhere on your granddaddy's property." His voice could not hide his discomfort with the conversation. It was clear that while he had taken on the duty of notifying Dodge of his grandfather's death, his father's was another matter entirely.

Dodge laughed bitterly. Henry stopped shuffling and looked at him. "She named me after my grandfather," Dodge said flatly, staring at the papers on the desk. "My mother told me she named me after my grandfather because my father hated him so much. And when I was born, she hated my father for leaving her." He wasn't stating this for Henry's benefit. He was stating it as if to hear it out loud for himself. It was something he had lived with his entire life. His fate was to carry the name of the man his father hated, because his mother had ended up hating him.

"It's getting late, and I wouldn't want you driving those dark country roads at night." Henry stood up. "I'm sure it's been a long day for you, so you can just come by tomorrow and we can start going through the documents then." He picked up the death certificate as Dodge continued to stare at it blankly, placing it gingerly back in the folder.

Dodge stood up stiffly. His father was dead. His father had died here six months before he was born. Why on earth had he come back to the town his mother said he had hated so much? The town she said he had run from, from a father he had hated? Was it because she had told him she was pregnant?

Henry was gently pressing Dodge toward the door and through the lobby. "The address is on the envelope with the keys. Do you need directions?" He asked, clearly hoping the answer was no.

"No." Dodge stared at the envelope in his hand. "I'll be fine."

Henry looked relieved. "Then we will see you again in the morning. Any time after ten o'clock will be just fine," he said as he maneuvered Dodge out to the sidewalk.

The door to the law firm shut firmly behind him and for a moment Dodge couldn't remember which direction to turn to get back to his truck. He stared at the envelope in his hands. It was as if his body had shut down momentarily while his brain continued to process the information it had just received. He stood for a few seconds and then looked up at the sun making its steady descent into the horizon. Every one of his family members was dead, including the father he had never met, and the man whose house he would call his own.

Chapter 2

The drive to his grandfather's house was not long, but the roads seemed to continue sluggishly on as thoughts fell through his mind like tiny drops of cold rain into one misshapen puddle. The sun had all but set behind him, casting one final crimson glow in the clouds above and a soft orange haze in the road ahead of him. Dodge saw nothing but the asphalt. His father was dead. He had died before Dodge was even born. He had not left his mother and gone on to live another life. His life had ended here, in the town Dodge was driving through, with the keys to his grandfather's house sitting on the seat next to him.

After leaving Henry's office he had punched the address of his grandfather's house into his GPS robotically. It meant nothing to him now, and whatever excitement he may have been willing to allow himself at seeing the birthplace of his father was gone. This was not just his birthplace, it was where he had died, leaving his pregnant girlfriend alone in New York City. He followed the directions of the soft voice from the GPS, without any awareness, or care, of where it was leading him.

His mother had spoken little of his father. "He was from the South," she would say off-handedly, not looking at Dodge directly. "Mississippi or Alabama or somewhere." He was never sure if she didn't know, or if she just didn't want to tell him more.

"But where?" Dodge would ask pleadingly. "Maybe I can find him." He imagined again the miraculous meeting of long lost father and son. "Maybe he's looking for me."

"He's not looking for you," she would say sadly. "He's not looking for you, or me, or us. He left us Dodge, and I know that it hurts you but it also hurt –". She would stop then, and continue on to whatever task she was doing in silence.

His young mind had slowly begun to understand. His father had left them, both of them, and he wasn't coming to find them. Which meant he didn't want Dodge to find him either.

One night, after yet another long day working too many hours for too little money, his mother had brought home a bottle of wine. It wasn't often that she drank, and when she did she was a quiet, sad drinker instead of the angry, loud, and sometimes violent drinker he later tended to be. She held the bottle tightly between both of her worn hands as she poured it, lest she spill a drop of the precious four dollar bottle her meager earnings allowed her the luxury of enjoying every other month or so, and sipped it slowly and deliberately from the same chipped mug she drank her coffee from.

"I named you after your grandfather." She crookedly held the mug of cheap wine as she sat at the table in their tiny kitchen, the fluorescent light above her casting an ugly shadow across her face. "Your father didn't tell me much about his childhood, but he told me his father's name. Said he was a farmer down in the South somewhere. He hated his father, and that's why your father left that town he was from as soon as he could and came up here."

She had poured the rest of the wine from the bottle into the still half-full mug. "Your daddy didn't hate anybody, except his own daddy. Wouldn't talk about him, just said he was never going to see him again. And when he just left one day and didn't come back I named you after your grandfather. I gave you the name of the man your father hated, instead of his own." She gulped the last of the wine, spilling some on the table before her. She tried to focus her eyes at the small spill before gently running her bare ring finger through it to push it off the table.

That was the most information Dodge had ever gotten out of her, and by then any hope he may have had for his father's return had begun to wane. He understood that someone didn't return to somewhere they never wanted to be in the first place.

He had helped his mother to bed that night, taking the empty mug gently from her hands. He was just fourteen years old, but he understood then that there would be no more questions, and no more answers.

"I love you, Dodge," she said, closing her eyes and laying her head on the pillow. "As much as I hated him for leaving me, at least he left me with the best thing I ever got in my life."

He pulled the covers over her and lay his head on her shoulder and listened to her breathe. He would never again ask her about his father. And if he ever found himself wishing again for his return he would instead remember how easy it had been for him to vanish from her life without so much as a goodbye.

"In point five miles your destination is on the right." The GPS voice cut into his thoughts. Dodge breathed in deeply. The sun had fully set and the road he had turned on was dark, the only lights coming from the few small houses set back from the road.

"You have reached your destination. Your total trip time is-" Dodge pushed off the unit as he turned from the road into the driveway. He couldn't see a house before him, just a long gravel driveway winding into total darkness. The long beam of his truck's headlights were the only source of light as he made his way slowly down the drive. He could hear the gravel crunch beneath the truck tires as he peered out the windshield into the darkness for some sign of a house.

To his left he could just make out the edges of a sizeable pond, its silent black water broken by a narrow wooden dock. A well-worn porch swing hung from the long branches of a tree near its edge, silently swaying

20

in the night's breeze. Tall, thin reeds and grasses encircled the water, and in the moonlight he could just make out a thin layer of algae coating the surface. He slowed the truck, rolling down the driver's side window. A chorus of frogs was the only sound that reached his ears, their high-pitched chirps breaking the dark stillness around him.

Five rows of thin metal strands of electrified wires wound their way along the edges of the drive. He slowed his truck and peered out at the movement of a misshapen mass of cattle, too far off in the dim light to observe the herd's actual size. Thick trees dotting the drive reached to one another overhead, like long-lost lovers whose hands had finally intertwined again after the winter to form a soft canopy of leaves.

He continued slowly forward and the faint outline of a large white building began to appear from the darkness ahead. His breath caught in his chest as he approached it. The size of the massive structure that stood before him was beyond the scope of anything he would have imagined. This was not merely a house; this was a mansion that had clearly stood for at least a century or more. The gravel drive ended in a wide circle in front, leading to a broad set of limestone stairs that ascended to a long porch lining the front. Six great white circular pillars reached upward to the roof where four columns of chimneys broke into the night sky. Two enormous black double doors lined on each side with broad windows made up the entryway.

Dodge turned off the truck and sat silently for a moment. The CD player continued to drone on, Chet Baker's trumpet sadly wailing its poignant, lonely tune. This was the place where his family had lived, and as he looked up the solid stone steps for a moment he envisioned his faceless father opening the two black doors and smiling at him while reaching out a hand to invite him inside.

Dodge opened the truck door and stepped out into the warm night air. There were no lights shining in or around the house. In the distance he could hear several quick raps of a gun being fired, and the long, slow sound of a cow calling for her calf to come home. From the darkness of the porch he could make out the silhouettes of a row of empty wooden rocking chairs running along each side. He pictured a person sitting in each one, laughing and rocking gently in the cool night as they watched him ascend the stairs.

He shook his head and pulled the key from the envelope Henry had given him and inserted it into the door. It creaked open, and Dodge could feel a blast of cool air hit his face as he entered. He looked to his left and found a set of switches on the wall. As he flipped the first one up the front entry instantly illuminated from a large chandelier hanging overhead. He gazed up at what looked to be thousands of twinkling drops of glass tossing fragments of light back and forth to one another. At the end of the long entry hall stood a wide circular staircase winding upward to the second floor. Between the staircase and himself stood four wide doorways, two on each side, and the light from the chandelier crept stealthily into each of them, leaving an eerie dead space where the light met the dark.

Dodge shut the front door behind him softly. It wasn't just the newness of his situation or the size of it that left him feeling out of place in this house. After living in rental apartments his whole life he was used to treating places like they belonged to someone else. He took off his jacket and placed it on the coat rack next to the door where two coats hung already. He leaned in closer briefly, breathing in the wool coat hanging languidly before him. It smelled of a man. His grandfather. His throat caught unexpectedly and he stepped back quickly.

He started into the room directly to his left. Delicate pieces of upholstered wooden furniture filled the room, stark against the backdrop of a soft pink floral wallpaper. Elegant white lace curtains hung from ceiling to floor, all but covering the massive windows that lined the front. On each wall hung a grouping of paintings, their thick golden frames glowing eerily in the bits of light they caught from the chandelier. He fumbled for a switch on the wall next to him but couldn't find one, and something told him to keep moving on. There was something soft and serene about the house, like a mistress whispering in the dark to leave the lights off.

On the far side of the room loomed another wide doorway leading to the room directly behind it. This too appeared to be a sort of parlor, more masculine than the room before it. Heavy gold curtains rose upward to an ornately carved mahogany beam above each window. The furniture here was more sizeable, and the dark green wallpaper swallowed up any light that made its way through the open door leading back out to the front hall. Dodge did not stop here either, and quickly made his way to the door adjacent to this one across the entry hall.

This too was a man's room, a study or office of some sort. Four wide, overstuffed leather chairs encircled a massive wooden table in front of the fireplace. Assorted paintings of animals and hunting scenes filled almost every inch of wall space that was not taken up by three large bookcases. The light made its way through the double wide doors from the entryway chandelier and over a deep red wool carpet.

Behind the study he found a large dining room with another row of tall windows lining the back wall. On each hung long, white lace curtains from floor to ceiling, standing tall and still like ghosts waiting a silent guard. In the center of the room stood a small, narrow wood table surrounded by four chairs, its size seemingly out of place in the massive room. Dodge glanced quickly over the imposing hutch filled with fine bone china that stood across from a long sideboard table with mirrors lining above and below.

He made his way through the dining room into a long, narrow hallway that led to an enormous kitchen. As he flipped up the light switch the room immediately filled with light. The far wall above the long wooden counter was almost completely covered by three wide, six-foot tall windows, each of which were crowned with two-foot tall transoms. Thin strips of dark wood separated them into twenty panes of glass each. As in the rest of the house, the ceilings rose far above him, and he guessed them to be at least fourteen feet high. Light blue cabinets adorned with glass fronts held a myriad of plates, glasses, and bakeware. Here the large table could easily seat eight to ten people. A tall fireplace ran the length of the wall behind it, soot blackening the worn red bricks inside. The appliances were surprisingly modern, considering the state of the furniture in the rest of the house, as if this room was the only one that had been allowed to come forward out of the past.

He moved to the refrigerator and opened it, the bulb emitting a familiar light. He wasn't sure what type of contents he expected to find, but this one held just the basic necessities – butter, milk, an unopened plastic sleeve of cheddar cheese, and an assortment of condiments on the door. It occurred to him that these were the last things his grandfather would have eaten when he was alive. If he hadn't dropped dead of a heart attack three weeks ago he would have drank the rest of the milk, perhaps right from the carton. He would have eaten the butter, maybe on two slices of toast he would make in the morning.

Dodge shut the refrigerator door abruptly. Ever since he was a child he had had a distinctive habit of imagining the details of other peoples' lives and how they lived among the things that to them would be ordinary and routine. It reminded him of visits to friends' houses where he found closets filled with the toys that no longer interested them or boxes of undersized clothes their mothers could not bear to part from. Having grown up on many forms of public assistance and moving every year or so to a new place and a new school whenever his mother found work, he did not have this excess surplus of belongings, and found it oddly comforting that he did not feel the need to.

He moved through the kitchen and dining room and returned to the front hall. He paused as he peered up the circular staircase that led to the dark upper floors. He could not shake the feeling that he was an intruder in someone else's home, or even a child accidentally locked in an abandoned museum, now able to touch all of the treasures without the persistent reprimands of an adult. He had to remind himself again that this was his. *This is my front hall, and those are my stairs*, he repeated to himself as he moved toward the staircase, knowing it would not make a difference.

On the wall at the bottom of the staircase he found another row of light switches. With each sharp click a brighter flood of light rained down from the floor above. The winding circular nature of the stairway did not permit a clear view upward, and he could only see the small circular ceiling at the top. In its center hung another chandelier, less grand and ornate than the one in the entrance hall but still a considerable size. The light fell in small diamond clusters against the curve of the wall, twinkling madly as if in delight that someone had finally turned them on again.

He slowly made his way up the stairs, grasping the smooth, solid wooden banister. Halfway to the top a small oval window was set into the wall, and he paused, peering out into the black darkness on the other side of the pane. *Who has stood here,* he thought to himself as he leaned into the small alcove and pressed his hand against the cool glass. *Who has stood here, was it him?*

He followed the steps up into a wide second floor hallway that contained another set of doors identical to the ones below. The hall itself was as big as a room, its wide, wood paneled floors stretching out before him toward a large window at the end.

He peered into the first room, barely able to make out the outline of the solid bedroom furniture. A massive canopied bed stood against the wall, surrounded by tall armoires and long dressers between overstuffed chairs. Across from the bed stood a fireplace wrapped in shiny marble. He made his way to the next room and found similar furnishings to the first. Dodge could not remember ever being in a house with rooms this large, at least not one that had been lived in most recently by just one person.

He crossed the hall and peered into the third bedroom. The moonlight cast an eerie glow across the room, turning the bedspread into a colorless ash under the fluffy snow-white canopy. He told himself he should go into these rooms and open the drawers, peek in the closets, and peer under the beds. But he still felt like an intruder viewing someone else's life from behind velvet ropes. He made his way back around to the first door on his left from the stairs. This was the only door that was closed.

He placed his hand on the cold metal knob and twisted. He could hear the slight click from the inner latch echoing into the room before him announcing his intended intrusion. He let go abruptly, stepping back. It was as if the open doors to the other rooms had been inviting him in, while this closed door said, *You're not welcome here.* His jaw tightened as the hairs on the back of his neck curled up.

"Dodge, what are you doing there?" His mother's voice called out *from somewhere dark and small.*

"Nuthin," he replied, quickly closing the lid on the box of photos he had found tucked far back under her bed.

"You don't touch that, Dodge," she said, as she pulled the box angrily from his hands. *"You hear me? That's not for you. Get out of my room."*

He took another step back and turned from the door. *What am I doing here,* he asked himself. He stood motionless, staring at the walls of the large hall around him, broken only by the three hollow doorways and the black window at the end. *I can just get a hotel room in Birmingham,* he thought. *I don't need to stay here. I don't want to stay here.* He turned and made his way back down the stairs quickly, hurriedly flipping off the light switches at the bottom so once again only the darkened silence remained.

He made his way out of the house and shut the door behind him, not stopping until he had descended the steps to the drive below. He breathed in deeply. *I am Dodge Montgomery,* he said to himself, standing on the gravel. *I am Dodge James Montgomery,* he corrected himself. He breathed in again. Then he opened the door to his truck, where he knew he would spend the night.

"Dodge." He heard a voice calling from somewhere far off. It was a woman's voice, sweet and high, splitting his name into two soft syllables. He turned his head in his sleep and burrowed his face deeper into the sweatshirt he had pressed against the seat cushion as a makeshift pillow.

"Dodge Montgomery," came the lilting voice again. He opened his eyes and stared at the truck dashboard. He rummaged beneath him and pulled out his phone to check the time. 7:30 a.m. He had spent many nights sleeping in his truck, some after a long night of drinking and some because he had had nowhere else to go. *Where am I,* he asked himself as he groggily looked at the light streaming through the truck's dusty front windshield. He shook off the remnants of a dream of dark rooms and hallways with dancing bits of light rambling across gold flecked walls. *It was a dream.* He sat up quickly, placing one hand against his chest and running the other hand across the top of his head.

"There you are!" The woman's voice came again, closer this time. He looked out the driver side window to find a petite blonde woman standing on the porch steps holding a square glass baking dish covered in aluminum foil. The hem of her sundress had been perfectly mended to reach mid-thigh while the top was cut low enough to entice but not endanger the demureness of its flowery pattern. Her golden hair was pulled back into a sleek ponytail away from her perfectly made up face, and for a moment Dodge wasn't sure how someone could look, or sound, so cheerful and positive at this hour of the morning.

He opened the driver side door and slowly made his way out. He was a foot taller than the woman at least, and as she stepped down from the stairs she looked up at him with wide eyes, the gleaming white smile never leaving her perfect pink stained lips.

"My goodness, Dodge Montgomery! What are you doing sleeping in your truck!" She giggled, extending a hand to him while still holding the glass baking dish effortlessly in the other.

Dodge took her hand and smiled. "I got in late, and I must've just fallen asleep out here last night," he said, as she continued gazing up at him. He knew he was a handsome man, and was used to women staring at him. But this woman was putting him off slightly, standing so close he could smell her flowery perfume and a faint whiff of lemon from the dish in her hand.

"You are just too much." She let go of his hand slowly. "I'm Millie, and I just brought you over a little something to welcome you to town." She waved the glass dish in the air.

"Thank you. I appreciate that." He began pulling his sweatshirt over his head.

"Oh you think nothing of it," Millie called behind her as she made her way up to the porch, the tall heels of her dainty sandals making a small clicking noise against the smooth stone steps. "I am just sorry I couldn't be here yesterday when you got in, but it was late, and it would have just been rude of me to show up here that time of the evening unannounced." She opened the front door and turned to look at him standing beside the truck, the hood of his sweatshirt rumpled over his head.

"You're coming in, aren't you?" She paused for a moment as she looked behind her, and Dodge watched her walk in, more casually and comfortably than he had the night before.

He followed her voice through the front hall as she headed directly back to the kitchen, placing the glass dish down on the center island. She turned to take down two plates from the glass cabinet behind her, and opened a drawer and picked out a butter knife, her chatter never ceasing.

"We are just so excited to have you here." She pulled the foil from the top of the dish and began slicing into its contents with the knife. "When we heard that old man Montgomery had a long lost grandson it was like something out of a movie, you know?" She cut two bright yellow squares and placed them delicately on the plates before her.

"I just love these plates. They have been in your family for generations, and they are so lovely. They don't even make this set anymore." She walked over to Dodge, who had seated himself at the kitchen table. He watched her without a word, not that he could have gotten one in anyway, as she set a plate in front of him and took a seat at the table.

"These are my world famous lemon squares," she said, pushing the plate toward him with a smile. Dodge smiled back and picked up the square, holding it gently in his hand. "Well I suppose not really world famous, since I don't know that anyone outside of Alabama has tasted them just yet. Except now you of course!"

Millie was looking at him, waiting for him to take a bite of the bright yellow square he held in his hand. Sharp, sweet lemon melded together with the thick layer of buttery crumb crust in his mouth, and his stomach gurgled appreciatively as he swallowed.

"They're very good," he assured her, wiping his mouth with the back of his hand.

Millie sat back proudly, nodding her head. "It's actually my grandmama's recipe, but she wouldn't share it with anyone but me, not even my mama. I was named after my grandmama, Mildred. My parents did not believe in giving children unique names like everyone else at the time. But I think they realized that Mildred wasn't really a suitable name for a child. So they took to calling me Millie. Not that I minded Mildred, of course, but it's true, it really doesn't suit a child."

Dodge nodded as he took another bite, not as fascinated by Millie's family name saga as he was about her familiarity with his own grandfather's house. "So you've been in this house before I take it," he said, seeing an opportunity to speak as Millie took a delicate bite of her own square.

"Oh heavens, yes." She set down her square and wiped her hands together. "Many times. Your granddaddy used to let us show the house every year for the Annual Parade of Homes. That's where the finer homes in town are opened up to the public. This house has always been one of my favorites," she said eyeing the kitchen around her as she spoke. "It's been in your family for so many years. Your granddaddy's granddaddy built it. Not with his own hands of course," she laughed, and touched Dodge's arm gently. "Your family could afford the finest things, so everything is just top notch. The furniture is almost all original. It's all so well-built you would just never know it has been sitting in here for over a hundred years."

Dodge watched her take another dainty bite. "I don't know anything about it really," he said dryly.

"Of course not, you just got here, didn't you?" Millie asked, standing up. "C'mon, I'll take you on a tour!" She giggled excitedly. "I was a guide here for the last three years of the Parade of Homes so I know all about this house." She stopped. "Your house."

Dodge stood up and followed as she made her way back through the dining room and study to the front hall. She stood, her back to the front door, hands clasped in front of her as she waited for him to join her.

"The Montgomery estate was built in 1879, by Robert Pierce Montgomery," Millie began. "He was a wealthy landowner here in Shelby County, as well as a lawyer who worked for the state government. That's his picture over the mantle in the front parlor." She moved into the room to her left. Dodge followed, moving to the fireplace and staring up at the large painting above it. The man in the painting was dressed in a white shirt and dark velvet jacket, his dark black beard almost covering his upturned collar and silk bowtie. He gazed serenely forward, his green eyes studying the room before him.

"Look at that, you have his eyes!" Millie was abruptly standing next to him as he leaned closer to the portrait.

"It's hard to tell." Dodge moved over slightly.

"This would have been the ladies' parlor," Millie continued. She pointed to the various pieces of furniture around the room as she spoke. "This was where Mr. Montgomery's wife would have entertained ladies of social stature, while he and the other men had drinks and cigars in the men's parlor just beyond this one." Dodge could see Millie's eyes widening as she stroked the furniture. He imagined she was picturing herself in this room, seated in the best spot on the rich, beautiful furniture, surrounded by equally rich, beautiful women.

She paused as she knelt over to adjust a throw pillow lovingly. She stood up and made her way to the second parlor.

"And this, this would be where the men would entertain themselves." She spread her arms as she entered the next room. "See," she said as Dodge entered, pulling two doors out from the walls behind him. The thick wooden doors rattled loudly on their tracks. "These are pocket doors, so the men and women couldn't overhear one another." She closed them tightly with a conspiratorial wink.

In the light of day the rooms felt much different than Dodge's first visit through them. Tall, wide windows lining the back wall allowed in an abundance of sunlight, and while the rooms were still not what Dodge would call comfortable, they at least had lost their ominous tone from the night before.

30

Millie broke into his train of thought. "Can you even imagine what went on in here?" She quietly lifted her brows.

"I can't," Dodge said flatly as he looked around him. He couldn't imagine the people who would have stood in this room. The painting over the mantle was the first time he had ever seen any of his family members on his father's side.

"Well, I can." Millie was already moving through the second door and back out to the entrance hall. "The parties and the gatherings and holidays in a big house like this. I'm sure they were just about the most fun you could have back in that day." Dodge could hear a wistful dreaminess in her voice. "I'll bet you could throw a fantastic party here. One that would rival the mayor's fete any day."

Dodge laughed. "I'm not much of a party thrower," he said as he followed her out of the room.

"Of course not, silly," she laughed. "You would hire help to do all of that."

They passed by the circular staircase as they moved into the front room. Millie took her place beside the doorway. "And here is the study, an important part of genteel country living in the late nineteenth century." She spoke as if reading from a cue card. "This was where the landowner would conduct business, selling and purchasing goods, livestock, and grain. Most of the money in Shelby County came from wealthy landowners like those in your family. Our town is the county seat of Shelby County-"

"How much land did my family own?" Dodge interrupted her.

"Let's see," Millie took a seat on the long velvet lined sofa beneath the window. "At their peak in the early nineteen-hundreds, I believe the Montgomery land was just over a thousand acres. Most of that was sold off over the years, but your granddaddy kept the house and the land surrounding it."

One thousand acres of land. Dodge wasn't sure he even understood what that meant. He had always counted space in city blocks, or miles on the road. He had never had to count anything in acres in his life.

31

Millie sensed Dodge's interest. "Your granddaddy was very active in the community. Not so much so in his later years though, as his health started to fail. But I would still see him around town sometimes. Everyone knew who he was, and everyone always had something nice to say about him."

"Not everyone apparently," Dodge said as he absently fingered a pile of papers on top of the desk and remembered his mother's voice recalling his father's words.

"What's that?"

Dodge looked up at her, pausing for a brief moment. "Nothing."

She stood up and moved into the next room. "This is of course the formal dining room." She waved her hand around her. "The table extends to seat sixteen people." She pointed to the small wooden table in the center of the room. "See, that's what the extra chairs are for," she said, pointing to the chairs lining the walls and in each of the corners. There were two more on each side of the buffet table and the glass fronted hutch. "The table would be left in its smaller form for more intimate gatherings."

Dodge moved to the long china cabinet and Millie was standing beside him again as he peered inside. He could again faintly smell her flowery perfume. "Your family's silver," she said softly, almost adoringly. Dodge wasn't sure if he had ever seen genuine silver in his life, let alone this much of it sitting out in the dining room of someone's house. "And that's porcelain china." She tapped a long pink fingernail against the glass as she pointed to a row of delicate plates, saucers, and bowls. "It belonged to your great grandmother." Dodge turned away from the cabinet, feeling more like he was in a museum instead of what was his own house.

"Look there." Millie was pointing under a long side table. A wide mirror lined the base, a soft brown patina mottling its surface. "That mirror was there so the ladies could check the length of their skirts when they were seated, to make sure they weren't improperly revealing any ankle to the gentlemen." She moved closer to the mirror and twisted her leg with a smile. Her legs were tan and smooth, and Dodge speculated that her skirt length had never once in her life reached her ankles.

She moved through the dining room to the long hall that led to the kitchen. "This hallway is not original to the primary house." She gently slid a hand along the wallpapered wall as they walked. "In the late eighteen-hundreds, when this house was built, the kitchens were separate from the main houses. That way if there was a fire it would burn the kitchen and the house would remain. Your great-grandfather added the hallway in the late twenties, just before the tornado came through." She touched the walls soundly. "It's held up nicely, wouldn't you agree?"

Dodge nodded, oblivious to the wall. "A tornado? It hit this house?"

Millie nodded. They were back in the kitchen again, and she sat down at the table, clasping together her manicured hands. "Yes, you'll hear the sirens go off whenever there's a chance of one. But the last big one that hit was back in the early thirties I think. They stay north of here mostly. It's not like anything exciting could ever happen around here." She dryly picked at a cuticle before looking up at him. "I mean, they are a terrible thing of course, just awful." She shook her head, as if for effect.

"What about the upstairs?" He leaned against the doorframe, realizing that Millie could probably provide him with more information in a ten-minute tour than he could learn wandering around on his own for hours.

"Oh, I don't know about the upstairs." She began clearing the plates from the table and taking them to the sink. "Your granddaddy wouldn't let the tours go upstairs. At least not by the time I was old enough to start doing them, which was after your daddy…" Her voice trailed off as she placed the dishes in the sink gently, not turning to look at him.

"After my father died," Dodge finished her sentence and thought about the closed door on the second floor.

She turned to look at him. "Yes, I'm not sure why but that was what I heard. When your daddy died your granddaddy stopped the tours for a few years, and then when he started allowing them again he didn't want anyone going upstairs." She shrugged her shoulders, as if to indicate that when there were things not spoken about they were better left unknown.

"So you don't know much about my father then I guess?"

Millie shook her head. "No, I'm sorry I don't. I wasn't even born yet when he..." Her voice trailed off again as she began to study a fingernail intently.

"Apparently I wasn't either."

Millie frowned. "I'm sure there are more than a few people still here who knew him. Even Butler would have been around then I suppose."

Dodge's ears perked up at the name. "Did you say Butler?" He remembered the gruff man from the gas station the day before.

"Yes, he did some sort of work here for your granddaddy. He used to hang around during the home tours, giving people sour glances. Like he owned the place instead of your granddaddy." She frowned. "But I'm sure he would know something about your daddy. He's not exactly the chatty type if you know what I mean."

"Yeah, I got that yesterday."

"Oh, so you've already met," Millie said with surprise.

"Sort of. When I was coming into town I stopped at a gas station and he was there. Hanging out." He left out the part about Earl's gun and leaving before the sheriff arrived.

"Sounds like Butler. I don't like to say an unkind word about anyone but he's not exactly a man of character. At least I don't care to find myself in the same social circle as him," she sniffed. "Anyway, everyone in this town knows everyone else. Or they know someone who knows someone else. I'm sure you'll be able to find someone who can tell you about your daddy."

They stood for a few moments in silence before she turned back to the sink and began rinsing the plates. She wiped her hands on a small towel on the counter. "I should be getting along. I'm sure you have a lot to do today." She smiled at him again. "And I'm sure I'll see you again soon. I will leave my number in case you find yourself needing anything." She pulled a small leather notepad and silver pen from her purse. "Absolutely anything you need, you just let me know." She handed the piece of paper to Dodge with a smile.

34

"I appreciate that, Millie." She was very pretty, and while she appeared to be around his own age he wasn't one to make friends easily, and he certainly wasn't looking for a girlfriend in this town.

Millie made her way out of the kitchen to the front door and again Dodge found himself following her. "Think nothing of it." She paused as she opened the door and turned back to him. "Maybe someday I'll get to see the upstairs after all," she said, closing the door behind her.

Chapter 3

Dodge watched from the front door as Millie glided down the steps to her car, one hand trailing lightly against the handrail. He turned the door's heavy lock with a loud click. He was not accustomed to unannounced visitors and didn't need any more today. Turning, he contemplated the stairs behind him at the end of the empty entry hall. A narrow beam of sunlight had begun to slip its way through the window on the landing he had stood before the night before, falling into a bright zigzag pattern on the bare wood steps.

He climbed the stairs, moving hurriedly past the open doorways to the closed door. Sunlight flooded in from the heavily adorned window, and while it made the hall less imposing there was still an emptiness to the space. He took a breath, turning the cold metal knob and gently pushing the door open with a long, lonely creak.

The room before him was completely bare of carpet and furniture. Particles of dust stirred by the opened door danced on the streams of sunlight that shone through its unclothed windows. The stark, naked walls were the inverse of the brightly colored wallpaper in the other bedrooms and highlighted its cold emptiness. This was a room stripped and exposed, unembellished and left raw.

He stepped in hesitantly and moved to the door at the far left corner. He opened it to find a small closet, empty of even a solitary hanger. He moved quickly to a door at the opposite end of the same wall, and turned the tarnished knob. It opened to reveal a narrow wooden staircase, and as he peered up he could see light coming from a third floor. He carefully made his way up the stairs, each step announcing his invasion with a short creaking moan.

Before him a large attic extended across the entire length of the house. Warm, stagnant air hit his face as he ascended the last few steps. He paused at the top, his eyes adjusting just enough to make out a collection of trunks and boxes, massed from floor to ceiling. Between these sat the remaining fragments of past lives: a set of wooden chairs stacked precariously atop one another in a corner, an old bicycle propped against an equally rusted metal bed frame, and barren, golden picture frames tucked into one another along the walls. A thick layer of brown-grey dust rested like a blanket over the room's contents and coated the floor before him.

Dodge made his way down the narrow strip of bare floor that led like a forgotten path through the discarded belongings. These possessions, which had once belonged to people who were strangers to him, were now his. The last years of the Montgomery family's existence remained here in a few shabby old boxes among items not even fit for a garage sale, all that was left of his family, discarded and alone.

He sat down on a large leather chest beneath the window and stared at the tower of boxes before him. *Open them, they're yours*, a voice whispered inside his head. These forgotten objects and unwanted belongings that had been demoted to an attic were his, and it would take him days, if not weeks to go through all of it. Perhaps somewhere within them were his father's belongings, the last items he had touched before they had been packed up and pushed away above.

He let his mind wander for a moment as he breathed in the stale air. Would he have played amongst these boxes as a child, perhaps during a game of hide-and-go-seek with his father? Would his grandfather have sat him on his lap, proudly showing him the contents of each box, pulling out the things his own grandfather had owned, and touched, and cherished? *"These things will belong to you someday, Dodge,"* he might have said to him with a smile, and Dodge would have smiled back up at him.

He stood up abruptly and made his way hastily back down the attic stairs and out of the empty room. He knew this had been his father's room. It was the room his father had grown up in, and the room he had left when he had escaped from this house all those years ago. It was a room that had once held his father's belongings, but was now empty and bare, any memories that had been kept within its drawers removed. *What kind of a monster would strip bare his deceased son's room, leaving it empty and forgotten?*

Dodge closed the door and made his way back downstairs. He glanced at his watch and saw it was just before ten a.m. He would need to shower and change before heading back to Henry's office to sign the paperwork. As he made his way to his truck to gather his bags a movement off in the distance caught his eye. It was the large mass he had come upon the night before - a herd of enormous gray cows gathered together, their heads slowly moving as they tore bits of grass from the field beneath them.

Farther behind them stood the hulking frame of a bright red barn, its two top spires reaching up into the blue sky above. Its width and height rivaled the house itself, and from where he stood he guessed it to be three or four stories high. The slate gray roof stretched over the red wood walls built upon thick layers of solid stone and mortar. Beside it stood a tall metal structure covering a large tractor and several heavy, round bales of hay.

He made his way forward, keeping a close eye on the large cluster of cattle. Kneeling down he tucked himself between two thin metal strands of fence, careful not to touch the electrified wires. As he made his way across the pasture his sneakers sunk into the damp earth and left a shiny, dark trail in the grass behind him.

As he neared the entrance he peered upward at the gaping dark hole of a large square door two stories above. The rusted hinges that held open its heavy wooden door gave a long, shrill wail before it thumped gently against the barn's exterior wall. He could hear the echoing ping of metal being brought down against metal coming from inside. He opened the barn door and stepped forward, keeping hold to the door frame as his eyes slowly adjusted to the dark, hollow interior. It was lit only by a few bare bulbs that hung at varying intervals from the wood beams overhead, their feeble glow unaided by the sunlight's futile effort to make it through the layers of dust and dirt that clung stubbornly to the panes of each window.

He walked carefully across the dirt floor that separated the stalls, stepping gingerly around the clumps of hay and straw that littered the wide floor. He followed the ringing sound of metal to the far end of the barn where a man stood hunched over a long table, his back turned. The wide barn doors at the other end stood open and Dodge immediately recognized the stout silhouette as he watched the arm fall toward the table with another ringing blow. *Butler.*

"Hello?" Dodge yelled out as he neared, unsure if Butler had seen or heard him as he entered.

The mallet dropped to the table with a loud clang. "Morning." Butler turned without a smile or trace of welcome. He leaned back against the table and crossed his arms against his chest, looking Dodge up and down. "Didn't realize you'd be arriving in town so soon. I'm just finishing up, then I'll grab my tools and get out of your way." He turned his back to Dodge and picking up the mallet began pounding once more, the metal ringing more sharply and louder than before.

Dodge took a step toward him. "You work here on the farm, is that right? You worked for my grandfather?"

The mallet stopped in mid-air, and he could see Butler's shoulders tightening as he said the last word. "I've been working on this farm since I was ten years old with Mr. Montgomery," Butler said forcefully, barely turning his head.

"Yes, I understand." Dodge immediately caught Butler's tone and his obvious lack of interest in being on friendly terms with him. He stood up straighter, lifting his chin slightly. "I was hoping you might stay on since you're familiar with the place, at least for a little while. I don't know anything about cattle, or farming really-"

"That's right, you don't." Butler interrupted him with a forceful swing of the mallet and the metal ring echoed loudly against the barn walls.

Butler shook his head slowly, his back still turned to Dodge. "I can't stay on and work for you. I've got another job lined up. You can go down to the feed store and talk to Jake Ewen. He can recommend someone for you." He turned from the table to a toolbox on the floor. He shoved the mallet into the box and slammed down the lid. "I'll come back in a few days for the rest of my things."

Dodge watched him pick up the toolbox and make his way out a rear set of double barn doors to a battered, yellow pick-up truck. A large semi-transparent confederate flag decal covered its back window, the wording beneath stating that one could have Butler's gun when they pried it out of his cold, dead fingers. Butler tossed the toolbox into the truck bed and jerked open the driver side door. He lifted himself into the cab and stared out the windshield. Dodge could see his knuckles whiten as he gripped the wheel.

"You don't look nothing like your granddaddy." He sneered at Dodge, slamming shut the driver-side door. He stared at him through the open window and spat a large brown spot of chewing tobacco on the ground. "But I guess you already knew that." The truck started up with a roar and lurched down the driveway, leaving a haze of dust on the road between them.

Dodge stared at the empty barn doorway and breathed out deeply. Unbeknownst to him his body had instinctively gone into fighting mode while he had stood listening to Butler speak, arms crossed over his chest, shoulders back and legs slightly apart. He tucked his still shaking hands

40

into his pockets and made his way back up to the house, slamming the barn doors closed behind him.

Thirty minutes later his truck was winding down the driveway. His body was still tense from the conversation with Butler. He understood that Butler's issues were not with him personally as he had just met the man less than twenty-four hours before, but it didn't much matter. He was a stranger in a small town, and a childhood spent moving from one town to the next and trying to fit in had taught him that having even one enemy was one too many. He would get the legal documents straightened out with the law firm and get out of this town as quickly as possible. Maybe even tonight. He could put the house up for sale when he was back in New York. What did he need with a dead man's old mansion in Alabama anyway?

He turned the truck out of the driveway and onto the road, rolling down both windows to get a better view of the surroundings he had missed in the dark the night before. A curious assortment of houses dotted the road, each built to its owner's distinctive specifications. Cows and horses scattered themselves in groups behind long lines of wooden fence across green pastures, in some places the animals standing within a few feet of the house itself. Small hand-painted signs boasted a diverse assortment of homegrown businesses including towing, dog grooming, fresh eggs, firewood, and local honey.

As he neared Main Street the houses grew larger and closer together, their wide white porches lined with wooden rocking chairs and flower boxes. He slowly made his way past a white columned courthouse and an enormous Baptist church that was only rivaled in size to the Episcopalian church across from it. It was quiet in mid-morning as he parked in front of the drugstore and walked into Henry's office.

Henry sat waiting for him in his office. "Dodge." He rose from behind his desk and extended his hand. "How was your first night in your new place?" He motioned for Dodge to sit down.

"It was fine." He didn't feel the need to share with Henry that he hadn't actually slept in the house, rather in front of it.

"It's a grand old place, isn't it? One of the finest houses in Shelby County, maybe even in the whole state of Alabama. It's on the historic register you know. People can't just build a place like that anymore." He paused. "Well, I suppose they could." He looked straight at Dodge. "But they'd have to buy the furniture from you." He chuckled at his joke as he opened a file.

"It's certainly nicer than any house I've ever lived in. And a bit larger than what I'm used to." Dodge continued quickly, "I'm not sure that I will be living in it though."

Henry paused and looked at him, nodding his head. "You'll get used to it." He slid the thick manila folder toward Dodge as he put on a pair of reading glasses and picked up his own set of papers. "Here's the first part of it."

Dodge opened the folder. The first page included an itemized list of his grandfather's possessions and holdings. He glanced through the list, his eyes widening at the bottom. *Eight million, three hundred and sixty-four thousand dollars.* He stared at the figure at the bottom of the page and felt his jaw slackening.

"That's an itemized list of all of the major items that encompass the estate." Henry was peering over his reading glasses at a copy of the same document in his own hand. "Those that we know of and have been able to evaluate as of yet anyway."

Dodge could not shift his eyes from the figure at the bottom of the page. It was far more money than he would have ever thought he would see in his lifetime.

"This is what my grandfather was worth?" He shifted uncomfortably in his chair. The soft leather felt like it was swallowing him. "Eight, eight million dollars?"

42

"That is the total of your grandfather's estate," Henry corrected him. He leaned over the desk slightly. "That is what you are now worth." He sat back. "Minus the estate taxes and lawyers' fees of course."

"What did my grandfather do exactly?" Dodge scanned the list of items listed on the first page. *Main residence: $890,000; Contents of house: $550,000; Livestock holdings: $250,000. Stocks and bonds: $1.4 million; Real estate holdings: $2.8 million.* The list went on into unfamiliar financial terminology and it occurred to him that the largest list of assets he previously owned sat in two black duffel bags in the back of his truck.

"Most of the money in your family has been there for generations, increased by sound investing and smart spending. You could say your grandfather was a cattleman by trade, and a darned good one at that. But the Montgomery men have always been smart money investors and managers. It doesn't hurt that the last three heirs were all only children, males to boot. Yourself included."

"I had no idea." He hadn't prepared himself for the house or this amount of money, and suddenly felt awkward sitting before Henry in a t-shirt and jeans, his sneakers still damp from his walk to the barn this morning. "My grandfather didn't have any siblings either?"

Henry shook his head. "No, no he did not. His father died when Dodge was young, eighteen or so I believe. He inherited all of his father's wealth, and his only son James." He paused. "His only son James would have inherited all of his wealth." Henry raised his eyebrows. "We don't like to talk figures over the phone, you see, for our client's privacy." He could see Dodge's minor state of shock, and he spoke slowly. "I hope it's not too much of a surprise to you, or that maybe you weren't expecting there to be more liquid assets. A lot of it is tied up in real estate and other holdings of course."

"No, no, not at all," Dodge said quickly, still staring at the piece of paper in front of him.

Henry took off his glasses. "Dodge," he said softly as he leaned in over the desk, "Montgomery's have been in Shelby County as far back as anyone around here can remember. Your grandfather's house has been on

County Road fifty-five since before there was a County Road fifty-five. You have to understand that there is a community here that your family has been a part of for many years." He spoke slowly, as if to a small child. "We're not interested in having someone come in here and just sell off a piece of our town's history, if you understand what I'm saying."

Dodge looked up at Henry as he continued. "It's not just a house or a piece of land, or a list of items on a piece of paper, Dodge, do you see?" Henry was staring at him over his glasses, still holding the piece of paper in his hands. "I know your daddy didn't want anything to do with it when he left here, but it was his whether he liked it or not, just like it was his daddy's and his daddy's before him. And now it's yours. Do you understand what I'm saying to you?"

"I suppose. I just don't really know what that means." He looked down at the list again. "To me, I mean."

Henry smiled. "You'll find out. In fact, I would be honored if you would attend our town's annual Garden Party this Friday evening." He held up his hand before Dodge could protest. "I know you are thinking of high-tailing it out of this sleepy little town and back to New York City as soon as possible. But you'll need a few days to get your affairs in order anyway. You'll want to have those papers reviewed by your legal counsel of course." He paused, lowering his head, more than aware that Dodge would not have known until now the vast extent of the estate. "Not that everything isn't on the up and up, but it would be to both our benefits to have an impartial third party review them. As your family's attorney I wouldn't advise you leaving town before everything is settled here. Besides, you can meet some of the townspeople and introduce yourself. Learn more about our town and your family's history."

Dodge nodded his head. "Yes, my lawyers will need to review this of course." He thumbed through the thick stack of papers and shifted uneasily in his chair.

"Good, good. Then it's settled. You'll be able to come to the Garden Party. It's held at the mayor's house, which is just a few blocks from here. I'll have our receptionist email you the directions. In the meantime, you have some of your lawyers look over that paperwork and then we'll schedule an appointment to get it all signed and notarized in the next few weeks or so."

"A few weeks?" Dodge looked at him. "No, I need to get this done as soon as possible. I have some," he paused, "prior engagements that I need to attend to." He thought back to his restless night's sleep in his truck and compared it to the thought of sleeping alone in the imposing old house. Even the thought of one night made him uneasy, let alone sleeping there for the next few weeks. "I'll have this looked at right away."

"We are here to work to your schedule," Henry said standing up. "Say, why don't I take you to lunch?" He glanced down at his watch. "Davidson's Drug Store is just next door and has an outstanding cheeseburger plate." Henry was lifting his suit coat from the back of his chair as he spoke.

"I don't think I have time." Dodge glanced down at his phone, wondering how he was going to find an impartial law firm to review the documents so he could leave as quickly as possible.

"Nonsense, it's just next door. You must try some of our local cuisine while you're here." He laughed and patted Dodge on the back. His tone had changed from the evening before, and he now seemed like a gentle old uncle rather than the standoffish lawyer who had rushed Dodge uncomfortably out the door.

"I suppose I could." He reluctantly agreed as he followed Henry out to the street. He did not, however, relish the idea of eating at a drugstore counter.

"Did you know that our town is the county seat of Shelby County?" Henry pointed up the road toward the large, white building standing at the end. "That there is the original courthouse built in eighteen fifty-four. They built the new courthouse in nineteen oh-six." He pointed at the other end toward an imposing marble building Dodge had passed on his way into town. "It was quite contentious, you see, where to hold the county seat. Lots of other towns wanted it, but we won out in the end. And to celebrate, the citizens packed an old pine tree with gunpowder and blew it up – they

45

say you could hear the sound of that explosion for miles." Henry's hands went up in the air. "We like our celebrations to be lively you see, and for everyone else around to know about them, even if they can't attend. Or, even if they don't want to." He opened the door to the drugstore and motioned for Dodge to enter.

Henry took a seat at the counter, raising a hand to wave at the two waitresses standing behind it deep in conversation. They both looked up and nodded, taking an extra moment to steal a glance at Dodge. The older waitress made her way toward them, wiping the counter with a large white dishrag without looking up.

"What's good today, Fay?" Henry smiled at her. Her graying brown hair was pulled back into a sharp bun at the back of her head, two pens sticking out like needles in a taut pin cushion. She looked to be in her late forties or early fifties judging from the lines around her eyes and mouth, which did not appear to turn up in a smile very often.

"Same thing as yesterday, Henry," she replied dryly. Dodge could tell this exchange had happened before, and Fay did not find it as amusing as Henry.

"My friend here is going to need a menu as this is his first time in your fine establishment." Henry patted Dodge on the back with a nod.

Fay reached behind her and set a sheet of shiny plastic in front of Dodge without a word. The menu consisted of just one laminated page that included the usual grilled cheese, burgers, and fries. At the bottom in big block letters it stated, *"Voted Best Hot Fudge Sundae in Shelby County"*. Dodge wondered who the other competitors were and exactly who had been doing the voting.

A bell rang out from the flat, narrow window in the wall behind the counter, followed by the cook's shout. Fay turned from them and picked up two plates before making her way out to the small seating area dotted with laminate chairs and tables.

The second waitress made her way toward them with a wide smile. She appeared to be a few years younger than Fay, her cheerful demeanor the exact opposite of her co-worker's. "Well, Mr. Wallace, what a surprise to see you here," she said brightly, winking at Dodge and setting a large glass of cola in front of Henry. He immediately began sucking down its contents through the wide straw that poked out from its plastic lid. "What can I get for you all this afternoon?" she asked brightly as she pulled a pen and a small tablet from the pocket of her apron.

Henry came up briefly from his soda for air. "Dottie, I am going to take my usual." He turned to Dodge. "You have to try the burgers, Dodge, they are just about the best you'll find anywhere. Not like that fast food garbage they serve out on highway two-eighty, either. And save room for dessert," he added, immediately leaning over his straw again to suck up the remainder of the sugary brown liquid.

Dodge nodded at Dottie. "I'll take a burger. And a water please."

Dodge looked around the busy room. The drugstore was much livelier than he would have expected judging from the outside, with people packed tightly around the small tables and others coming and going hurriedly from the front door to the counter. The diners Fay made her way slowly around in the dining area consisted of older retirees, while those who rushed in for their take-away orders appeared to be mostly business people in suits and ties. He watched Dottie smile as she handed them their crisp white bags of takeout burgers, without the need to ask their name or order before doing so.

Henry finished his soda and jingled the ice cubes in the empty cup toward Dottie. "Fay and Dottie have been working here for as long as I can remember. You want to find out anything in this town all you need to do is just ask them, because they hear it all." He leaned in toward Dodge. "Not that everybody else won't know as well, they just know it first."

Dodge watched as Fay leaned down toward the table she had just brought the plates to and listened to the diner carefully, glancing over at Dodge and Henry seated at the counter. As she made her way back to the counter Dodge shifted in his chair, and continued to watch her as she silently began scooping ice cream from a large tub into a long silver bowl.

Dottie set down a fresh glass of cola in front of Henry and handed Dodge his water. "What's news, Henry?" Dottie asked offhandedly, one hand on her hip, the other wiping the clean counter in front of her.

"Oh you know, just the usual." Dodge guessed this was some sort of game the waitresses would play with their customers, or perhaps their customers played with them. Dottie would ask for the news while Fay stood busy at her side within earshot of any fresh gossip. Henry put a hand on Dodge's shoulder. "Did I introduce my friend?" he asked, clearly knowing he had not.

Dottie held out a hand to Dodge as Henry smiled. "This is Dodge James Montgomery." He emphasized Dodge's middle name. "The grandson of Mr. Dodge William Montgomery."

"Is that right." Dottie shook Dodge's hand slowly across the counter. "Your granddaddy used to come in for lunch a few times a week. Tuna salad on white with the soup of the day. Didn't much care what the soup was, he always had a bowl. He also liked our sundaes of course, but as he got up in age he quit them."

Dodge nodded his head politely, not sure what he was supposed to make of his grandfather's lunchtime eating habits.

"Yup," she continued. "Quiet, but always polite. He never said more'n a few words, but always left a good tip. You can tell a lot about a person based on their tips, you know what I mean?" She made her way behind her to pick up the two plates that had just been brought to the window and set them down in front of Henry and Dodge. Henry immediately took a bite of his cheeseburger.

"You just get into town?" Dottie watched as Dodge took a bite of his own burger. He nodded and swallowed.

"Yesterday." He quickly took another bite to fill his mouth with food so as to not have to elaborate on an answer.

Dottie nodded her head. "My aunt used to work behind this counter, thirty years ago or so. She liked your granddaddy very much. Said he was quite a looker when he was a young man." She gave him a wink. "Said he must have lucked out and gotten his looks from his mama's side of his

48

family, because his daddy was a small, wiry man." She wrinkled her nose. "Your granddaddy was tall, like you. And handsome." She added, "Like you."

Dodge nodded, filling his mouth with another bite of his burger. He was not much interested in hearing a stranger's thoughts on a grandfather his own father hated, who had stripped his own father's room after his death and had forgotten all about him.

Dottie leaned in toward him from over the counter, brushing the white cotton cloth over the counter absently as she lowered her voice until he could barely hear her. "My aunt told me your grandaddy's daddy was a very cruel man. Didn't know how to treat his own kin or even his own wife. She may have lucked out when that tornado took her instead of leaving her with him." Dodge stopped, his jaw clenched open in mid-chew. Dottie straightened up and continued brushing the soft white cloth over the counter as she slowly moved to greet the next customer.

Henry worked on his burger in silence. Fay made her way back and forth from the window to the diners as Dottie worked behind the counter, making small talk from time to time with the other customers.

Henry finished his burger with a pat of his stomach. "Yes sir." It was the first time he had spoken since the plate was set down in front of him. "When I was younger I could eat four of these in one sitting. That was back in my college days playing ball though. Metabolism just isn't what it used to be I suppose."

"What kind of ball did you play," Dodge asked absently, only halfway through his own burger but unable to muster any more appetite after Dottie's odd words.

"Football, what else?" Henry said incredulously, as if shocked that he had needed to ask. "The only ball there is down here." He looked at Dodge. "Come fall that's all you're going to hear about around here. And rightly so. You need to have a team." He finished his second glass of cola. "Roll Tide or War Eagle?" He peered at Dodge intently.

Dodge shook his head as he swallowed a bite of his burger. "Excuse me?"

"Roll Tide or War Eagle," Henry repeated louder. "Alabama or Auburn?"

"I'm not really much into college football. Although I did have a roommate once who liked Michigan State, so I would watch them play every once in a while."

Henry threw his hands in the air. "Big Ten?" He snorted, slapping his hand down on the counter. "No, no, no. You need to pick a *team*, an SEC division team that's worth watching. And don't go pickin' one of them Georgia, Florida or Ole Miss nonsense teams. It's either Alabama or Auburn around here." He leaned in toward him. "I mean, Alabama is really the only team, of course."

Fay piped up from the end of the counter. "You better watch your mouth there Wallace." She pointed the metal ice cream scoop in his direction. "Everyone knows Auburn is going to take Alabama this year. Now that we have the quarterback to do it."

Henry waved his hand at her. "Y'all don't have no such thing. You just wish you did." Henry's voice had slipped into an even softer drawl, his demeanor clearly more relaxed when discussing football rather than dead relatives.

Dottie was standing before them again as well, ready to add in her own two cents. "Alabama is going to take it all the way to the National Championship again." She switched places with Fay and began scooping ice cream from the large tub on the counter in front of her. "I mean, everyone knows that," she added as she pumped warm hot fudge on top. She placed a bowl in front of both Dodge and Henry.

"This one's on the house, sugar," she said to Dodge, smiling. "You can't come to town without trying one of our famous hot fudge sundaes." She watched him intently as he took the first bite. Dodge was almost full from the burger, but he nodded his head in appreciation. Henry had quickly started in on his sundae, waving his spoon as he continued his banter with Fay on the Alabama-Auburn dispute.

"Y'all don't have but one good running back Miss Fay," he was continuing. "How you gonna get the ball down the field with just one

50

player to get it there while the rest of the team is back trying to figure out which end zone is their own?"

Fay shook her head. Dodge tuned out their conversation and began to eat his ice cream. He couldn't remember the last time he had had a real hot fudge sundae, and he savored the warm, dark chocolate mixed with the creamy white vanilla ice cream. Thinly sliced curls of glossy chocolate slid down from the top, melting into the hot fudge like bits of volcanic crust dissolving into warm, oozing lava. He pushed aside the gleaming pink cherry that Fay had perched atop a light mound of whipped cream and tunneled his spoon directly into the core, watching the dark liquid melt its way into the center of the silver bowl.

Within a few minutes Henry's spoon clinked against his empty metal bowl. He stood up and made his way to the register. "Lunch is on me." He laid a twenty-dollar bill on the register with a nod toward Dottie.

The afternoon had grown warmer, and Henry loosened his tie as they made their way down the sidewalk toward Dodge's truck. "Thank you for lunch, Henry. And I'll get this paperwork back to you as quickly as possible."

Henry waved his hand in the air. "No rush, no rush. You take your time. I will see you at the Garden Party, any questions you have we can go over then. That is, if you can remember by the time the evening is winding down." He laughed and opened the door to his offices. "Never mix business with pleasure, that's what I always say, but it should always be a pleasure doing business."

Dodge laughed silently to himself as he watched Henry amble down the sidewalk to his office. Dottie's words stuck out in his mind as he made his way to his truck. *She may have lucked out when that tornado took her instead of leaving her with him.* What kind of person would say such a thing? He shook his head as he climbed into his truck, the one safe, familiar place he still had in the world.

Chapter 4

Dodge switched off the GPS unit's robotic voice and relaxed into the seat as he began to drive aimlessly across the winding county roads leading out of town. Warm, sweet-smelling air, unspoiled by floods of exhaust, breezed in through the truck windows, mingling with the sharp scent of fresh cut grass and the soft hint of some wild blossom. A band of cotton white clouds hovered just above the horizon before him, silently slipping eastward across the sapphire sky.

All around him were shades of emerald and indigo broken only by the long gray pavement of road before him. As he drove he passed several large white wooden signs advertising nearby branches of local churches, their painted arrows pointing the direction to salvation to aimless wanderers like himself. Paint flecked mailboxes standing on thick wooden stakes marked the beginnings of long gravel drives leading to houses set too far back from the road to be observed.

What would it have been like to have grown up here, he wondered to himself. *To have grown old here. To die here. To have lived in one dwelling, the very same that your own father had been born in, and his father before him. Why had his father hated such a beautiful place so much that he had fled from it at just eighteen? And what long-forgotten secrets did the great aged house conceal in dust covered boxes and empty rooms?*

He turned the truck back towards his grandfather's house, thinking that perhaps he should take Earl up on his offer to stop by and meet his wife, Miss May. Earl had said he knew his father, and could possibly provide him with more information about his family. Even if his stay here was to be brief, he should at least make a proper introduction to the neighbors whose land abutted his own. Especially one that was such a good shot with a rifle.

He turned the truck into the drive next to his own, a small cloud of dust stirring up from the soft crunch of loose gravel under his tires. Mature trees spread out along the property, their branches pushing up and out at peculiar angles from thick gnarled trunks, some limbs missing altogether from old age, high winds, or strikes of lightning. The driveway wound up and along a daffodil-dotted hill leading to a small white house at the end. As he neared, two large brown dogs awoke from their noonday slumber to receive him, jumping from the porch and circling the truck with tails flapping and yelps of excitement.

On the porch sat Earl, a cigarette dangling from his lip as he squinted toward the truck as it made its way up the long drive. Dodge waved an arm out the window as he pulled closer, hoping Earl remembered him, and also hoping there wasn't a hunting rifle tucked behind one of the chair cushions if he did not.

"Get out of der boys," Earl yelled to the dogs as they jumped up to greet Dodge through his open window as soon as the truck came to a stop. Dodge slid from the driver's seat slowly and ruffled the thick fur on the dogs' heads.

"Those two knuckleheads. Be sure to check your back seat before you leave or you might find one of them with you when you get home." Earl stood up, pointing at the dogs. "Not that they won't make their way back like they always do." He swatted one of the dogs lightly on the rump as it bounded up the stairs to the porch. "C'mon in." He smiled to Dodge as he held open the rusty screen door behind him.

Inside, he followed Earl down a dark narrow hall that led toward the back of the house. The sound of Otis Redding and the smell of baking both floated from the bright kitchen at the end. In front of the stove stood a middle-aged woman, a faded yellow apron tied tightly around a cloud of housedress that billowed around her as she moved from the large steaming pot on the stove to a mound of vegetables on the counter. "Who is it, Earl?" she asked without turning. Earl moved a stack of newspapers from a kitchen chair and motioned for Dodge to sit.

"Why, it's mister Dodge Montgomery," Earl replied. She turned from the pot, wooden spoon in hand, her mouth gaping open and turning into a large smile when she saw Dodge.

"I don't mean to intrude on anything." Dodge gave Miss May a small wave as he entered the room.

"Well, I just." Miss May stammered as she looked down at the spoon in her hand and wiped her other along her apron. "My goodness. My goodness," she repeated, staring into his eyes.

"Don't you worry about intruding." Earl opened the refrigerator and pulled out two cans of beer. "Miss May's just concocting another one of her *secret* family recipes she gets out of one of them old cookbooks her mama gave her." Earl's shook the cans of beer in the air at the word "secret".

"You hush," she said sternly as she turned back to the stove. "I have told you before that these are just the simple recipes that require my refinement to make them into world-class dishes." She laughed haughtily as she peered over the pot into a worn cookbook propped up on the stove behind it. "You'll be sorry when I win one-million dollars in that baking contest and leave you for the life of *lux-u-ry*." She said the last word slowly, emphasizing each syllable with a wave of the wooden spoon over the pot.

"Aw, hush, Yankee," Earl said over the pop of the opening beer can. "You ain't winnin' no contest and you sure ain't livin' no life of," Earl paused for effect. "Lux-ur-eee. If it hadn't been for your mama leaving you those cookbooks, you wouldn't know the difference between a sweet potato casserole and a sweet potato pie."

"I don't seem to recall hearing you object when your mouth is full of my food."

54

Dodge looked at her quizzically as he sipped his beer. "Yankee?" He asked as he took a seat at the table across from Earl.

"Mm-hmm. He calls me a Yankee whenever he's fussin'. Or when he knows I'm right."

"Why is that?"

She smiled as she dried her hands on a worn kitchen towel tucked into her apron and moved toward the table. She began talking excitedly as she placed her hands on the back of Earl's chair.

"Mama was a huge fan of Jim Reeves – you know who he is." Dodge wasn't sure if she was telling him or asking him, but shook his head nonetheless. Miss May's jaw dropped as her eyes narrowed. "That man had a velvet voice that mama just loved. Oh, she was so tore up when she heard he had died in a plane crash up in Nashville. Flew right into that rain they said. So sad."

Earl cleared his throat.

Miss May shot him a glance before she continued. "Mama used to call into those radio shows when they ran their on-air contests. You know the ones, where the hundredth caller or what-not gets entered into a grand prize drawing for a chance to win tickets or something?" Dodge sipped his beer and nodded his head.

She sat down at the old worn table, pushing aside a pile of old Tupperware bowls and their haphazardly perched lids.

"This time it was a Jim Reeves concert in New York City including airfare, hotel, concert tickets -they were just givin' away the whole hog. Mama called every day and finally got through as the one hundredth caller. She was just so excited but she had to wait for the *big* drawing to take place to see if she was the *grand prize* winner of course."

She paused, looking at Dodge, as if he couldn't have already guessed who had indeed been the big winner. "And what do you know, she won!" Miss May clapped her hands together as if she herself had been the big winner. Earl rolled his eyes and took a long sip from his can.

"Well, mama hadn't even ever been outside of Alabama, let alone to somewhere like New York City. Problem was she was eight and a half months pregnant with me at the time. But that wouldn't stop mama. Daddy begged her to skip the concert and keep put but she would hear none of it. And Mama couldn't fly with her being so late in the pregnancy, so she and Daddy packed up his truck and they drove all the way up to see that concert."

Her eyes shone as she spoke. It was clear she had told this story many times before, and that it brought her immeasurable joy with each retelling.

"Mama musta been so excited at the concert after all," she continued. "Because what do you know, she starts getting labor pains right there. At the concert!" She leaned forward pressing both hands flat against the table. "Daddy near pitched a fit and was rushin' her to the truck yellin', 'I'll be darned if any child of mine is born outside of Dixie!'" Miss May waved her fist in the air in imitation of her father. "And he had to just about drag her to the truck with mama howling that she didn't want to miss the rest of the concert - Jim couldn't have gotten through but just a few songs by then - but Daddy was ready to high-tail it out of there."

"They made it as far as Pennsylvania and mama said, 'I just can't hold it in anymore!' and that's when Daddy got pulled over by the state trooper. Mama always said if it wasn't for that trooper catching up with them she would have near well had her first child in the back seat of Daddy's pickup truck." She let out a large laugh. "He got them to the hospital just in the nick of time, and out I come at four in the morning in Bethlehem, Pennsylvania." She was smiling brightly as she sat back in her chair breathlessly. "Can you believe that? Not only was their first child born in the North, I was born in the city named after the birthplace of our Lord and savior!"

Miss May looked at Dodge as if waiting for all of this to sink in. But she was not finished. "Of course Daddy begged mama not to tell anyone that their baby girl was born up North. He wanted her to tell them I was at least born in West Virginia. But mama was so proud that her baby girl had been born in Bethlehem, and just after a Jim Reeves concert that she just couldn't keep it to herself." She slapped the table as she let out another laugh. "And that's why that old coot calls me a Yankee. But I'm proud to say where I was born. Not like this old redneck." She patted Earl's hand gently.

"Pish." Earl waved his hand as if swatting away an annoying fly. "Don't matter what the name of the town was, you're still a Yankee," he said to her, but Dodge could see a faint smile on his face as he sipped his beer.

"And you." He pointed toward Dodge forcefully. "You, sir, are what we call a damn Yankee." He sat back in his chair with a smile.

Dodge looked at him quizzically. "How so?"

"Yankees are people who are born up North and come to the South for a visit. Damn Yankees are the ones who don't go home." Earl leaned back and slapped his knee soundly.

"Oh you hush," Miss May said with a shake of her head as she stood to make her way back to the stove.

Dodge nodded his head with a grin. "Actually I'm not sure how long I'll be staying around here anyway," he said. "So I may just be a regular old Yankee like you Miss May."

"What do you mean," she asked, her hand on her hip. "You got all that decent land, a nice big house, and a solid herd of healthy livestock that your granddaddy left you."

Dodge winced involuntarily at the reference to himself and a man he had never met. He traced his finger down a drop of condensation on the beer can. "I don't know anything about farming, or cattle, or any of that stuff. I think the best thing may be for me to just sell it off."

She set down the wooden spoon and looked at him. Earl had suddenly taken a deep interest in the list of ingredients on his own can and studied it carefully.

"Why, that land has been in your family for generations," Miss May said quietly. "Your granddaddy and his granddaddy. Montgomery family has always been there. That's your family's land. It belongs to you. You belong to it." She paused, turning back to her simmering pot and continuing to stir.

Earl looked up from his can. "You won't get much for it soon anyhow," he said with a sigh. "It's not like land around here is in high demand. Developers started buying acreage up off the highway about ten years ago and building their fancy developments. Four thousand square feet of house on a half-acre lot of good land that they tore all the top off just to replace with sod," he said with a push of air. "But that all fizzled out anyhow. They can't give that land away anymore. You drive back there behind those fancy gates and all you find is a few houses and a bunch of empty lots full of weeds and nothin'. I'm sure one of them will pay you something for that land, but seems a shame to give it away for nothing just to be rid of it." Earl nodded his head toward Dodge.

"I'm not really sure what I'm going to do with it, that's all." He wasn't up for a conversation about his newly acquired property, or the recently deceased person he had acquired it from.

Miss May pulled open the oven door and slid out two golden topped pies. She turned back to Dodge. "What you need to do is get down to the feed store and talk to Jake. He's been there for years, and knows all about livestock and what you're going to need for that cattle. I know Butler has been taking care of them by himself since your granddaddy passed, but you're going to need to get stocked back up on supplies."

"Butler is very good at what he does but he has his own peculiar way of doing some things," she continued as she set the pies on a wire rack on the counter. "I'm not saying he isn't correct, but I am saying that boy has had to make do with what the good Lord gave him and the good Lord did not give him much if you understand what I mean."

Earl laughed. "That's an understatement."

"You know it's most likely because of his mama and her not taking proper care of herself while she was pregnant," Miss May said as she cut into one of the warm pies. She turned to Dodge and lowered her voice. "She always liked the bottle more'n she liked her own children."

"As did his daddy," Earl said. "For as long as he was around anyway."

Dodge shifted uncomfortably in his chair. "I saw Butler this morning, in the barn outside the house. He said he can't work on the farm anymore, that he's got some other job lined up." Earl and Miss May exchanged a quick glance before she turned back to the pie. She began placing thick pieces onto small yellow plates. Dodge looked at Earl as he caught the look between them. "What?"

Miss May set the plates of pie on the table before them, and Earl quickly filled his mouth with a large bite.

"You're better off without him, anyway," Miss May said as she brought a plate for herself and sat down at the table.

Dodge picked up his fork and took a bite of the warm pie. The sweet taste of vanilla mixed with buttermilk melted in his mouth. "I figured he must know more about the place than I do, and I asked him to stay on, but he didn't seem too enthusiastic about the idea." Dodge recalled Butler banging the heavy mallet into the toolbox. *You don't look nothing like your granddaddy.* He took another hard bite of the pie. "Maybe he's just still shaken up over my grandfather's death. He said he's been working on the farm since he was a kid."

Earl nodded his head as he moved the fork around his plate. "Your granddaddy was usin' him more often when he started getting up in years. To do the heavy lifting and things around the farm he couldn't do anymore. Before then, he just mostly hung around the farm doin' odds and ends as far as I know. Seemed like he was always just around when he was younger." Earl stared at the wall behind Dodge's head as he continued. "That boy did not have the best life at his own home, and your granddaddy gave him something he never had, and wasn't going to have neither. A place to go, somewhere quiet where there wasn't all that drinking and yelling like at his place." Earl took a bite of pie and added offhandedly, "'Cept between him and James as he got older but it still wasn't nothing like what Butler had to deal with at his house."

Dodge looked up at Earl as he said his father's name. "Butler and my father?"

Earl looked up from his plate to Dodge's face and blinked once. For a brief moment as their eyes met, Earl stared at him blankly, as if his mind was recalling a scene from somewhere far off.

"You're a big strong man, you don't need the likes of Butler, anyway," Miss May interrupted. "That boy thinks he knows everything there is to know about anything, and in reality he doesn't know nuthin' about anything. Anyway, what you need to do is get yourself down to see Jake. Just don't wait until it's too late and he's out of hay for the season." She pointed her fork at him. "He'll help you out with finding someone to replace Butler."

Dodge finished his last bite of pie and looked back at Earl. "What else did you know about my grandfather? I mean, besides about the farm and all that." He looked at Miss May, who was staring at her own plate intently, then back at Earl who had gone back to reading his empty beer can, turning it in his hands against the kitchen table.

"Your granddaddy was a solid man," he said slowly. Dodge wanted to ask if he meant solid in build or in character but he waited for Earl to continue. "Folks around here tend to keep to themselves, but we still stick together as a community. Your granddaddy went to Four Mile Church every Sunday, and if a neighbor needed a hand he was there to help. He was a quiet man, and he kept to himself mostly. Especially after your daddy left." Earl stopped and looked at Dodge, his words saying perhaps too much and not enough.

Miss May sighed. "Don't nobody know what happened in that house after your grandmamma passed, and it ain't nobody's business, anyhow." She looked at Earl sharply. "Your granddaddy did the best he could after she died, but just as soon as your daddy could get gone he did, and he never came back. Except once." She said it sadly, as if it were her own son who had abandoned his family. "Lots of people around here like to talk about the past, like it's somewhere they can get back to. Your daddy wanted to forget the past altogether. That made him different than most folks around here and probably why he left in the first place."

"You knew my father?" His mouth was suddenly dry and he took a long swig from the beer can.

"Sure," Earl said carefully. "Your daddy was a friend of mine." He smiled and Dodge thought he saw a slight bit of sadness in his eyes. Dodge tried to picture the man in front of him with his father, a boy of just eighteen when he had left. "I'm sure there must be some pictures of him up in that big old house," Earl said quickly as he stood up and moved to the fridge to withdraw another can of beer.

"None that I've seen." Dodge pictured the large oil painting over the mantle. Now that he thought about it other than the painting he hadn't seen a single photo anywhere in the house. His mind wandered to the boxes sitting in the attic above the empty room.

"I am sure we can dig some up from somewhere," Miss May said brightly as she picked up the empty plates and took them to the sink. "Lord knows lots of people in this town knew your daddy and someone must have at least one photo of him for you."

Dodge realized that they knew as little about him as he knew about his own father, and suddenly he felt like the stranger he was sitting in their kitchen. "Thank you for the pie Miss May," he said standing up. "I think I should get back to the house and keep getting things in order." He wanted to make it sound like he was busy, when in reality there wasn't much of anything to take care of, except paperwork from lawyers. Again the image of the boxes and other dust laced items in the attic flashed through his mind.

"You come by whenever you like," she said, smiling as Earl stood up. Dodge followed him back down the hall to the front door. Once outside Earl sat down in the wooden rocker and reached for a pack of cigarettes on the table next to it.

"Thank you, Earl," Dodge said as he pulled the truck keys from his pocket. The dogs had awoken from their slumber with a surge of energy, moving around Dodge's legs with tails wagging as they bumped their thick heads against his thighs. "I appreciate you letting me drop by. And I appreciate any information you can give me about my family. I don't know much." He stopped and shrugged. "I don't know anything, I guess. But I'm not sure how much I really need to know."

Earl stared out at the land before him and took a long drag from the cigarette. Dodge squinted to make out the roof of his own house through the thicket of tall trees next to them. Earl blew a long stream of blue smoke from his mouth and stared at the dogs.

"You know those dogs don't even need to make a sound to communicate with one another," he said. As if sensing his gaze, both dogs stopped their bouncing and lay down lazily on the porch floor at his feet. "They say animals don't understand language, 'cept maybe that gorilla they gave that kitten to." He let out a short laugh and stared at his cigarette. The end glowed red as he inhaled deeply and blew a long line of smoke out into the air.

"Seems to me, what people don't understand is that animals don't need to be talkin' all the time. Chatterin' away about nuthin' the way humans always do. Animals know what's important in life. Food. Shelter. A good mate. What else is there to be talking about all the time anyway?"

"You hear these dogs barking in the middle of the night, it's 'cause there's somethin' out there in the woods, and they're lettin' whatever it is know it's best not to come around here. They ain't even tellin' each other – 'cause they know the other one already knows it too. They're not talkin' nonsense with one another, 'cause they know the more time they spend makin' noise that's time they're not listening." He sat back in his chair. "And if they ain't listenin' they ain't gonna hear that pack of coyotes before it's too late."

"Listen." He looked at Dodge carefully. "There are a lot of stories in this town. Some of them you might want to hear, and some of them, well…" He stopped and looked out across the porch again thoughtfully. "Unfortunately, you may not always get to decide which ones you get. Folks around here like to talk. About themselves, about one another, about just about anything." He trailed off as he flicked his cigarette absently from the porch. "Go talk to Jake about the livestock. The first thing you need to do is make sure those animals are taken care of. Your granddaddy would've wanted that. The rest you'll learn when you need it."

Dodge nodded and walked down the steps toward his truck. He turned to wave as he opened the door but Earl had already gone back inside, the screen door slamming shut behind him.

Chapter 5

The sun was beginning its languid descent into an auburn liquid horizon as Dodge slowly pulled the truck into his grandfather's drive. In his haste to depart that morning he had neglected to leave on a single light, and he felt the same unease from the evening before as he slowly made his way up the darkening drive.

As he opened the door he paused before switching on the imposing chandelier overhead. It was as if with each entrance he expected someone to come rushing from one of the darkened rooms to protest his arrival; that this was their place and he had no right to be in it. But again he was met only with silence as he shut the heavy door slowly behind him.

He made his way upstairs, a duffle bag tucked under each arm. Turning on the light in the first bedroom he set the bags on the bed, still made up neatly for its last rightful occupant. He sat on the edge of the crisp white duvet and opened the drawer of the nightstand. Inside sat a pair of reading glasses and a heavy black bible, the edges of its leather cover worn with wear. As he picked it up a small yellowed card fell from its pages to the floor and he reached down to retrieve it. On one side was a majestic winged angel, her arms outstretched and a soft yellow glow surrounding her head. He turned it over to read the inscription on the back.

In Loving Memory of Fiona McKay Montgomery, it read. *February 20, 1943 – June 29, 1968. We celebrate your life and your love, as you are welcomed home into the arms of Jesus Christ, Our Lord. Waldronson Funeral Home.*

Dodge rubbed his thumb gently across the worn face of the card. He did not know who Fiona Montgomery was, or why his grandfather had kept her memorial card in a bible next to his bed. He gently tucked the card between the pages and placed the heavy book back in the drawer before shutting it soundly.

As he brushed his teeth he mused over who Fiona could be. It occurred to him that other than his father and grandfather he didn't know the name of a single other relative from his father's side of the family. Could she have been his grandmother? The date of her death was just five years after his father had been born. Had his father lost his own mother at such a young age? *Your granddaddy did the best he could after she died.* Miss May's words floated hauntingly in his ear. Dodge remembered the pain of his own mother's passing when he was just twenty-three. Had the two of them lived here together with that same hurt?

He made his way from the bathroom back into the bedroom before falling into the soft bed. The thought crossed his mind of changing the bed sheets, but after his uncomfortable sleep in the truck the night before his exhaustion prevailed over rummaging through closets. As he lay his head on the cool pillow he expected his mind would be racing, but he found it was not. The room was quiet and serene, the only sound the gentle whoosh of air from the air-conditioning coming from the floorboard. *Fiona.* The name wandered softly through his head, and was the last thing he thought of before drifting off to sleep.

No bothering alarm broke through to lift him from dim smoky dreams. He opened his eyes to muted rays of sunlight gently summoning him to day. The room was no longer heavy, and as he sat up from under the supple cotton sheets that had enveloped him during the night he realized he had slept through without waking, something he hadn't done in a long time. He fell back again into the pillow, and lay for a few moments, the only sound a soft tapping from the bathroom as water dripped slowly from the faucet into the sink.

He made his way groggily to the bathroom and opened the linen closet to search for fresh towels. On the shelves sat the remains of a man's personal care items; an electric shaver, a tall green bottle of aftershave, boxes of toothpaste and soap. More reminders that this place had very recently belonged to someone else. Dodge did not touch them, or line his items up neatly beside them, instead leaving his own in the duffel bag on the floor.

After fumbling with the coffee maker he stared out from the kitchen's wide windows at the land before him as he sipped the bitter black coffee. He did not, as he had told Henry, have any actual prior engagements to get back to in the city. From the paperwork Henry had provided he knew that the land surrounding the house totaled seventy acres, most of it pastures and woodland. He was not, by nature, one prone to long walks through forest and meadows, but perhaps a walk could help shake the lingering feeling that he was an awkward trespasser intruding on someone else's property.

As he descended the front steps, he paused to listen. To his left, beneath the eaves, hung a set of long, delicate wind chimes. This was the first time he heard them as they gently swayed with a breeze, the long, hollow shafts of metal gently brushing against one another to create a soothing sound. From the trees overhead a pair of large black crows shrieked out warning cries to one another as a hawk lazily circled the blue sky above them. Far off a cow bellowed a long, low wail, and closer he could make out the gentle humming of fat black bees that hovered over bright yellow flowers lining the porch railing. Unlike the bleating horns,

65

bells, and sirens that vehemently intruded into his thoughts when he was in the city, these sounds did not assault his ears, rather they combined into one harmonious agreement.

He followed the wide porch along the east side of the house. A long, thick row of hydrangea bushes clustered against its side, their fat blue clusters of delicate blooms imploring one to lean down and breathe in their heady scent. Farther beyond the house a worn wooden fence rambled its way around a small pasture. Here stood yet another barn, smaller than the one he had met Butler in the day before. As he entered, the biting aroma of animal urine and manure struck his nose and he involuntarily grimaced. Inside, four straw covered horse stalls lined each side. Large halters and ropes hung from rusted metal pegs on the walls.

He made his way hesitantly across the concrete floor, peering into each stall to find it empty, the only sign of its inhabitants a pile of hay in each corner. As he poked his head from over the half door of the last stall he turned to find himself standing face to face with an enormous brown horse, its dark, glasslike eyes watching him intently. He fell back instinctively, catching himself against the wall behind him.

"Whoa," he shouted loudly as he steadied himself against the wall. The horse did not move, continuing to stare at him silently as it flicked its ears back and forth. Dodge stood still as it leaned its nose in to smell the collar of his shirt and let out a small snort. He had never been this close to such a large animal, and certainly not alone. The only horses he could recall were the ones in Central Park, silently and obediently tethered to carriages. They did not roam free, silently creeping up on people from behind and scaring the wits out of them.

"Whoa there, buddy," Dodge said, slowly pushing himself up from the wall. The horse turned its head slightly as he did, but still did not move its massive body. He gently put his hand out toward it. "What's your name?" Dodge asked as he ran his hand down the animal's long nose. The horse stood motionless, watching him calmly. "Yeah, that's a good boy. Girl?" Dodge said as he moved slowly around to the horse's side. The horse's eyes followed him, and he gently patted its silky hair.

66

He looked up through the doorway behind them to see three more horses, each watching him with the same silent glaze, their tails flicking at the air behind them. Their stance did not convey any nervousness, rather a slight curiosity about the man in their barn. Dodge slowly crept his way along the wall, slipping back out the way he had entered. As he crossed the pasture he noticed a large black trough filled with water and behind that a large round bale of hay in the middle of a metal feeder. Dodge surmised that Butler had at least made sure the animals had food and water before he had left so abruptly the morning before.

He made his way past the barn, crossing through the fence to a sloping field behind it. A narrow stream trickled down toward a line of trees that thickened into a dense wood. He paused and pulled out a piece of paper from his back pocket. It was a survey of his grandfather's property that he had found in the paperwork Henry had provided. He followed along the edge of the creek, moving toward the far north side of the property. Before entering the dark woods, he turned to look at the house behind him, sitting imposingly at the top of the gently sloping hill. Its dark windows gaped back at him, caring not whether he stayed or went.

He picked his way gently through the overgrowth and the tall, gnarled trees around him. The only sounds were his own, the crunch of brittle leaves and the snapping of small twigs and branches beneath his shoes, and his own heavy breathing as his lungs pushed out and pulled in the warm air around him. He soon found himself on a quiet tree lined road and again pulled out the paper to assess where he was. Country Road 43. He walked along the edge of the road running alongside what he guessed to be the western edge of the property. It was quiet here on the road, no cars thundering along to their destinations.

He stopped, squinting forward at the road ahead of him. Farther up, a deer stood silently on the side of the road, dipping its head to chew on tufts of bright green grass. It raised its head and chewed silently, watching him approach. As he drew closer it did not move away, and he slowly realized it was not a deer after all. While he was certainly no nature enthusiast, he could tell this animal was much larger, its patches of dark brown and white fur unlike that of any deer he had ever seen on television or in the movies.

He continued walking toward it, slowing his stride. The animal lifted its head to gaze up at him now and then, still unfazed at his approach. When he got within a few yards the animal turned its elongated neck to stare at him with large, bulging eyes. Bits of grass stuck out from its mouth while it chewed thoughtfully, as if it too was assessing the situation before him.

From behind he heard the gravel crunch of an approaching car. The animal lifted its head higher to peer at it curiously. He turned to see a small silver Toyota making its way slowly down the road toward them. Dodge waved his arms to alert the driver to the animal's presence, and the car came to a slow stop. A middle aged man emerged from the driver's side door, his suit and tie peculiarly out of place against the background of this location.

"Is that your llama?" the man yelled to Dodge, standing behind the open door of the vehicle.

Dodge turned back to study the animal. "No," he yelled back. He thought quickly, "At least I don't think so." Up until this morning he didn't know that he owned four horses. Maybe he did own a llama.

The man yelled back to him. "Looks like the same one that got out a few weeks ago." The man reached back into his car. He pulled out a long leather dog leash and walked slowly towards Dodge, keeping a watchful eye on the llama. It continued pulling small clumps of grass into its mouth, entirely uninterested in their conversation.

"Listen, I've got a dog leash here. See if you can get it around its neck." The man approached Dodge slowly and threw the leash toward him. "Make a loop out of the end of it. Keep it up high by his ears though."

Dodge stepped over and picked the leash up from the road. He hesitated for a moment, wondering if he was really here, standing in the middle of a remote country road trying to lasso a llama.

"Put out your other hand as you approach it! Make it think you have a treat or something and it should come right up to you."

Dodge moved toward the animal slowly, one arm extended out with his palm upright as the man had instructed. He held the dog leash tightly behind his back.

"That's it," he could hear the man say. "Talk to it softly as you approach. And don't let it see the leash."

Dodge continued walking forward slowly, one arm extended, as the llama continued to chew casually on the grass in its mouth, seemingly unconcerned with Dodge or his plan.

"OK, now stop. Keep your arm out, make it come to you."

He was less than a few feet from the sizeable animal. It raised its head, towering its height to match his own. From afar he had not realized how massive it actually was, and standing this close he was having second thoughts about his ability to persuade it into the leash.

He kept his arm out straight as the man had instructed and the llama turned toward him slowly. It circled him, keeping its head held high, and slowly made its way closer to his outstretched hand. It reached its head down and sniffed, then moved closer to place its face next to his. Dodge took the opportunity to gently wrap the leash around its neck.

"Keep it up by its ears, and don't pull too tight. Just make sure you stay calm." The man made his way over to Dodge, standing on the side of the road holding the leash while the again apathetic llama bent down to continue his brunch.

"You did real good!" He patted Dodge on the back.

Dodge nodded, letting out a long breath. "Yeah, for my first time apprehending a llama." He watched the enormous animal as it continued to eat. "Is it yours?"

"God no," the man replied, shaking his head. "I had to catch it on this same road a few weeks ago while I was on my way to work. Little bugger didn't let me get that close to him that easily though." The man extended his hand. "Martin Pearson. I live just a few miles from here."

"Dodge," he replied as he shook his hand. "I guess you're familiar with these animals?" The adrenaline coursing through his veins was slowly beginning to die down.

"No sir," Martin shook his head. "That little bastard spit on me the first time I tried to catch him."

"Thanks for the warning." Dodge took a small step away from the animal.

"Sorry, I don't have as much experience with animals as you all do out here. I just moved out this way a few years ago. To get away from the city." He smiled again at Dodge. "I'm a professor at UAB," he said, then explained when he noticed Dodge's perplexed look. "University of Alabama at Birmingham. You know, in Birmingham?" He looked at Dodge quizzically.

"And you live all the way out here?"

"Yep. It's just a bit more peaceful out this way. I bought a little house on a few acres a couple of years ago. Nothing big, just enough for me and some room for my dogs to run. I do consider myself an animal lover though. That's why I caught and returned this guy last week." He moved toward the llama and patted its side. It raised its head, pushing its nose up in the air while it looked down at him and he took a step back.

"What do you teach?" Dodge continued to watch the llama, still unsure of the large creature.

"Biomedical Engineering," Martin replied as he leaned over beside the llama and peered underneath. "Yep, this is the same one as last week. It's got the same bald patch on its stomach. See here?" He pointed at the underside of the animal.

Dodge pretended to peer at the animal's stomach. "Biomedical Engineering sounds pretty intense."

Martin shrugged as he stood up. "The first year is a lot of chemistry, engineering, calculus, physics. Then we get into the bio-imaging, biological transport phenomena, biomechanics. You know, the usual."

Dodge shook his head. "Sounds… interesting."

Martin nodded. "Oh it is. Did you know that in the early eighteen-hundreds a French doctor couldn't place his ear on a young woman's bare chest to listen to her heart? Back then that would have been considered immodest. So he took a newspaper, rolled it up, and took a listen. And that young doctor ended up inventing the stethoscope. Pretty neat, huh?" He shrugged. "It's all about knowing the human body and applying engineering applications when needed. Speaking of..." He looked down at his watch. "I've got to be headed to work."

"What do we do with this?" Dodge held up the end of the leash.

"It probably lives just up the road. A woman there owns a bunch of them. Her name is Anne. It's just a left onto fifty-five and her place is about a half mile up on the right." He motioned toward the road ahead of them.

"So how do we get him back?"

Martin laughed. "You get to walk him up there," he said, moving back to his car. "Sorry my friend, I had to take him back last week and I have a class I need to make."

"What about your leash?" Dodge yelled as Martin quickly started the car and slowly started to roll past.

Martin did not appear to hear him, and gave a quick wave out the window as he drove off.

Dodge watched as the car turned onto the road ahead of him. He stood for a moment and looked around, half expecting a camera crew to burst from the bushes and let him in on the prank they had just filmed. The llama stared at him as it slowly chewed a mouthful of leaves, its bottom teeth protruding out of its mouth like an old man's ill-fitted dentures.

"Well, buddy, I guess it's just you and me." He tugged lightly on the leash as he started walking. The animal seemed to understand, and slowly followed along behind him, stopping at intervals to refill its mouth with grass and leaves.

They made their way out to the road and turned left as Martin had instructed. He walked along the edge of the road on the right hand side, as he had been taught to do when riding a bike. He wasn't sure what the procedure was when one was walking their llama, but assumed it to be the same.

As they neared the first drive, Dodge could make out a cheerful llama decorating the mailbox. Like the surrounding properties this too started with a long winding gravel drive that led toward the back of the property. They slowly made their way up the drive, the llama walking next to Dodge as if it was showing him where to go.

Farther up the drive he could make out a brightly colored barn, and as he neared several llamas crept from its interior, their tall pointed ears pushed forward as they stared at the duo with uncertainty. Unable to curtail their curiosity, they lumbered slowly from the barn toward them. Dodge's llama sniffed at them, his head held high in the air in a stately manner, and the entire herd followed them slowly along the fence toward the house.

As they approached the house the front door burst open and a small woman rushed down the steps toward them. "William!" she yelled out. Dodge paused, unsure if perhaps she had mistaken him for someone else.

Her long brown hair was pulled back into a tight ponytail, and her smiling face was a mixture of concern and relief. Her grass-stained jeans were tucked into her worn leather boots, and in her hand she held a long lead rope and a small halter, which she gently placed over the llama's nose, fastening it behind his ears. "You are just so mischievous, aren't you, William Henry Harrison?" She spoke to the llama in a mock stern voice. She continued to talk soothingly to it as she fitted the halter in place and removed the leather dog leash from behind his ears, handing it to Dodge.

"Thank you so much. He just keeps escaping. He must be jumping the fence." She spoke rapidly, all the while caressing the llama's neck as it hummed quietly at the others. "Do you know I put in a five-foot high fence just because of him, and they're not even supposed to want to jump over it, but I guess you just never know what an animal wants to do or where they want to go." She wiped a few stray hairs from her makeup-less face as she looked up at him.

"I wouldn't know," Dodge said to her as he tucked the leash into the back pocket of his jeans. "This was my first time catching a llama." He held out his hand. "I'm Dodge. I'm staying just down the road and I found him..."

The woman cut him off as she took his hand tightly in her own. "Dodge Montgomery's grandson! They have been talking about your impending arrival for weeks down at the feed mill," she said, shaking his hand vigorously. "Oh my word, I can't believe you had to catch my llama your first week here," she said, covering her mouth and laughing. "That is truly embarrassing."

"It wasn't any trouble at all, really," he said, caught off guard that even more people had known of his coming when he himself had made the decision so hastily. "I was just out for a walk around the property when I spotted him in the road."

"I'm Anne," she said, moving the llama away from a cluster of wildflowers he was chewing on contentedly as the others watched enviously. "Listen, let me put him in the barn and I will be right back." She pulled the llama gently away from Dodge. "Don't go anywhere!"

Dodge looked around him. The llamas that had followed him up the drive were still clustered along the fence next to him, eyeing him warily. He took a step back, careful to keep his distance after the warning from Martin about the spit.

Anne returned and stood beside him. "Aren't they gorgeous?" she asked as she stepped forward and stroked one on the nose. "That there is Millard Fillmore, and that's Franklin Pierce, and the tan one is Chester Arthur." She pointed at each llama as she spoke.

"You named them after presidents?"

Anne nodded her head. "That's right. The boys at least. The ladies are named after the presidents' wives. Of course." She pointed toward a small patch of land behind the house. "They're wandering around here somewhere." She paused before adding sheepishly, "It's a little quirky, I know."

She turned from the group of llamas and looked up at Dodge, her arm hooked over the fence. "I really am so embarrassed to be meeting you for the first time like this. How did you know where to bring him back to?"

"I met Professor Pearson. He said he caught him and brought him back last week."

Anne laughed. "What are the chances? I guess maybe that little bugger is out finding me men. "What did you think of Martin?"

"He seemed nice enough."

Anne nodded. "He struck me as one of those egg-head types, but I guess he should. He teaches at UAB you know."

Dodge nodded. "Yes. Biomedical engineering."

"Is that right?" Anne said slowly as she looked out at the pasture. "I did not know that." She looked up at Dodge. "Listen, c'mon inside," she said as she moved from the fence. "I would very much appreciate it if you would join me for lunch to thank you for bringing my llama back."

"You don't have to do that, really." Dodge suddenly felt awkward as yet another stranger offered him food.

"No really, it would make me feel better, since you had to walk him all the way back," she said, moving toward the house. "C'mon, it's always good to meet a new neighbor. And I can let you in on a few things around here," she said as she made her way up the steps and opened the front door. "We foreigners have to stick together," she said with a wink.

"Foreigners?" Dodge asked quizzically as he followed her up the steps.

"Why yes, darling," she said as they entered. Her house did not appear to be as old as other homes in the area, and while it wasn't large the interior was comfortable. "When it comes to people around here if you're not Alabama born and bred you might as well be from another country."

As they entered the smell of food wafted from the kitchen. Anne made her way to the oven and lifted out a small casserole dish. "I don't cook a whole lot, but when I do it's nice to have someone to share it with. Please sit." She motioned toward the round kitchen table next to him.

"How long have you lived here?" Dodge asked as he took a seat.

"Oh, not long." She paused, as if trying to remember. "I guess nearing on ten years."

"That's quite a while." Staying in one place for ten years was almost unheard of to him.

Anne shook her head. "Not to the folks around here. Most of them have lived here their entire lives, and they're generations from being the first." She set the plates down and sat opposite him, scooping heaps of

74

casserole out of the dish. "As you can probably tell from the lack of a southern accent I am not an Alabama native. It's always a dead giveaway. There's just something that reverberates in that southern speech that you just can't acquire, no matter how long you live here."

"I suppose," Dodge said as he picked up his fork and took a bite of the casserole. "This is really good."

"It's spectacular," Anne said, smiling. "Chicken Spectacular actually. It's a recipe I found a few years ago."

"So how did you end up here?" Dodge asked as he continued to eat. He looked up from his plate. "If you don't mind me asking."

"It's actually kind of a funny story," Anne said as she slowly took a bite of casserole. "I don't generally tell a lot of people. Although around here you don't need to tell a whole lot of people anything in order for everyone to already know." She looked at him as she trailed off. She set her fork down next to her plate and leaned in. "I won the lottery," she said in a hushed voice.

Dodge sat motionless for a moment, a forkful of casserole resting in mid-air. "Like, *the* lottery?"

"Yup. Not here in Alabama though. They don't have a state lottery. I think gambling is too close to the devil's work for them." She laughed.

"I was born in Ohio. At the time I was," she paused, trying to choose or exclude her words carefully. "I was in a relationship that I just couldn't seem to get out of." She looked up from her plate at him. "My boyfriend liked to drink and hit things." She stated it factually without elaboration, no hint of a desire for pity. Dodge could feel himself tense.

"I was young then," Anne continued. "I didn't know any better." She paused and looked up. "No, that's not true, I knew better. You can't put out a fire out with gasoline just because it's a liquid."

"Anyway, I was working a typical dead-end job, not enough to live on but not enough to leave. But I liked it. I went home one Friday night after I had pulled a double." She picked up her fork and moved the food around her plate absently. "My boyfriend had gotten home from yet another night of drinking. We argued and he started," she paused and stopped pushing

75

the casserole around her plate. She looked up at Dodge. "You know when you realize that there's a moment when you've had enough?" Dodge nodded slowly. Anne continued. "For me that moment was when I had yet again locked myself in a bedroom, listening to furniture crashing and walls being punched in. I had had enough. Not just the drinking and the screaming. Enough of everything right there in that room."

Anne paused and looked down at her plate again. "So when he finally passed out I grabbed my purse and my keys and I got the hell out of there. And I decided there was no way in hell I was ever going back. Not ever."

"So there I was, with just the money I had in my purse, nowhere to go, and less than a half a tank of gas. I just got on the highway and kept driving. I headed south, thinking I would just keep driving till maybe I hit Florida. It was winter, and Florida sounded nice right about then." She looked up at him, her sad hint of a smile not able to hide a concealed ache. "It was so cold, and I just wanted to be warm again."

He could see the traces of a memory in her eyes, and for a brief moment felt a familiar commonality with her. "I made it all the way into Kentucky before I started running out of gas. So I pulled into a gas station and I turned off my car and I just sat there. I didn't know what I was doing, or where I was really going. I hadn't been outside of Ohio except maybe a handful of times. And never by myself. So I started praying. Now I was not, and am not, a religious person, mind you. It was just…" She paused and looked around the room, shaking her head. "There was nothing else left to do."

"So there I was, sitting in my car praying to God to just give me a little something, anything." Anne looked at Dodge again and smiled. "And that's when, I swear to the Lord above, the neon lotto sign in the store window right in front of my car just started going haywire. Zapping away, sparks flying everywhere, like a thousand bugs hitting one of those bug lights all at one time. For a second I thought it was going to explode right in front of me and I was going to die right there in the car. I figured, wouldn't that be something, if I had asked God for a sign and an actual sign exploded and killed me? And in the next second I thought, *Dear Lord that is not what I meant, I don't want to be taken from this earth."* She laughed and took another bite from her plate. "And then it just went out. Just like that." She snapped her fingers. "So I figured I should go in and buy a lottery ticket, and that's just what I did. I got one of those scratch-off kinds, the real expensive ones no one ever buys. *'Millionaire Spectacular'* it was called."

Dodge sat back in his chair. "And you won?"

"And I won. One million dollars off of that little ticket."

Dodge whistled. "That's a lot of money." He remembered his own shock at the staggering figure on the piece of paper Henry had handed him the day before.

"You're darn right it is. I filled up my tank with all the money I had in my purse and I took that ticket and drove as far as I could get that night. And guess where I ended up? In Alabama. I think I was supposed to go into Georgia to get to Florida, but I didn't know where I was going and I was just so excited and overwhelmed that I had just kept on driving. The sun was coming up and I headed off the highway to try to turn around, but for some reason I just kept going. And then I saw the most beautiful place I had ever seen in my life." She was looking off over Dodge's shoulder again as she spoke.

"It was this land right here. I figured my boyfriend would never guess that I would move to Alabama of all places, and he didn't know about the lotto ticket. So I went back up to Tennessee to cash it in, then I came back and bought myself this little piece of land and I built this house on it. Then I went and bought some llamas, just because that's what I wanted, and no one could tell me I couldn't. And I've been here ever since." Anne finished and looked at Dodge.

"That is an amazing story."

Anne nodded her head. "Kind of a little like yours I suppose. I heard your grandfather didn't even know he had a grandson, and now here you are, in Alabama of all places."

Dodge stared at the table, tapping his fork against the side of his empty plate. He hadn't even known the names of the neighbors in his apartment building who lived on the other side of the wall, let alone whether or not they had a long lost grandchild or eight million dollars to give him. "What I don't understand is how everyone knows so much about my family?"

Anne shook her head with a smile. "Everyone in this town knows everything about everyone. You can't blow your own nose without someone telling you what color it's going to be. Seems like everyone's been waiting to see what the young Dodge Montgomery looks like."

"I really wish they wouldn't. I mean, I'm not that interesting." His voice was flat. "Is there so little going on around here that I'm the big news?"

"Oh you'd be surprised at how much goes on around here," Anne said, raising her eyebrows. She shrugged. "It's different here Dodge. People have to pay attention to each other out here. I mean, look around. Everyone lives so far from their neighbor you need to find somewhere to meet up with some folks and chatter a little gossip every now and then. It just happens that you're the best gossip this week. This year maybe." Her face broke out in a wide grin. "But that'll change. A few weeks from now someone's bull will get loose or one of the ladies in the bridge club will leave her husband and you'll be pushed to the back burner."

Dodge shook his head. "I hope so. I don't have any interest in being anyone's gossip, that's for sure."

"Oh but it's not just gossip. People here have a lot of pride in their community. It's important for them to know what's going on, and to share information with each other. Think about it. You have all that cattle up there on your property. Mr. Hilton up there behind you, he's got cattle too. What if his cows started dropping like flies, from some sort of disease or parasite? What if there was a pack of wild dogs killing young calves? You'd want to know about that, wouldn't you?"

"Of course," Dodge replied, although it occurred to him he hadn't yet had time to even think about the care of his grandfather's herd.

"See there, if you head over to the feed mill, why you might meet up with Mr. Hilton, and you might get to talking about those things. And of course you might throw in a little gossip of course." Anne winked at him.

"Listen, when I got here," she continued, "people thought I was nuts. A woman from up North building a house on a piece of land way out here? I'm pretty sure it was almost unheard of. I had never even shot a gun before I got here." She sat back and folded her arms across her chest. "But they didn't realize that I was way more afraid of going back to living the life I had been living than whatever might get me out in those woods."

"What could get you out in the woods?" Dodge shifted uncomfortably in his chair.

"Wild boar, a pack of coyotes. Some people around here swear there's a mountain lion roaming around. Plenty of people claim to have seen it with their own eyes. And that's not even taking into account the fire ants, or the black widows, and brown recluse spiders." She continued rattling off predators like ordinary shopping list items. "Then there's the copperheads and the cottonmouths. Oh, and rattlesnakes, of course."

Dodge felt a shiver race down his spine as he recalled his leisurely walk through the woods earlier. Anne noticed and laughed again. "See, sweetie, it's not just the southerners that want to keep the northerners out. The whole eco-system is set up to destroy us."

"Everyone has been friendly enough to me so far." He hoped to change the subject while making a mental note to take the road home rather than going back through the woods.

"Oh sure, they're friendly. Just about the friendliest people you'll ever meet. It's just..." Anne's voice broke off. "If you're not from here then you're never going to be from here. It'll be different for you though, because your family has lived here for so long." She paused and added softly, "Must be weird having the same name as your grandfather, though."

"You have no idea. Everyone seems to know everything about my family, except me."

"I met him, once," Anne said as she scooped the last bit of casserole from her plate into her mouth.

79

"You mean my grandfather?"

She nodded her head. "Yes, at one of the Garden Parties. It was a few years ago. I don't think he went every year. He seemed like a very nice man. Quiet, but polite. I remember I was heading to the bar and asked him if he needed a drink. He smiled and told me he didn't drink anymore. Seemed like he said it in sort of a sad way, though." Anne looked up at Dodge. "I don't know much about him. I would see him around town every once in a while. He was always by himself."

"Sounds lonely."

Anne shrugged. "I don't know. No one ever said a bad word about him that I heard. I think he just kept to himself. All alone in that big house up there." She shook her head as her voice trailed off. "I can't imagine one person living there all alone."

Dodge nodded as he thought about the large rooms empty of sound and body. "Tell me about it."

"Is it spooky?" Anne asked with a mischievous smile. "It's like a hundred years old or something, isn't it?

"Older than that, apparently." He recalled Millie's story about his great-grandfather. He also remembered his first visit to the house the night he had arrived, and how he had slept in his own truck. "It's not that bad really," he added, feeling a sudden twinge of guilt at not defending the grand home's honor.

Anne nodded her head. "You'll do alright here Dodge. You'll start meeting people, and they'll tell you everything you need to know. And then some." She stood up from the table. "If you think women like to talk, you haven't met a cattleman. Let me tell you something, those are real men. They can lift a bale of hay over their head like it was a baby, rope an eight hundred pound cow, and shoot a coyote from a hundred yards away. But you get them started gossiping and they will start clucking like a bunch of hens." Anne laughed again. "But don't you worry, they're good people."

Dodge wiped his mouth with a napkin. "Like I said, I'm not one for gossip. I think I'm going to try to keep to myself as much as I can while I'm here."

Anne laughed. "Good luck with that, sweetheart." She picked up his empty plate from the table. "If there is one thing a Southerner loves about as much as Jesus it's a good story. Sometimes I wonder how anyone down here even has a conversation, 'cause once you get one of them talking nobody can get a word in edgewise."

"I guess I'll be meeting some of the town people this weekend. I got an invite to that Garden Party you mentioned."

"Oh, yes. It is *the* social event of the season. Look at you getting an invitation so soon upon your arrival," she teased him.

"The lawyer suggested I go. I'm guessing everyone wants to see the new Dodge Montgomery in the flesh," he said dryly.

"Oh, I'll bet they do. Don't worry about anyone..." she paused awkwardly and looked at him, "...not accepting you."

"Because I'm a *foreigner,* like you?" he asked with a smile.

"Right." Anne laughed gently.

"I'm not worried. I'm not sure how long I'll be here anyway. I'm just stuck here until the estate stuff gets settled."

"That should be just enough time for you to meet a few people. And who knows, you just might like it here Dodge. I did. I'm never going back," she said, looking off again.

"Will you be at the Garden Party?"

She nodded. "Yes. I usually hate those types of events, but they really go all out for it. You did bring your tuxedo, didn't you?" Anne smiled. Dodge frowned and shook his head. A tuxedo was not an item of clothing he owned, or ever planned to.

"Don't worry, you can go down to see Mary. She'll have one available this late. She owns the consignment shop in town, right on Main Street, which also serves as the only formal wear store in town as well. You do not want to show up to the Garden Party in a tuxedo that was not provided by Mary. You will most definitely be the talk of the town if you do that."

Dodge looked at her quizzically. "Consignment shop? Like used clothing?"

Anne nodded. "Only the very best in town. You'd be surprised at her store though. Very fashionable. I think she brings in her formal wear from Paris or something. She's a very stylish old broad."

"I guess I'll have to add it to my list of places to go." He sighed as he glanced down at his phone to check the time. "Thank you for your time, Anne, really. It's been nice to talk to someone here who can empathize a little with my strange situation." He stood up, looking around the small, warm kitchen Anne had built in this small, strange town.

"Anytime." She followed him to the door. "Do you want me to drive you back to your place? It'll only take a minute."

"Nope," Dodge said, opening the screen door. The afternoon air was even warmer, and the sun was still high in the sky. "I think I'll walk off that spectacular chicken." He rubbed his stomach with a smile.

"You know where to find me if you need anything. And where to bring any escaped llamas back to," Anne joked, waving as he headed down the drive.

"I certainly do," he said as he waved and made his way back home.

Chapter 6

The next morning Dodge moved through the lower floor of the house unlatching the windows and sliding each open one by one. The heavy curtains remained stoic as a warm breeze made its way through the front windows and out the back, refusing to bluster about like stuffy old maids enrobed in heavy clothes. He inhaled deeply as the scent of new grass and wildflowers stole its way through each room, mocking the stale heavy air with their aroma.

When he reached his grandfather's office he paused and sat down at the large wooden desk. Neat rows of papers and books lined the edges on each side. There was no computer, just an ancient adding machine with a thick roll of paper yellowing along the edge. He picked up one of the stacks and leafed through what appeared to be mostly bills. Each was marked *PAID* in his grandfather's shaky handwriting.

He slid open the top drawer and to find more papers, a checkbook and a thick green ledger. He picked up the checkbook and opened it. On the bottom of the carbon copy of each check he could just make out his grandfather's signature scrawled atop the black security background. He stared oddly at his own name written in someone else's hand.

"Dodge Montgomery. Now what kind of a name is Dodge?" The newest teacher would ask in mock politeness as he stood before yet another sea of strange faces in yet another new classroom.

"It's a family name," he would reply awkwardly, hoping she would not ask any further questions, although they always did.

"And where is your family from?" The teacher would continue on as he stood nervously gripping the battered and worn textbooks she had just handed him. The other students would be listening now, their ears tuned from their conversations and their eyes turned to stare at him.

"I don't know. It's my grandfather's name."

"Well, you don't look like a Dodge." She would shrug, pointing to an open desk in the back corner of the room.

"Dodge," one of the other students would laugh as he made his way down the row of staring eyes. "What a stupid name."

The papers on the desk ruffled slightly with the breeze from the window. With it came the soft tinkling of the wind chimes from the porch, the sound gently breaking into his thoughts. He rose and made his way outside, the checkbook still in his hand. He looked up at the swaying chimes and noticed an inscription on the small flat piece of wood that hung from the center. He reached up and grasped it, squinting in order to make out the message etched on the front: *For Father – From James*. Not, *With Love James*, or even a simple but heartfelt, *Love, James*. Just from James. He held the piece of wood against his palm, imagining his father's hands as they had not so lovingly created it.

His cell phone vibrated from his pocket. He answered, immediately recognizing the area code as New York.

"Mr. Montgomery, this is Ellen from the law offices of Stark and Young, we received your email inquiry regarding speaking to someone about an estate and one of our attorneys would be able to meet with you next week if there is a day and time that work for you I can check his calendar." The woman on the other line spoke briskly, each sentence rapidly following into the next without pause.

"I'm not in New York City at the moment. I would prefer to speak with someone over the phone, and if I could perhaps send some paperwork to you for-"

"That would be fine," the woman cut him off. "I can see if we have someone available, or would you prefer a call back at a later time that would be more convenient for you?" He could hear the sound of computer keys tapping hurriedly in the background. He sighed.

"Now would be fine, I suppose." He watched the chimes swaying lazily above his head.

"Hold please," she said as the line went silent.

He made his way back into the office and absently leafed through papers on the desk while he waited. Within a few minutes an attorney was on the line, his tone as brisk as the woman's before him.

Dodge slowly opened and closed the desk drawers as he listened to the attorney drone on about diversified wealth management and the taxable estates of the deceased. He opened the bottom drawer to find a pile of thin leather bound journals. Each cover was marked with a different year, beginning with 1950. He absently leafed through the most recent, glancing at the various statistics and figures relating to the property, all in the same shaky handwriting as the bills and the checks.

"March 16th – Two heifer calves born each to #3675 and #2497. Health: Good. Nursing: Good. Weight: Excellent." He absently flipped through a few more pages. "May 9th – Spring vaccinations completed." "June 15th – Bermuda seed laid in south pasture."

"You don't understand," Dodge said into the phone, breaking into the attorney's prattle. "I need this taken care of right away. This weekend if possible. Money is not an issue. The sooner I can get this paperwork verified the sooner I can-" he stopped himself from saying the last word. *Leave.* "The sooner I can return to New York."

"That's not a problem sir. If you overnight us the paperwork I can have someone here review it as soon as it's received. We can call you as soon as Monday to decide next steps."

"I can have the paperwork to you tomorrow." Dodge placed the journal back in the drawer and shut it tightly. He quickly found a pen and paper and wrote down the information provided by the receptionist he had been transferred back to.

"Is there anything else you need today, sir?" the woman asked brightly.

"No, I think that's it. Thank-"

"No trouble at all," she said, and ended the call.

After a quick stop at the town's tiny post office, he made his way to the feed mill. "Just through the stop light and over the train tracks," the woman behind the counter had casually directed him as she entered the address into the computer. "New York City," she read aloud from the priority mail label. "Hmph," she murmured as she handed him his receipt.

The feed store was easily identifiable by the towering sign in the parking lot advertising the sale of baby chicks and John Deere boots. A line of pick-up trucks faced the red checkered awning, under which sat pallets piled with bags of animal feed and grass seed.

He entered to the high-pitched chirps of hundreds of baby chicks stacked in cages atop one another next to the front door. Behind the counter stood an older gentleman, a wide-brimmed, well-worn cowboy hat atop his silver hair. "What can I help you with," he asked with a friendly smile as Dodge made his way inside.

"I'm not sure exactly," Dodge said, making his way over to the counter, where another customer already stood, leaning idly against the counter. "I've, um, just come into some property. With some cattle," he said, then quickly added, "and some horses." Dodge looked at the man and shrugged his shoulders resignedly. "I don't know exactly what it is I need and was told to come talk to Jake."

"You're talkin' to him," the man said with a wide grin as he extended a large, weathered hand over the register toward Dodge.

"Right, of course," Dodge said as he shook his hand. "I'm Dodge Montgomery." He knew from his conversation with Anne that no further explanation would be needed.

Jake nodded his head. "If it isn't the new city slicker." Dodge smiled uncomfortably and glanced at the man standing against the counter. "I'm just teasin' you. I figured Butler would be taking care of the animals over there." He looked at Dodge questioningly.

"Butler said he had another job lined up, and couldn't stay on. He didn't seem too keen on staying on under the new ownership I guess," he added dryly.

Jake looked at Dodge carefully. "Is that so." He glanced at the man in front of the counter. "Seems a bit odd, seein' as how he's been workin' on that farm since he was a young boy." He picked up a pad of paper from the counter in front of him, flipping through its pages idly.

"I don't think Butler thought much too highly of my coming to town. Besides, I'm not sure how long I'll have the place anyway, so if he's found something else it's probably just as well."

Jake looked up from the pad. "What's that?"

Dodge stared at him blankly.

"About you not having the place," he repeated.

Dodge shrugged. "I'm not really a country guy is all. For now I just need to find someone to take care of the animals. Until some things get settled and I can figure out what I'm going to do with it."

Jake smiled. "You know, your granddaddy built a hunting blind right there in the back of his woods, about a quarter mile from the house. You find that yet?" he asked Dodge.

Dodge shook his head. "I'm not really much of a hunter," he explained absently, wondering why they were talking about a hunting blind when he just needed some feed for a few horses and some cows.

Jake nodded. "He said he used to go up there at night and wait for the coyotes to come through. Then he'd pick 'em off with his rifle. Not sure why though. He didn't have any animals that were small enough for a coyote to take down." Jake looked at him. "I think he just liked bein' out there, sittin' out on his own land. Such a nice piece of property, I bet it's pretty peaceful bein' when you're out there alone." He shrugged. "Course he didn't have anyone to sit out there with him. Maybe he just wanted to make sure those coyotes knew it was his."

Jake straightened up over the register. "I can see if the Vincent boys, Connor and Davis, can come out to your place to take care of the animals. They're good boys, live just a few miles from your place. They're young, but their mama taught them well. They won't charge you much more than what Butler was makin' for the two of them. They can at least make sure the cows and horses are fed until you decide," he paused. "Until you decide what it is you're going to do with it."

"I appreciate that. And if you know of anyone who might be interested in buying the property I'd appreciate that too."

"Ain't no one here gonna want to buy that land," the idle customer said, pushing himself off the counter. "That land is cursed."

Jake put his hand out to him. "Just you hold on a minute there, Jackson."

"He should know, shouldn't he?" Jackson asked. "It's his family's land. It's their curse." He eyed Dodge. Jake shook his head.

"What curse?" Dodge asked, looking back and forth between the two men.

Jackson shrugged his shoulders. "Your great-grandmama died on that property. So did your grandmama, then your daddy. All under suspicious circumstances, every one of them."

"Hold on Jackson," Jake said. "A tornado is not 'suspicious circumstances'."

"It is when that tornado didn't even hit that house. Everyone knows that. How's a woman gonna die in a tornado that ain't even hit her house?"

"Tornado?" Dodge asked, remembering his conversation with Millie.

"E-F-4 tornado. You know what that means?" he asked Dodge doubtfully.

Dodge shook his head.

"It means total destruction. But after it went through town your family's house was still standing, not a single window pane broken. Your granddaddy was just a newborn baby in the cradle, still tucked in safe and sound. But his mama, they found her body a half a mile away. My grandmamma told me all about it, said it was because the Montgomery house was cursed."

"For crying out loud Jackson, that was over eighty years ago. Besides, she wasn't the only casualty of that tornado. Thirteen other people here lost their lives," Jake clarified. "Were their houses all cursed?"

"Not a scratch on the whole darn house?" Jackson asked him incredulously. "A baby sleeping inside? And she just happens to get snatched up and taken away?"

"No one knows where she was when that tornado hit," Jake sighed.

"So she was killed, the year my grandfather was born," Dodge asked absently.

"Yup. Then your daddy's mama died when he was just a young'n, and then your daddy dies right there on that property before you were even born," Jackson said, shaking his head. "Cursed."

"My father died on the property, just like all of them," Dodge reiterated slowly. He stared at his hand resting on the counter next to him. It had been a long time since he had asked anyone about his father, and it did not come naturally for him to do so now. To him it did seem like an unrealistic number of deaths in one place.

Jake snorted. "Jackson, you know good and well that every family has their fair share of difficulties," he broke in, and for a moment Dodge thought he had read his mind. Jake looked at him. "Your granddaddy lived eighty years in that house, and his father before him lived to a ripe old age there too. Ain't no use talkin' about curses and any of that nonsense. And Fiona's death was not under suspicious circumstances nor was your daddy's." He turned to Jackson. "And you need to learn to watch what you're sayin' about other folk's family, Jackson," Jake said to him forcefully with a glare.

"Fiona?" Dodge remembered the prayer card that had fallen out of his grandfather's bible.

Jake nodded. "Your daddy's mama. She was a beautiful girl."

"How did she die?" Dodge asked, stepping closer to the counter.

Jake shook his head. "She just got sick is all. One day she was here and the next," he again toyed with the pad of paper on the counter. "She was gone. God rest her soul. Your granddaddy took it real hard. He was never the same after she died. But don't you go thinking there's anything wrong with that house or that land. Montgomery's have done just fine on that land for generations."

Jackson snorted. "Yeah, just fine," he said under his breath, yet loud enough for both men to hear.

The door behind Jake swung open and an older woman emerged holding a small silver pan with a white cloth towel over it. "The cornbread is cooked fellas," she said with a large smile, placing the pan proudly on the counter and lifting the towel. She leaned over the pan and breathed in deeply. "Fresh from the oven." As she stood up she looked at Dodge. "Oh, hello," she said, a faintly puzzled look on her face.

Jake placed his hand on her shoulder. "This here is Dodge Montgomery's grandson." He nodded toward Dodge. "Dodge, this is my wife, Diane, who also happens to be the best baker of the best cornbread in Alabama."

Diane laughed. "You hush," she said as she swatted Jake's arm lightly. "It's nice to meet you, Dodge." She began slicing into the bright yellow bread methodically.

"We stone grind all of our own corn meal, right here on the property," Jake said to Dodge, his eyes glued to the pan on the counter. "That's the trick, see, you have to start with the freshest ingredients. None of that garbage they sell in a box over at the Pig." He took the large slice of bread Diane handed him.

"This bread is made from the finest organic stone ground corn in the county," Diane said as she handed a crumbling piece of the warm bread to both Dodge and Jackson. Dodge knew by now that resistance was futile when it came to Southerners feeding him. "And with our own fresh eggs taken right from under my ladies this morning."

Dodge took a bite of the bright yellow bread lined with a thin, crisp brown edge. The middle was a spongy mixture of buttermilk and cornmeal. It was not sweet like the store bought cornbread he was used to; rather it had a hearty, rustic flavor to it.

"So, Dodge," Jake said between mouthfuls of cornbread. "How many head of cattle does your granddaddy have out there at his place? Uh, your place I suppose," he corrected himself.

Dodge looked up from his cornbread. "I don't know, to be honest with you. I've only been here a few days." It had not occurred to him to actually count the cattle he had seen on the property.

Jake nodded. "That's not a problem. You'll want to do a full inventory of course, although I'm sure your granddaddy has all of the information written down somewhere. They'll be fine on the pasture for a bit, and the Connor boys can take care of making sure they have water and any other feed. I'll check our records here to see what Butler bought most recently for them. Then we will-"

He was interrupted by the opening of the front door and a holler from the tall, wide-shouldered man who stepped inside. "I smelled that cornbread cookin' all the way from my place and had to hop in my truck to come over and get some," he said with a booming voice and warm grin as he made his way toward the counter.

Diane placed her hand on her hip. "Wade, you old rascal. You live ten miles from here as the crow flies," she said, shaking her head as she began cutting a piece for him.

"It's my sixth sense, then," he said as he took it from her. "A man knows when a fine woman is baking a fine batch of cornbread." He took a bite and rolled his eyes. "Ooo-eee, Diane, as wonderful as always."

Jake looked at him from behind the counter, taking the last bite of his bread and wiping his mouth. "Wade, this here is the new Dodge Montgomery. Just got into town a few days ago." He motioned to Dodge. "Dodge, Wade lives right down the road from you, 'bout four miles."

Wade pulled his eyes from his cornbread to look at him. "That so? How're things out there at your grandaddy's place?" he asked Dodge. He continued before Dodge could answer. "Beautiful piece of land he's got out there. I helped your granddaddy out from time to time, working with Butler on some fence repairs and other odds and ends. Heard he won't be staying on, which is a shame, but people are gonna be the way they're gonna be, you know what I mean?" he asked as Dodge looked at him blankly.

"Yup, that Butler is somethin' else. Real close to your granddaddy. It was like his own daddy had died when he passed. Took it real hard, though I suppose he had to have known ol' Dodge couldn't live forever, what with his heart and him getting up there in age. But I think that Butler thought he'd be around forever. Or, at least maybe that he would get a little of that land from him after he'd gone." Wade trailed off as he took another bite of his cornbread.

Dodge looked away and tried to seem interested in the dozens of baby chicks squawking away in the stacked metal cages. He wasn't interested in hearing anything else about Butler, and certainly not how close he had been to his grandfather, the man he had never been given the opportunity to meet. He bent over and peered into the bottom cage. "What are these big striped ones?" he asked Jake, pointing to the large, fluffy chicks huddled in the center of the cage. Each bird had several dark brown stripes running from its bright orange beak and over its head.

"Guinea fowl," Jake answered. "The babies are called keets. If you're looking for a good alarm system you should take a few of them home with you," he laughed.

"Alarm system?"

Wade nodded, swallowing the last piece of his cornbread. "That's right. You don't need a guard dog when you got guineas 'cause they'll make a racket if anything comes into their territory or when just about anything suspicious comes around. In fact," he said, wiping his chin with a paper napkin, "old man Hylton's guineas saved his life. He had a whole flock of 'em, treated 'em like they were his pets. His wife Margarite used to complain that he spent more time with those birds than he did with her. Not that you can blame the man. Margarite is one heck of a woman in the kitchen but sadly for her she must not have had enough time to get in line when the good Lord was handin' out the looks, if you know what I mean." Wade nodded at Jake and Jackson.

"Wade," Jake said with a sigh. "You were tellin' a story?"

"Right, right," Wade continued. "So one day Margarite hears those birds makin' some kind of fuss right outside the front door. She's not a big fan of the guineas, probably seein' as how they're more attractive than her. Anyway, she comes out of the house to find Mr. Hylton lying face down on the ground. The man had had a heart attack right in his own garden. Margarite said she wouldn't have gotten to him in time had it not been for those birds making such a commotion."

"Wow," Dodge said, imagining the ugly Margarite standing over her husband's lifeless body while a bunch of strange birds squawked around them.

Wade nodded. "You ever had chickens?"

Dodge shook his head. "Not any live ones."

Wade laughed. "If you ever come home and your wife has purchased a wood chipper and a bunch of chickens you just turn your truck around and keep on driving. 'Cause chickens will eat anything." He nodded at Dodge and then toward the tiny chirping birds next to him. Dodge took a step back from the cages.

"Wade, what you got goin' on at your place this weekend?" Jake asked, trying to change the subject. He leaned over the counter toward Dodge. "Wade has quite an establishment over at his place," he said with a wink.

Wade put down his napkin and pulled his wallet from his back pocket. He removed a business card and handed it to Dodge. On the front was a large red *W* over which was written, *Red Neck Rock Club*. Above that in neat blue script was, *Top Soil – Brush Disposal – Fence Repair*, along with Wade's phone number.

"That's right," he said as Dodge peered at the card. "It's the best place to drink a cold beer on a warm Saturday night in Shelby County."

"This says top soil and fence repair." Dodge flipped the card over in his hands to the blank back.

"Of course it does," Wade said, picking up his bread and popping the last bite into his mouth. "Got to be an established businessman." He looked over the counter at the cornbread. "Mrs. Ellis, what does a man gotta buy in this place to get another slice of that bread?" Diane waved her hand at him as she cut into the pan of cornbread and handed him another slice.

Wade continued. "Dodge, you gotta get yourself over to my place. In fact, you can come on by this Saturday night. We'll have a live band and plenty of folks for you to meet. I'll make sure to introduce you to the right people, none of that riffraff that shows up just to drink beer and party. Though I suppose quite a few of them won't be coming around again anytime soon, seeing as how they got the law called on themselves shootin' off their guns last time they were at my place."

"Shooting off guns? Is that illegal?" Dodge asked.

"It is when you miss and hit my neighbor's trailer," Wade replied seriously.

Dodge cleared his throat. "I've already agreed to attend a party at the mayor's house tonight. "Two in one weekend may be a bit much for me."

Wade raised his eyebrows. "An invite to the Garden Party. Well, la-dee-da. Are you gonna tell me you're gonna take yourself to the mayor's party and not mine?" he asked him in mock indignation. "Now then, you go ahead to the mayor's place and then you'll be ready for a real party at my place tomorrow night. The good folks over at the mayor's don't even know what a party is, what with their pink drinks and servin' food on those little plates you can't even fit a quarter slab of ribs on." He waved a hand in the air. "You stop by my place and get yourself some real food – barbecued ribs, pulled pork, and chili that'll stick to your bones. You see," he said, as he finished the last bite of his second piece of cornbread, "You gotta live your life so when you get to heaven you look around and say, 'Yup, it was almost just like this'. That's how I live it."

"I appreciate the invite," Dodge said, however unsure he was if he would take Wade up on his offer.

Wade nodded. "Alright then, it's settled. Can't miss my drive, just look for the black and white checkered race flags hanging on the fence." He placed the wadded up napkin in his pocket and turned to the door. As he opened it he turned back to Dodge. "And you're gonna want to get yourself some better footwear," he said, nodding at Dodge's sneakers. "You never know what you're gonna step in."

Chapter 7

As his truck rambled back toward Main Street Dodge mulled over the conversation at the feed mill and Jackson's blunt assertion that the house was cursed. He reminded himself that he didn't believe in those types of things, and was more concerned with the dilemma of selling a house and land tainted with an enduring legacy of misfortune in local lore.

He recalled the way his mother would move through each new apartment, gripping a cluster of smoking dried sage in one hand. *"Places hold negative energy Dodge,"* she would say to him as she moved through each room, the white smoke wafting around her. *"You have to displace the negative energy so your positive energy can move in."* He would vaguely nod at her insistent nonsense, keeping his head buried deep in a book, as he followed her from room to room. For him any "negative energy" would be encountered not in some random new apartment but at school, where he would again be the fatherless, latch-key new kid with the strange name who didn't seem to fit in with everyone else.

Dodge pulled onto Main Street, parking again in the familiar space in front of the drugstore. Once again the town was silent, the storefront windows reflecting little movement other than his own, and this time he did not bother to lock the doors to his truck.

He opened the door to Mary's shop and stepped inside to the sound of Patsy Cline's voice floating out from a speaker directly above the door. Shiny metal racks bulging with colorful clothes were a stark contrast to the dark wood paneling of the walls and ceiling of the interior, which appeared to have been suspended in time decades ago. Small wooden cubicles filled with antique hardware goods occupied the wall behind the counter while chic clothing and handbags sat piled neatly atop heavy dark wooden counters and tables. On the opposite wall a tall rolling ladder stretched to the top of the fourteen-foot ceiling, providing access to a row of small, numbered drawers along the wall that looked as if they had not been opened in years. Large metal fans circled lazily on the ceiling above, barely moving the air around them.

As he made his way farther into the store he passed a rope-operated elevator adjacent to a pile of brightly colored sequined purses cheerfully arranged atop an ancient black Franklin Stove. Behind this he paused, peering quizzically at an antique desk enclosed in a box made of thick acrylic panes. A worn office chair, the seat cushion fraying at the edges from years of use, sat empty before it. He leaned over and peered at the contents of the desktop, making out an old invoice among the ledgers, envelopes, and other papers. Atop each item was stamped '*Harris Hardware*'. It looked like a small shrine to a previous owner who had simply stood up one day and never returned.

"If it isn't the most eligible bachelor in Shelby County," a soft voice said from behind. He looked up to find a tall, smartly-dressed, silver haired woman smiling at him. Her right hand played with the strands of thick gold necklaces that hung from her neck, complementing the rows of bracelets and bangles that jingled down her arm from her delicate wrists.

"I don't know about that," Dodge said as he stood up from the desk.

"Aw, c'mon darlin'," she said, walking toward him, "Every single lady in this town has heard all about the new Dodge Montgomery," she teased. "Why I heard that Miss Millie has already paid you a proper visit," she said, raising her eyebrows. She lowered her voice. "I'll tell you what, if that girl had a signature scent it would be called *Desperation*."

Dodge laughed. "Is that right? What if I told you I was gay?"

"Darling," she looked him up and down over her glasses. "You don't dress well enough to be gay."

Dodge shook his head as he too looked down at his frayed jeans and running shoes.

"I have been waiting for you to arrive." She made her way past him and behind the counter. She held up a hand immediately. "Now you don't even need to tell me, I know why you are here already."

He looked at her. "You do?"

"Why of course. You need to lose those t-shirts and jeans and start dressin' like the rich southern gentleman you now are!"

Dodge laughed silently again and shook his head. Mary was as warm and colorful as her store, so much so that he did not mind her gentle mocking of his lack of style.

"I'm teasing you of course. You need a tuxedo for the Garden Party this evening. You think the new Dodge Montgomery is going to arrive in this town the week before the biggest event of the season and not get an invitation? It was just a matter of time before you showed up. But let's not get right to business." She reached under the counter. She pulled out a small round metal tin and opened the lid.

"C'mere sugar," she said, patting a purple velvet-lined stool in front of the counter. From the looks of its well-worn fabric it appeared many people had enjoyed a long sit in it. Dodge sat down as Mary reached into the tin and handed him a delicate butter cookie.

"Your store is very…" he paused as he took a bite of the cookie. "…interesting."

Mary nodded her head. "It most certainly is. The space belonged to my dear husband, Lyle. It had been in his family for generations, since eighteen ninety-seven to be precise. His family ran it as a general store, and in later years converted it to a hardware store. It was left to him when his brother Arthur died, and when Lyle passed, God rest his soul, it was all left to me." She looked around the store wistfully.

"I had no interest in running a hardware store of course. Goodness gracious for our entire marriage all I heard about was this store," she said with a wave of her hand. "But I couldn't bring myself to sell it. Lyle would have most certainly rolled over in his very grave had I done that. So I turned it into my own shop. Other than the stock itself I kept most everything just where Lyle had left it, right down to his desk." She pointed a pristinely manicured finger toward the enclosed desk and chair at the back of the store.

"People of course thought I was being quite foolish, a middle aged woman trying to sell clothing out of a dusty old hardware store. But I told them I was no fool. With the new Brown Hardware being built down on Highway 25 there wasn't any need for a hardware store on Main Street anymore. But there is always a need for fashionable clothing my dear." She nodded her head at Dodge's outfit with a smile.

"Some of the men in town were not too keen on an old lady like myself taking over one of the oldest establishments and turning it into a clothing boutique. They came to see me and said, 'Mary, we know your husband was the brains of this business, perhaps it would be best for you to sell it to some of us to continue his legacy'." Mary scoffed. "His legacy my left foot. They wanted to get their hands on his inventory and sell it off to the highest bidder of course. So I politely declined their offer."

"They asked me, 'Mary, what're you gonna do with all this junk?' And I looked them in the eye and told them, 'Leave it right where it is'. And that's exactly what I did. Then I went to the Shelby County Historic Society and told the ladies that we needed to preserve the store's history, which was in essence a part of the history of our town itself. And we also needed somewhere to buy and sell fashionable clothing of course. So we added the store to the town's historic places. And those gentleman never did bother me again."

Dodge laughed as he took a bite of the cookie. "It looks like you did just fine."

99

Mary lowered her voice. "Now, it is my understanding that you were not aware of your daddy's passing until recently, so I must give you my condolences." She laid her hand on his, each finger shining with a large jeweled ring. "I myself know the heartache of losing a loved one. My Lyle, God rest his soul, died when I was just a young woman of fifty-two," she smiled. "Almost twenty years ago. I'm sure the news of your granddaddy's death must have been quite a shock to you."

Dodge shook his head. "Not at all. I didn't know the man. Or my father either, so it wasn't a great shock really." He shrugged his shoulders to impart his indifference. "From what I've heard my grandfather was a quiet man who kept to himself, and he and my father didn't get along. So my father left. That's it." He spread his hands and clasped them together, staring at them to avoid Mary's gaze.

Mary's eyes narrowed. "I can tell you it's true that your granddaddy was quiet and reserved. Quite the opposite of your grandmamma. She would have loved to have gotten a chance to meet you," she said, smiling at him sadly.

"You knew my grandparents?" Dodge asked, surprised but not as shocked as he would have been just a few days ago.

Mary nodded and leaned over the counter. "I was there the very day your grandparents met." She wiggled a finger toward him. Her bracelets jingled along in conspiratorial glee.

"Really?" Dodge asked, cupping his chin in his palm as he too leaned forward on the counter.

She nodded. "Fiona and I waitressed together that summer at the drugstore, just across the street. We were so young then, just seventeen. Oh she and I had so much fun together. She could make me laugh like nobody else," Mary's eyes glimmered as she spoke. "We had just started to get the hang of serving burgers and milk shakes at lunch to a bunch of fussy old-timers when one day your granddaddy came in with a few of the others," she said, staring off. "I had never seen Fiona so nervous. She was a beautiful girl. She could have had just about any of the boys our own age and Dodge had to be in his late twenties by then. But Fiona was always

100

much more mature than any of us. I personally didn't know what she wanted with someone so much older, but you could just tell, something right there, that she just knew."

"Don't get me wrong, your grandfather was a very handsome man. He didn't look anything like his father's side of the family, thank goodness for that. Everyone said he must have gotten his good looks from his mother's side, but she died just a few days after he was born and we never did see any pictures of her to tell for sure. He did look something like a movie star though, tall and rugged with piercing eyes just like yours."

"I'll tell you what, most folks in this town had just about given up on your granddaddy ever finding a wife. A man of his age and stature being single was just unheard of at that time. Everyone thought he would find a girl at college, and when he came back after graduating and still didn't show any interest in the eligible ladies tongues started to wag of course. But I think he knew he was waiting for someone. And that someone was Fiona. When the two of them were together it was like just before fireworks go off, when you're sitting outside on a warm night and everyone gets quiet and just watches and waits. It was just like that, everyone in this town watching them to see what would happen next. Funny how it works, isn't it?"

Dodge nodded his head.

"James, your father, was just five when Fiona died," Mary continued. "Oh, your grandfather was just devastated. All he wanted was her, and then all he had was a child that he just didn't know what to do with. I tried to go by there, to help. I had two little babies of my own by then. But your grandfather was such a proud man. He wouldn't take anything that in any way resembled charity, even a good woman's time to try to give his son a little motherly love," she said sadly. "I don't fault him for it, it was the way he was raised, without a mother. He just didn't understand that a little boy needs that kind of love, and he never understood it." She looked off again. "Or maybe he did, and he was trying his best to get it out of your father."

"I will tell you this, Dodge. Your grandfather wasn't a monster. He was a plain old human being, just like the rest of us. He did what he had to do, what had to be done to just keep on living. Even when there may have been times he didn't want to, and there were many of those. No, he wasn't perfect. He took to the drink more than he should have there for a little while. But he stopped. Picked himself up and kept moving forward again."

"So he was an alcoholic?" Dodge asked, remembering his own bouts of liquor-soaked nights.

"He most certainly was not," Mary replied firmly. "He never touched the stuff until Fiona died, and then after James died, well," she turned her head. "But I don't like to talk about things I don't know about. What I can tell you about is me and Fiona. Let me see," she said tapping her finger on the counter. "Nineteen sixty it must have been when we worked at the drugstore. She had just moved here from Montgomery after her parents died. She had an aunt who took her in. This town was quite sleepy back then, as you can imagine. If you think it's slow now, sugar you have no idea. There wasn't even a stoplight on Main Street back then. The whole county was chicken farms and dairy pastures, and the most exciting thing you could do was drive to Birmingham to go see a movie."

"And was she a spitfire! Why that girl wouldn't take no for an answer. Or yes for that matter if it didn't suit her." Mary laughed. "She was just so full of life, always wanting to be going somewhere or doing something. James was just like her. Why that boy gave your granddaddy a time of it, just like Fiona would have continued to do if she hadn't passed so soon."

"Maybe that's why they hated each other so much," Dodge said absently.

"Hate? No, not hate. But Fiona did tell me something once…" Mary said, looking down at the counter. "I thought it was odd then, but…" Her voice trailed off.

"What was it?"

Mary shook her head. "She told me when she was pregnant that Dodge didn't want a son. He only wanted a daughter. When I asked her why she said he just didn't feel much like a Montgomery, that was all. Something about not wanting the Montgomery name carried on any longer. Seemed like an awfully odd thing to say. Maybe it was because he didn't look much like a Montgomery, being so tall and handsome. I wouldn't think Dodge would have cared about that kind of thing though. Anyway, when your daddy was born Dodge wasn't quite the proud father you would have thought he would have been. Seemed like he just didn't know what to do with a son."

Mary straightened up. "And then he ended up having to raise him on his own, without the one person he loved most in the world. I think your daddy might have felt the same. They were just too much alike in some ways, and not enough alike in others. Just like Dodge and Fiona."

Mary took another cookie from the tin. "It was a different time back then Dodge," she said. "Why a black man couldn't sit at this counter, couldn't sit at any counter with a white woman serving him," she said as she handed him another cookie. "But Fiona, she was different. She didn't see color. She always told me, 'Jesus made all of us and he loves all of us just the same'. She just wasn't one to believe what someone told her just because they said it was true. She was a very big supporter of civil rights," Mary said, raising her eyebrows. "Which was of course quite unheard of for girls our age back then."

"My grandmother?"

Mary nodded. "That's right." Her voice dropped. "One time she and I were hanging around on a Saturday afternoon and she had the idea to drive into Birmingham. I had a car that my daddy had just bought for me, and she knew that if he found out we had gone into Birmingham, two young girls all by ourselves, he would tan both of our hides. But you couldn't say no to Fiona. And off we went."

"It was nineteen sixty-three, just before Easter. We drove into downtown Birmingham. It was nothing like our sleepy little town. And oh lord, the city was changing, even then. The city parks had been closed by the mayor that year, after a federal judge had ordered the city to desegregate them. The black folks had started boycotting the businesses downtown. They had been struggling against segregation in Birmingham for years at that time. We hadn't seen anything like that here, and

Birmingham seemed so far away from us. I am ashamed to admit this," she said quietly, "but I didn't think much of any of it. But Fiona..."

Mary's voice trailed off, and for a brief moment they sat silently, listening to the ticking of the fan above them as it picked along to a snare drum and the floating strains of Patsy Cline.

"Birmingham then was a volatile place, and certainly not one where two young ladies from Shelby County should find themselves alone. I thought we were going that day to see a movie or do some shopping, but not Fiona. She knew full well what was happening and she wanted to see it for herself. The whole ride down there she talked about change, and how people had lost their ability to just be kind to one another." Mary looked him in the eye. "I really thought that was all she wanted. People to just be kind to one another. But for Fiona it was more. So much more. I never understood it until years later, and she had been long gone by then."

"So there we were, two young girls walking around the big city. We both had money just burning in our pocket books from our waitressing jobs. We went into Loveman's. Oh what a grand department store that was in its day. It was just magical in there for two country girls. Fiona and I were trying on hats in the ladies' section when we overheard one of the salesgirls speaking with an elderly white woman. 'Shame what they're doing to the businesses, not spending any money in these stores, and just before Easter,' she was telling the woman. The old woman nodded her head. 'It's just such an un-Christian thing to do. The Lord Jesus wouldn't have wanted negroes taking their business away so close to the anniversary of the day he was risen, I just know it,' she said to her."

"Fiona walked right up to them and asked them what they were talking about. 'The boycott of downtown businesses, by the Negroes dear,' that saleswoman sniffed at her. She seemed to be quite uppity. She could tell we weren't city-folk I suppose."

"'Well,' Fiona said to her, 'My Lord Jesus loved everyone just the same, and he wouldn't have just stood by and watched the injustices that are being done to people just because of the color of their skin,' she told her. That saleswoman's jaw just dropped, and the old woman left the store. I had to pull Fiona out of there."

"'What on earth are you doing?' I asked her. 'Are you trying to get us in trouble?' Fiona pulled her arm from my grip. 'I will never stand by and let others spread lies. Not about coloreds, and certainly not about Jesus.'"

That was when we heard the voices of two women coming from the alley next to the store. It was two black ladies. Fiona took my hand and pushed me against the wall as we listened.

"'So I told her, No'm I ain't heard nothing about no boycotts downtown. And she asked me if I was participating with the troublemakers. And I told her, No'm course not. I wasn't about to let her know that I knew everything about it. You know how she is. I would've lost my job for sure. So she reaches in her pocketbook and pulls out a ten-dollar bill, and she tells me to go on down to Newberry's and buy two new Easter dresses for the children, along with new Easter bonnets. You know she picks out everything for those children to wear herself, and ain't no way she would have ever had me go by myself to purchase somethin' as important as their Easter wear. And she looks at me, and she says, of course you won't have any problem with that, will you?'"

"Fiona looked at me and I just knew what she was thinking. 'C'mon Fiona, this isn't any of our business,' I told her. But she just put her hand out and pressed me back against the building as she continued to listen.

"The black woman continued, 'What am I going to do? She knows if I come back without those Easter dresses that I was lyin' to her, and I'll lose my job for sure. But I can't go into that store. Reverend Stone told us just last Sunday we was to continue the boycott. That woman knows exactly what she doin' to me.'"

"Fiona stepped into the alley then, dragging me with her. I could tell those two poor women were just scared to death that we had overheard their conversation. And Fiona says to her, 'I'll buy the dresses. You give the money to me and tell me their sizes and I'll go in there right now and bring them back out.' Those black ladies just looked at each other and lowered their eyes. I don't know what they must have thought, maybe that

Fiona was just going to take the money. But Fiona reached out and placed a hand on the woman's arm. 'Please, let me help,' she said to her. 'It will just be one white woman buying dresses for another white woman's children. And my friend will stay out here with you,' she said, pushing me toward them. 'So you know I'll come right back.' I couldn't believe her!"

"The woman gave her the money, and told her the dress sizes, and we stood there in such awkward silence for what seemed like forever while Fiona went back into the store. I just didn't know what to say of course. And then out comes Fiona with two bags and she hands them to the woman with her receipt and her change. They didn't say a word."

He sat still, staring at her. "Wow," he said. "That was my grandmother?"

Mary nodded. "She wasn't afraid of nothing or nobody that girl," she said with a smile. "She settled down a bit after she married your granddaddy a short time after that. But not at all as much as people would have liked. Fiona just saw things differently, or maybe things affected her differently. I don't know. There were things that we saw then, things that some people just wanted to close their eyes to."

"What do you mean?"

She sighed, shaking her head. "I don't know why I'm telling you all of this." She set her partially eaten cookie on the counter. "An old lady sharing her old stories," she said dismissively.

"It's nice to hear. I don't know anything about any of them, my family, except what people tell me. They're all just ghosts to me."

She smiled and patted his hand as she continued. "I suppose I thought Fiona would settle down after she met Dodge. That maybe she found what she had been looking for. Especially after she got pregnant with James. She was just so happy, and she had everything she could ever want. Or so I thought."

"One day, a few months later, she asked me to drive her into Birmingham, to buy some clothes for the new baby. We hadn't gone back since that first trip, and I was reluctant, of course. The city was even more dangerous than when we had been there, with people setting off bombs in

106

the black churches. But I could never say no to Fiona. So we drove into Birmingham, both of us laughing and just having such a good time. I parked the car and we got out and there was just something in the air," she said. "Do you know what I mean, when you can just feel something, but you can't put your finger on what it is exactly? That's what it was like. I shrugged it off. I hadn't been in Birmingham but a handful of times, and I thought maybe it was just the energy of the big city."

"We walked around the downtown shopping district, looking in the store windows. It felt to me like Fiona was looking for something, but it wasn't in those shops. She was just looking around her, and I could feel an excitement or something coming from her. You could never tell with Fiona though."

Her eyes darkened, and she placed the half-eaten cookie down on the counter before her. She clasped her hands together and looked at them.

"I haven't told anyone this story, Dodge. Not even my own husband, God rest his soul. It was something indescribable. Sometimes there are just no words that man has made that can convey what you see and feel."

She stared off out the large window in the front of the store. Dodge could see her body tensing up.

"We turned the corner and in front of us was a large church, and in front were hundreds of black children all around, on the steps, the sidewalks, in the streets. I said, 'Fiona, we can't be here, this must be the black part of town,' and she just shushed me. We peered out from the corner of the building, watching them. And then they started singing, all of them holding hands and moving forward together. I'll never forget the sound of their voices, it was so beautiful and powerful, all of them as one, making their way down that street."

She began to softly hum their cry of freedom from hatred and injustice, the song of the little children marching together toward a promised land.

She stopped abruptly and looked at Dodge, as if in embarrassment. "Oh Dodge, it was like nothing I had ever seen or heard before in my life.

Those children, some of them had to be as young as seven or eight years old, just singing at the top of their lungs."

"They made their way to the street corner and turned right onto the street we were standing on. I just stood there holding onto Fiona as tight as I could. The sound of their voices was all around us, and we just leaned against the wall, watching them. That's when I looked down at the other end of the street. The white folks were all standing on the sidewalks, and the police had barricaded the street at the end. They were trying to contain demonstrations to the Negro sections. As we watched three fire trucks pulled up to the barricades, and the men jumped out quick and started pulling out the hoses. I just..." Mary's voice trailed off.

She looked at Dodge. "I just stood there Dodge, I didn't know what else to do. I thought for sure my daddy was going to find out we had gone into the city, and that he was certainly going to take away my car, and I said to Fiona, 'We have to run,' and she didn't even look at me. She just said, 'No, we have to watch,' and she gripped my arm and stood there, just like she was rooted to the ground. I was shaking then, seeing all of those police officers and firemen, and the white people were shouting and the black children were singing. It was just too much. And Fiona said to me, 'We have to watch, someone has to know what happens here,'. I didn't understand then what she meant, I had no idea what was going to happen there. I just wanted to go back and pretend like we had never been there. I knew then that something was going to happen, and I wanted no part of it, and I didn't even want to see it."

Dodge could see Mary was in a different place. He reached out and placed his hand gently on her arm. She looked up at him and smiled, and placed her hand over his.

"They turned on the fire hoses then." Her voice was flat and far away. "I had no idea what those fire trucks were there for. It had not occurred to me that they would use them on people. On children. I don't know if it was me just being naïve, or that I didn't want to think that something like that really happened, or, that maybe, deep down inside, I just didn't really care to think about it. And when they turned on those hoses and those children started sliding across the street and the sidewalks, it was..." she stopped again. She breathed in. "Then they turned the dogs out on them, those beasts ripping at clothes and skin, and again I told Fiona, 'We have to go,' and that time I meant it. I pulled her from that corner and we ran as fast as we could back to my car. And all the time," she paused, "all the time I could hear those little children singing that song. They never stopped singing Dodge, they never stopped singing. I still hear their little voices singing that song in my dreams sometimes. And every now and again I find myself humming it, and I don't even know why."

Mary stood up and shook her head. "After seeing such violence I just couldn't bring myself to even listen to anyone who brought up the civil rights movement. I would have to excuse myself from the room. I am not proud to admit that Dodge, but to me it was someone else's fight, not mine. But to Fiona, for some reason, she felt it was her fight, and she just couldn't let it go."

Dodge stopped chewing his cookie. "What do you mean?" he asked her.

Mary traced a finger on the glass top counter. "She always said to me, 'I hope my baby doesn't grow up in a world of hatred, but one full of kindness.' I think she went into Birmingham that day somehow knowing full well what was happening. The men in the drugstore were always talking about what was going on in Birmingham. I just tuned it out entirely. But not Fiona. She listened to what they were saying. I wasn't as strong as your grandmamma you see," she said. "You have to understand, I wasn't raised the way she was, I hadn't lost anything in my life yet," she trailed off. "We were so young but she was so," she looked at him. "different. Different than all of us. I think that's why I loved her so. Because she wouldn't stand for any injustice, whether it was some man kicking a dog or someone..." she trailed off again.

"Was she actually involved in the civil rights movement?" Dodge asked eagerly. "I mean, did she actually take part in meetings or marches or anything?" He found himself getting excited, learning of his own grandmother's involvement in a part of history he knew so little about.

Mary looked straight at him. "There were things you didn't talk about then," she said with a careful look in her eye. "I know how she felt about it, and I know your granddaddy knew how she felt. She and I never spoke of those trips into Birmingham, and we certainly didn't tell anyone else about them. But Fiona, it changed her. I know it did. She was quieter after that day, like there was something she knew that she couldn't tell anyone else, and she was afraid that if she opened her mouth it would just come right out."

Dodge shifted in his chair as he slowly let it sink in that his father's mother, a young white woman in Alabama, may have been involved in activities of the civil rights movement in the sixties.

Mary looked at him. "Tell me about your mama."

Dodge sat for a few seconds in silence, slowly turning the tin on the counter in front of him. No one had asked him about his mother since he had arrived. He had assumed it was because all anyone cared to talk about was the Montgomery side of his family, the side he knew nothing about. Which was just fine with him as he was not comfortable sharing details of his life with others, and felt the past was best left behind him.

"There's not much to tell," Dodge said, tracing the edge of the tin with his finger. "She was a single mother and she did the best she could." He looked up at Mary. "She died a few years ago. Cancer." He said the last word with a shrug, knowing it spoke its own inevitability without elaboration.

Mary nodded her head. "Were you close?"

Dodge hesitated, not sure how to answer. They had been close when he had been younger, when she could easily pick him up and move him about from place to place like a piece of furniture. As he had gotten older he had slowly started to pull away from her, both physically and emotionally. His teen years had been filled with minor troubles that, while they did not involve the law, included her rightful anger at his stupidity and disrespect. When he finally understood the pain he had caused her it was too late to repair the damage that reached even across the physical distance he had put between them.

"We were close when I was younger. But I've been on my own for a long time so I'm used to it."

Mary nodded her head, understanding his meaning underneath the words that came from his mouth. "Men are only what women make them. What their mama raised them to be – kind, respectful, and gentle. And what the woman they marry expects them to be – kind, respectful, and gentle. Men need to have both in their lives." Mary smiled again as she closed the lid over the tin of cookies and placed them under the counter.

"And I know what you need right now," she said, moving from behind the counter. "A tuxedo for the Garden Party. With a pink cummerbund to go with it of course."

"Pink?" Dodge held up a hand. "Just how southern do I need to be," he joked as he raised his eyebrows.

Mary laughed as she made her way into a back room. "Darling it's the Garden Party. All of the men wear a tuxedo with pink accoutrements. And the ladies wear pink dresses. It's been that way since the first Garden Party years ago."

Dodge followed the sound of her voice. "Really?" he asked, beginning to rethink his already reluctant agreement to attend.

He could hear her rustling through racks of garments in the back room. "Oh yes, darling" she called back to him. "The first Garden Party was hosted by the Culture Club in nineteen-fifty-nine. The country had just come out of a recession the previous year, and the ladies agreed that a grand affair was needed to mark the occasion. Oh shoot." Dodge craned his head at the sound of boxes crashing to the ground. "I'm alright, I'm alright," Mary's voice came again. "The gentleman agreed it was a tremendous idea of course, if only because it was yet another something to keep their wives occupied while the men went off to fish and hunt, or whatever it is that men do together. Here we are," she cried from the back room. She emerged holding a long, black garment bag.

"Here, this should fit you like a glove."

He unzipped the bag and pulled out the dark black tuxedo, fingering the soft pink cummerbund and bowtie looped around the shirt collar.

"Is this for real?" he asked her, holding up the pink bowtie. "Or are you just trying to haze the new guy from up north?"

"Of course it is for real," she said in mock indignation. "Would I lead you astray?" She gave him a mischievous smile. She stared at him as he looked over the tuxedo skeptically.

"My god you do look like her," Mary breathed suddenly.

Dodge looked up at her. She was still smiling, but Dodge could again see the touch of sadness in her eyes. "Maybe you will find the love of your life right here, just like she did."

Dodge shook his head. "I'm not exactly searching for my great love right now," he said, zipping up the garment bag.

"You never know, sugar. You've been in love before, haven't you?" She took the garment bag and moved back toward the front of the store.

He followed, scratching the back of his head. "Yeah, I guess. I'm not sure, really," he said uneasily.

Mary laughed. "Darlin', sayin' you're not sure if you've ever been in love is like sayin' you're not sure if you've ever been hungry. You know when you're hungry, don't you?" She hung the garment bag on a rack by the register and turned to look at him.

Dodge looked around him aimlessly, uneasy at Mary's directness in her questions.

"Ah, it's always the people who are most afraid of getting hurt who end up doing most of the hurting." She moved back behind the counter. "Sugar, I will be more than happy to open up a line of store credit for you if you'd like to pick out some additional clothing," she said as she again looked him up and down. "How about some nice slacks to replace those ratty old dungarees you've got on?"

Dodge shook his head. "That won't be necessary." He reached into his jeans for his wallet.

Mary held up her hand. "Oh no, sugar, this one is on the house. Why when the people in this town see such a handsome young man like yourself walking into that party they will all ask, 'Who dressed that dashing young man?', and that's when I will tell them it was me. You just promise to save a dance tonight for me." She gave him a wink.

"I will do that," Dodge said as he picked up the garment bag. "And thank you Mary. For your time and your kindness."

"That's all I got left darlin'," she said with a smile. "Time and kindness." She watched as he exited the store, reaching under the counter and pulling out the tin of cookies. "And I wouldn't have it any other way," she said to herself as she nibbled another sugar cookie.

Chapter 8

The directions Henry's receptionist had provided to the mayor's house were not the easiest to follow, directing him "past the Monroe's place just off of Collins" and then a "left after the Meyer's house". Luckily his GPS was more forthcoming with street names.

The borrowed tuxedo was not uncomfortable, but he felt awkward wearing it and had to continually remind himself not to tug at the brightly colored bowtie around his collar. His aversion for social gatherings meant that other than a handful of weddings he rarely even wore a suit, and as he glanced down at his torso he couldn't remember ever having worn a tuxedo with pink 'accoutrements', as Mary had so fashionably put it.

The mayor's house was just a few blocks off of Main Street in what appeared to be the more fashionable part of town. Here the houses were larger than those leading up to the Main Street's shops. Tall magnolia trees lined the sidewalks, their delicate flowers carelessly dropping their large petals across the pristinely manicured lawns while plump crepe myrtles fanned out their miniature fireworks display of pink and purple flowers.

As he approached the mayor's house he passed a long line of cars parked on each side of the street, and more idled in the grand circular driveway in front. Parking attendants in pink vests and bowties raced from car to car opening doors and accepting keys. Centered within the house's wide front lawn stood a massive concrete fountain, lights flooding upward at the pink water that flowed majestically from the top. The giant base of the fountain was swathed in green vines entwined with delicate pink flowers, whose combined fragrances blended together and floated into the open windows of his truck.

The valet rushed to greet him as he opened his truck door. "Good evening sir," he said, without the slightest indication that he noticed the truck was so unlike the Mercedes and Land Rovers that had pulled in before him.

"Good evening," Dodge nodded, straightening the jacket of the tuxedo. He handed the keys to the valet who quickly got inside, a line of cars already forming again behind them. He looked up at the imposing house. The steel gray siding was a striking contrast to the tall black shutters lining each window. The railings of the imposing white staircase leading to the front door were draped with what appeared to be hundreds of large pink flowers, their stems delicately hooked onto the intricately curved metal giving the illusion that they had grown there naturally. As he approached he stopped and stroked one of the flowers softly.

"That there is the state flower of Alabama." A man's deep voice came from a dark corner of the porch. "Camellia. Which also happens to be the same name as the tenth, and most difficult hole, of the Augusta National Golf Club." Dodge looked up to see a tall, neatly dressed man standing just off to the side under a small chandelier. The smoke from a long cigar billowed around him as he inhaled and then breathed out slowly. In his other hand he held a glass of clear brown liquor, the ice clinking delicately as he carefully held it away from the black tuxedo he wore, his cummerbund the same shade of bright pink as Dodge's.

"They're really beautiful," Dodge said, releasing the flower from his hand.

The man moved over to the edge of the porch railing, continuing to puff on his cigar. "They don't have any fragrance you see. Just like a very beautiful woman who doesn't need any perfume to attract a man."

The man continued on as he moved closer. "However the first official state flower was the goldenrod. Until a few ladies over in Butler County decided it was unworthy of such a role. Goldenrod is little more than a weed, you see, and back in nineteen fifty-nine they had it replaced with the camellia. Seems to me," he said as he flicked the ash from his cigar and moved closer to the stairs, "they didn't like the idea of our state flower growing along the side of the road in ditches, and in pastures where it could be defecated on by any passing animal."

"That's quite interesting," Dodge said, with little interest at all. He made his way up the steps and the man extended his arm.

"Archer Sterling." He introduced himself as he shook Dodge's hand vigorously. "President of the Garden Club."

"Dodge Montgomery," he replied, noticing the considerable gold watch that slipped out from Archer's cuff-linked sleeve as he shook his hand. He was perfectly polished from head to toe, his dark, slicked back hair gleaming as brightly under the chandelier as his glassy black shoes.

Archer's eyebrows went up. "The new Dodge, eh?"

"I suppose so," he replied. Archer was looking him up and down, and he was thankful he had made the trip to Mary's shop.

Archer nodded. "Your granddaddy was a fine man. A very good man indeed. And a good friend of the Garden Club."

"Is that so? I didn't notice a lot of gardens at his place."

Archer laughed. "No, a gardener he was not. No time for that between his cattle, his hunting, and his fishing I suppose."

Dodge watched as he puffed on his long cigar. He was tall, as it seemed most of the men in this town were, almost matching Dodge's six foot three frame. But there was most definitely something different about him than the men at the feed mill. The hand holding the cigar was smooth, not as tanned and coarse. His looked more like the hands of a man who spent his time tending camellias and playing golf rather than hunting and roping cattle.

Behind them a couple cautiously climbed the stairs to the front door. The woman held the edge of her delicate pink silk gown in one hand as she carefully ascended each step. The gentleman's long-tailed tuxedo was accented with a pale pink vest that accented her dress flawlessly. Her laughter rang out towards them as she held on tightly to her escort's arm. "Archer, darling," she cried out. "Have they relegated you to the porch already dear?"

Archer tipped his glass toward her and grinned. "My dear Savannah, it will be a sad day for Alabama when a gentleman cannot enjoy a bit of tobacco amongst the company of friends, I'm sure you would agree. I have taken it upon myself to greet our guests as they arrive. Why, Mr. Montgomery here was not even aware of the sordid history of our state flower."

The man beside her nodded toward Dodge. "That's because no one cares, Archer," he said as he pulled the woman toward the open door.

Archer frowned and turned back to Dodge. "It is not everyone who appreciates the importance of maintaining a semblance of gentility in this day and age. Your grandfather was such a man. And he was a great benefactor of our club. We do hope you will be as well, of course."

"I'm in the middle of dealing with his estate, so I'm not really sure what I'll be able to, um, benefit," Dodge trailed off as he turned his attention from the couple back to Archer.

Archer laughed and clapped him on the shoulder. "No worries of course," he said cheerfully. "I'm not here to hit you up for money the first week you're in town. That would certainly not be very genteel of me," he said, although Dodge was in no doubt that was exactly what he had just done.

"Go on inside, everyone's out in the back garden, just through the hall," Archer said motioning to the front door with his glass. "I'll catch up with you later this evening."

117

Dodge nodded and made his way through the wide doors to a brightly lit entry hall. Each was held open by a solemn tuxedoed waiter holding a silver tray of bubbling pink champagne in tall, delicate crystal flutes. Dodge picked one up with a nod, taking a sizeable gulp as he entered.

The interior of the home had been adorned even more enchantingly than its front. A grand mahogany table draped with hundreds of soft pink blossoms stood in the center of the immense hall beneath a glittering crystal chandelier, whose light was reflected brightly about the room with the help of two enormous gilded mirrors. Beneath each mirror sat a massive mahogany sideboard overflowing with lush cream and pink flowers. Garlands of greens and pinks circled the rails of the wide, circular staircase leading to the second floor.

Before him stood a set of ornate French doors opened wide to a terrace overlooking the back lawn. Laughter and voices mingled above the strains of Etta James' honeyed voice floating from the dark. He finished the last sip of champagne as he made his way across the entry, willing himself to flow into the crush of strangers before him.

He stood on the wide veranda and looked out at the scene before him. Across the rich green grass large round tables sat draped in crisp white cloths edged in pink silk. In the center of each stood a large bouquet of flowers, each massive arrangement distinct from the next and surrounded by small glowing pink glass votive candles. The chairs too had been embellished with strands of pink ribbons and flowers. Above, small white lights glittered from within the tree branches, lighting delicate blushing flowers that swept down as if to join the merriment below.

On each side stood a long bar with bartenders rushing from one drink to another, ice clinking into glasses filled to the brim with soda and bourbon. He chose the bar on his left and joined the small group of people laughing and waiting patiently with empty drink glasses in hand. He noticed that each man wore the same black tuxedo with pink highlight, and each of the ladies' dresses was some shade of pink, giving the appearance that they too had grown magically from the beautiful surroundings around them.

"Dodge!" he heard his name shouted from the lawn. He peered over the heads of the people before him to see Henry standing among a small group of men. "Get yourself a drink and come meet some folks," Henry yelled louder, the brown liquid from his glass spilling about as he waved it in the air. Dodge nodded his head toward him, speculating correctly that Henry had had several drinks already.

Several people turned to look at him as Henry called out his name. He could feel their eyes on him as he stood waiting for the bartender to finish the order of the people in front of him. "Montgomery's grandson," he heard a woman whisper behind him. "That's him?" another woman's voice asked. Two men to his left leaned in closer to each other, glancing at Dodge and murmuring in hushed tones.

The couple in front of him turned from the bar, fresh drinks in hand. The woman smiled up at Dodge warmly as she took a sip of her drink, and her husband took her arm and quickly pulled her away.

"What can I get you, sir?" The bartender scooped several large ice cubes into a tall glass. "We've got a very nice single malt scotch this evening."

Dodge shook his head. "Just a glass of white wine, please." He had sworn off hard liquor after a night of drinking in a dark Irish bar had left him with a busted nose, three broken ribs, and no memory of exactly why he had started the fight in the first place.

He took the glass from the bartender and made his way down the steps to the lawn. He could hear Henry's booming voice before he even joined the group.

"The Tide's got it this year, yessir," Henry slurred slightly. "Kelly at center, Steen on right guard and Williams on left, we can't be taken down with that lineup," he said before gulping down the last bit of his drink. He turned to Dodge as he approached. "Mr. Montgomery!" He shouted loudly as he waved the empty glass in the air.

Dodge extended his hand as Henry clapped him on the back soundly and began to introduce him to the men in the group before him.

"Gentleman, I would like to introduce you to none other than Mr. Dodge

Montgomery." He chuckled and slapped his thigh. "I still cannot get over saying that." He pointed clumsily toward the two men next to him. "Dodge, these are my partners at the firm." Dodge shook their hands and nodded hello. "And these," Henry said, pointing his glass to the other two, "are our town's other finest – Dr. Robert Thomas and our mayor, Stanley Haley."

While each of the men wore the same attire as Dodge, they looked far more comfortable in the stiff jackets and bow ties that seemed to want to choke him with every turn of his head. The well-manicured hands he shook were not worn from sun or labor, and their grips were firm. Each man gave him the same polite nod and half-smile as he tried in vain to commit their names to memory.

"Welcome to town," Dr. Thomas said to him as he extended his hand. He was a small man, and made even more diminutive next to Henry's hulking frame. "We're so glad you could join us this evening."

"Absolutely," said the mayor, smiling widely. "And someone gave you the dress code I see." He nodded at Dodge's tuxedo. The mayor's own pink silk vest was dotted with large camellia flowers, and his pink bowtie fanned out from beneath his chin in the form of the flower's petals. He continued to look Dodge up and down as he took a sip from his glass.

"Your house is… very nice," Dodge said awkwardly as he took a sizeable gulp of liquid from his glass. He could feel the stiff collar of his shirt digging into his neck, and found himself with few words among these finely dressed strangers.

The mayor waved him off with a short laugh. "It's not much compared to your family's house. How are you getting along in that big old place?" Before Dodge could reply he continued. "I don't know how your grandfather lived in it all by himself all those years. The man couldn't even cook himself a meal, I know that. I think he kept Barney's down on Main Street in business eating there as much as he did. Can't imagine how he kept it up without full time staff. Although I believe he had a cleaning service come in a few times a week, I'm sure we can get you their number."

"Cleaning service," snorted Dr. Thomas. "What that house needs is a nice big family." He tapped Dodge on the arm and nodded at him knowingly. "A place like that ought to be full of children. And lucky for you this is just the place for you to start meeting some of the most eligible young ladies," he said winking. "Unless of course you've already got a lady back where you come from..." His voice trailed off as he glanced at Dodge over his glass.

Dodge rubbed his neck, his collar suddenly feeling even tighter, if that was possible. "No," he said, shaking his head. "I don't, ah..." He looked down at his drink. The men were staring at him intently over their drinks. "I don't have anyone in my life right now," he said before quickly adding, "But I'm not really looking either."

"Doesn't much matter if you're looking," said the mayor. "If these gals are looking for you." The men around him laughed heartily. "You'll figure out soon enough that southern girls are polite enough to take no for an answer, but then they'll just figure out another way to ask until they get a yes."

Henry clapped him on the back and laughed. "That's right, my boy. You're young, you should be out and about, playing the field. Your granddaddy didn't marry until he was nearly thirty. You got plenty of time." Henry peered into his empty glass. "Looks like I need a top up." He jingled the ice cubes in the empty glass and made his way toward the bar.

The other men began small conversations among themselves as Dodge slowly sipped his wine and looked around. The lawn was quickly becoming more crowded, and he could barely hear the music over the sounds of floating voices and laughter. He caught a few lines of Patsy Cline's *Walking After Midnight* and watched as several couples moved across the makeshift wooden dance floor set up in front of the DJ booth.

"Dodge!" he heard his name called from behind him. He turned as Millie approached, flanked by two young women. She extended her arms as she approached and hugged him tightly.

"Oh I am so glad you are here!" she squealed, keeping her hands on his arms as she pulled away. "And look at you, dressed to the nines! Much nicer than that sweatshirt you were wearing when we first met," she said loud enough for her friends to hear. "Dodge, these are my dearest friends, Johnny Sue and Josephine." She nodded toward them as she slipped her arm through his.

Dodge shook their hands with his free hand. Both women were as attractive as Millie, with petite builds and perfectly coiffed hair and makeup. The fabric of their pink dresses hugged their slim bodies tightly.

"Johnny and Joe," he said to them. They giggled as they sipped their champagne.

"Johnny Sue owns her own catering company here in town," Millie said. "She makes the most delightful ambrosia cake." She squeezed his arm and moved in even closer. "Not as good as my lemon squares, which you have tried already of course. She would just love to get her hands on that recipe." Millie's eyes narrowed above her wide smile.

"It's because of my secret ingredient," Johnny Sue said to him cheerfully, throwing a sideways glance at Millie. She leaned in toward him secretively. "It's the bourbon."

"So," Millie said to him, as she tugged on his sleeve for attention. "I heard you caught a llama the other day!"

Dodge finished his drink. "I did, actually," he said as Josephine took a glass of champagne from a passing waiter and handed it to him brightly. "Thanks."

"Aren't they just adorable," Johnny Sue asked him. "The llamas."

"Ugh," said Millie snorting. "I heard they spit and kick."

"Well, so do you," said Johnny Sue, sipping her glass and looking around idly. Millie threw her a sharp glance.

"Dodge," said Josephine, "I heard that you are from New York. It must be so exciting there."

All three women looked up at him with wide eyes. He took a large gulp of champagne. "It's not all that exciting really," he said quickly.

"It certainly must be more exciting than here, that's for sure," Millie said with a snort. "I would just love to visit," she said as she looked up at him with a smile. He could again smell the same flowery perfume from their first encounter, its scent seemingly headier in the damp night air than it had been before.

"Have you ever been down to Mobile?" Josephine delicately stroked her fingertips along the beads of condensation from the side of her champagne glass. "It's absolutely lovely down there on the water. Very romantic."

"You would know," Millie said brusquely. "How many times have you been down there now, Josephine?"

"My family is from Mobile, Millie, you know that. Of course I have been down there many times."

"Funny," Millie said as she gripped Dodge's arm tighter. "I don't remember your mama going with you on the last few trips." Josephine's mouth dropped open as she stared at Millie darkly.

Henry reappeared over Josephine's shoulder. "If you ladies don't mind, there are a few people I'd like to introduce Mr. Montgomery to while the night is still young." He gently took Dodge's arm out of Millie's grip and began moving him through the crowd.

"Those ladies will fight over you like three hungry coon hounds rippin' apart a dead possum," he said to him as he steered him away from the girls.

Henry steered Dodge around the lawn, stopping at various tables to politely introduce him. With every hand he shook and every introduction he made he got the feeling everyone already knew exactly who he was. However, each person politely peppered him with the same questions: where was he from, how was he getting along at his grandfather's place, had he tried the burgers at the drugstore? Fortunately, no one asked how long he was staying.

While Henry was deep into yet another conversation about Alabama football, Dodge excused himself to make his way over to the bar for a refill. He found he always drank more when he was uncomfortable or nervous, and the third glass of high-quality wine went down as smoothly and easily as the first. After refilling his glass yet again Dodge made his way to an empty table and sat down.

"If it isn't my good friend Dodge," he heard from behind him. He stood up as Mary took a seat next to his, a large slice of ambrosia cake in one hand and a glass of sparkling pink champagne in the other.

"Mary," he said with a wide smile, helping her into the chair and sitting down next to her.

"Have you tried this ambrosia dear?" She took a large bite from the heaping mound on her plate. "It's just to die for."

Dodge shook his head as he took another sip of his wine. It occurred to him that he had not eaten anything since he had arrived.

"How are you liking the Garden Party?" She took another bite and twirled her fork lazily in the air around them.

"It's… ah…" He looked around the lawn at the stylish men and women in their finery. "It's nice," he said to her.

"Psh, it's a bunch of rich drunk people is what it is," she said, taking another bite of the ambrosia and washing it down with a large gulp of champagne.

Dodge laughed. "So why do you come at all then?"

"One has to go to the Garden Party, dear. An invitation is not an option. Besides, this is my clientele," she said to him, taking another large bite of her dessert. "See that woman over there?" She pointed to a tall, elegantly dressed woman across the lawn. "Just last week Mrs. Dryer came by with her Mercedes loaded full of her husband's clothes. She had caught him sending shameless emails to his secretary. So she decided to teach him a lesson. She was going to set all of his clothes on fire right there on their front yard. But she re-thought that idea, I mean what would the neighbors have said? And certainly the ladies of the Culture Club would have wagged their tongues at that. So instead she thought it might be a better idea for her to bring all of his clothes to my shop for me to sell. You see that way her darling husband could see all of the other men walking around town in his own clothes!" She let out a hearty laugh, almost spilling her drink on her pink flowered dress.

Dodge sat back. "Are you serious?" he asked incredulously.

"Of course sugar, why would I make something like that up?" she said with another laugh. "You can ask her yourself. But I wouldn't ask while her husband is right there next to her." She took a sip from her glass. "You know what we Southerners always say, 'Kindness is delightful, especially when it's spiteful'." She leaned back in her chair, laughing heartily.

"I was not aware of that saying," Dodge laughed, finishing his wine. As he did a waiter appeared, replacing his empty glass with a full one.

She stood, patting him lightly on the shoulder. "Don't forget you owe me a dance Mr. Montgomery," she shouted as she walked away into her next conversation.

Dodge made his way across the lawn toward the couple Mary had pointed out, who were in conversation with Josephine and Johnny Sue. The wine was beginning to catch up from his stomach to his head, and while he was sure Mary was pulling his leg he still wanted to get a closer look at Mrs. Dryer and her husband. He quietly sidled up next to the group while Josephine finished her story.

"So afterward he decides we are going to fly to Mobile in his plane for lunch, which was very romantic of course. We got to his plane, and it was just a little bitty thing, one of those Cessna's with one propeller on the front," Josephine was saying, holding her champagne glass in one hand and a plate of ambrosia cake in the other. "And he looks at me and he says, 'Darlin', I am supposed to ask each of my passengers how much they weigh, but lookin' at you I can tell you aren't a pound over one-oh-five'," Josephine took a gulp of her champagne. "Let me tell you, I haven't weighed one hundred and five pounds since my cheering days in high school, but I was darned if I was going to tell him that. That plane could have gone down in flames before I admitted my real weight to a man I was dating."

The four of them pealed with laughter. Dodge grinned and took a sip from his glass of wine. Mrs. Dryer turned to him.

"Hello," she said smoothly. "I'm Myrna Dryer." She extended a manicured hand and a smile to Dodge. The enormous diamond ring on her left hand glimmered in the candlelight as she drew her glass to her lips. She pointed to the man next to her brusquely. "This is my husband, Dick."

Dodge shook her hand and extended it to her husband. The wine was making his head swim, and he did his best to keep his handshake steady. "Oh, is that short for Richard?" he asked, shaking the man's hand.

He leaned in to him and said in a low voice, "My name is Charles actually. My wife is still angry with me apparently." He glanced at his wife with a furrowed brow.

Dodge bit his lips and tried to hold back the smirk that threatened to turn into a full laugh. As he did Charles turned to another man making his way toward the bar. "Ronnie," he said, stopping him. "Where'd you get those shoes?"

"My wife got them for me down at Mary's," the man answered. "Can you believe she was selling them for only fifty dollars? They've got to be at least three hundred retail, don't you think?"

"Three hundred and sixty-five to be exact!" Charles answered, following angrily behind the man. Dodge watched as Myrna chuckled to herself quietly as she gulped down the rest of her drink.

"Dodge," he heard his name being called. He turned, adjusting his gaze to focus on Martin.

"My llama roping friend," Dodge said louder than he had intended, and he set his wine glass down on the table beside him.

He and Dodge shook hands. "We're like old friends now, aren't we? How many men can say they've caught a wild llama together? Did you get him back alright?"

Dodge nodded. "I sure did. Anne was very kind," he added. "She joked that her llama was the only way she could get single men out to her place," he laughed.

"Is that right? Is she single herself?" Martin asked casually.

"Yes," Dodge said. "At least I think so. I'm pretty sure." He blinked his eyes as he tried to focus on Martin's face. "You should meet her."

"I have met her, remember?"

"Right, you took back her llama before me." He knew that the wine was catching up to him, and looked around him for a waiter with a glass of water. "Would you excuse me," he said to Martin as he made his way back toward the house. He needed water and a seat, and thought it best if he didn't try any new conversations for a few minutes at least.

He gratefully accepted a bottle of water from the bartender and made his way clumsily out onto the lawn, moving away from the twinkling overhead lights and amusement around him. He sat down at the thick base of a tall tree and took small sips of the cool water. From here he could see the cheerful party guests clearly, and still hear the music that wafted from the speakers, but he needed the quiet stillness of the dark for a moment. He rested the back of his head against the thick trunk of the tree and closed his eyes. The faces of the people he had met swept behind his lids, outstretched hands and women's pearly white teeth flashing through his head. While he didn't mind the company of other people, he also never minded being alone. He preferred to watch, rather than take part. He found that he always had little to say anyway, and would just as soon rather smile and give the occasional chuckle rather than join a conversation himself.

The music stopped abruptly. He opened his eyes and looked over the tops of the guests' heads to see Charles Dryer standing next to the DJ stand. "I am dedicating this song to my dear wife, Myrna," he slurred into the microphone he held shakily in his hand. "I love you my darling, you and only you."

Dodge looked over at Myrna. She stood apart from the crowd, and even from his vantage point in the dark he could see her throw back her head and roll her eyes in derision. A small crowd was forming outside the dance floor's edge as the strains of "*My One and Only Love*" began. Charles extended a hand toward his wife, who had seated herself cross-armed at a table next to the dance floor. Everyone listened to the raspy voice of Louis Armstrong, watching Charles' outstretched arm and waiting excitedly to see what Myrna would do.

Charles made his way across the floor toward his wife clumsily. She still sat, glaring at him from her seat. A thin smile spread across her face as she stood and slowly crossed the dance floor toward Charles.

The music continued, and Charles smiled, swaying slightly as Myrna approached. As he held out both arms for her embrace, she walked past him to the DJ booth. A hushed groan fell out from the crowd on the lawn.

As she leaned over and whispered in the DJ's ear, the music stopped abruptly.

"No, no, no," Myrna said, pulling the microphone from Charles hand. "I have a song for my dear husband." Charles' face fell as she placed the microphone back in its stand and made her way across the dance floor.

Dodge sat watching the two of them standing awkwardly in the middle of the dance floor. The DJ shook his head as the music started up again. The drumming started, and the horns kicked in to the sound of Aretha Franklin's husky voice letting Charles know he was no good, a liar, and a cheat.

Myrna took Charles' hand and placed it on her back, draping her arms around his shoulders. They began to move slowly across the dance floor, their eyes locked on one another's, as the guests around them murmured and sipped their drinks. Myrna's pink dress swayed as Charles gripped her hips and moved her lightly around the dance floor.

Dodge watched them dancing together with a small smile. He took another gulp from his bottle of water, toying with the plastic lid. He had committed more than his share of aches to the women in his life, and knew how just a few shallow injuries could turn to a deep wound that didn't heal.

Slowly the people around them made their way onto the dance floor, everyone forgetting for a brief moment Charles' emails and the misfortune of his clothes.

Archer Sterling's voice once again rang out from the darkness. "Dodge," he said, picking his way carefully across the tree roots in the dark, his arm tucked against the thin elderly woman next to him. Dodge stood up, feeling slightly less woozy after the bottle of water.

Archer turned to the woman as they approached, bending slightly to speak into her ear. "Mother, this is Dodge Montgomery."

The woman looked up at Archer and frowned. "Oh, I know Dodge. Archer, what do you take me for? Dodge and I go back to grade school together." She scowled at him before turning to Dodge with a smile. "Now Dodge tell me, did you ever find that cow you lost across the creek?"

"Um, I'm not sure," Dodge said, looking at Archer quizzically. "I didn't know I had lost one."

"Mother," Archer said exasperatedly. "This is Dodge Montgomery's *grandson*." He turned to Dodge and whispered quietly. "You'll have to excuse my mother, since the dementia started she has some good days and some bad days."

"Dodge Montgomery does not have a grandson!" Archer's mother cried as she pulled her arm from Archer's abruptly. "His only son James died when he was young." She gave Dodge a disdainful look. "James was not married and certainly did not have any children."

"Now, Dodge," she said, clasping his hands in her own. "How many of those cows do you have left? And how is that beautiful house of yours? I should get up to see it again. It's been so long."

"Mother, this is Dodge's grandson. GRANDSON." Archer explained even louder.

"I just told you..." she started but stopped. "Oh look, there is Theresa McMahon over there. I haven't seen her in ages." She took one hand from her grip on Dodge and waved. Slowly she moved, her other hand dropping from his.

Archer took his mother's hand and turned to Dodge. "I am sorry, again," he said as he began to turn her away toward the party.

Mrs. Sterling turned back to Dodge abruptly. "I know for a fact that Dodge had just one child, and that was James, from his only wife Fiona. Oh, that horrible young girl. Dodge did not even want to get married and there she went just floating into town from God knows where, and getting knocked up almost immediately by a man a decade her senior! Scandalous!

129

Poor Dodge had to marry her of course, he was a gentleman of the highest caliber after all."

Archer's jaw dropped, horrified at his mother's abrupt words. "Mother, look, it's Theresa and she's waving for you to come over," he said awkwardly.

"Why, it is!" she exclaimed, waving excitedly again.

Archer nodded at Dodge as he again steered Mrs. Sterling away from him.

Mrs. Sterling turned back to Dodge suddenly. "And he didn't kill her, either. No matter what people in this town like to whisper!" With that parting remark she turned, waving at Theresa and making her way back through the tables of laughing partygoers.

Dodge stood silently, the empty plastic bottle snapping quietly as he gripped it tightly in his hand. *Didn't kill her? Where would Mrs. Sterling have heard that?*

Archer shook his head as he watched his mother move away from them. "I just never know what that woman is going to say anymore," he said as watched Mrs. Sterling pick her way carefully between the tables.

"What did she mean? About not killing her?" Dodge pressed him.

Archer shrugged. "Who knows? Who knows what's real anymore in that mind of hers. She's still a bit outspoken, just like she's always been. Except now," he paused. "I'm the one who's left to explain exactly what she's talking about, and even I don't know sometimes." He looked up into the dark at the branches above their heads. "Funny how when you're younger you want your parents to live forever, to never leave you. Then you grow up and they grow old, and you're left with these people you never even bothered to get to know."

"I wouldn't know," Dodge said as he leaned back against the tree trunk. "Both of my parents are dead."

Archer nodded thoughtfully and then straightened up. "Tonight is not a night to dwell on the unfortunate. Come on, Dodge, let's rejoin the festivities and lighten this place up." He motioned toward the lights of the grand house. The music's tempo had picked up, and the dance floor was

130

again crowded with couples. As they approached Mary danced her way toward him.

"Mr. Montgomery you owe me a dance," she said as she took his hand. He let her lead him back onto the dance floor as Archer patted him on the back. They moved about the dance floor, laughing as they bumped into the other revelers and he delicately held Mary's hand in his own. She twirled slowly beneath his arm, throwing her head back with a laugh. For one brief moment as her eyes twinkled like the tiny lights above them he could envision her as a young girl, laughing gaily on the dance floor among her suitors.

The music slowed and she stepped toward him, placing her hand again in his. The couples around him pressed their bodies closer together to the cool voice of Otis Redding. "Dodge you are a wonderful dancer," Mary said to him.

"That's funny, I don't get much practice."

"Oh darlin', it's not about practice," she said with a laugh. "Some men are born with the ability to move while others are not. Why look at that poor soul right there," she said, nodding at Martin as he clumsily held Anne's hand in his own and shuffled around the dance floor, his feet unaware of the beat of the actual music. They both looked down at their feet and up again, Anne laughing as Martin shook his head with a lopsided grin.

"I guess her llama was bringing her a man after all," Dodge said off-handedly as he nodded toward them.

Mary looked up at him quizzically. "Dodge, have you been eating the ambrosia cake?"

Dodge laughed. "It's a long story, Mary," he said to her as they twirled off again beneath the glittering lights.

Chapter 9

The following morning his body begrudgingly consented to waking, his head heavy against the pillow as if the remnants of the wine and champagne had somehow left his stomach to occupy his skull overnight. As he brushed his teeth his mind chased after the names and faces of the people he had met the night before. Leaning over the sink he remembered Mrs. Sterling's outlandish remark, *"And he didn't kill her, either."* It was clear the old woman was not completely in her right mind, but her words had burrowed into his head like the echoing line of a song that his mind could not shake. Did she mean something by it, or had she perhaps confused his grandfather with someone else?

Downstairs he found the front door open, the screen door tapping the edge of the trim softly in the breeze. He puzzled for a moment, trying unsuccessfully to remember if he had left it open the night before.

As he moved to close it he caught sight of a small blue car moving quickly up the drive toward the house, leaving a long trail of white gravel dust behind in its wake. He squinted his eyes and tried to make out the model and year as he checked the time on his phone, a habit he had acquired living in places where one might be asked later to recall as many details as possible for a police report.

As the car neared he made out two male passengers. It stopped before the house and two young boys climbed out, their tall, lanky bodies extending from the car slowly at the speed only teenagers and old people moved. Dodge stepped out on the front porch, his arms crossed against his chest.

"Good morning, sir." The young boy pulled his lanky body from the driver's side and made his way around the car toward the steps. "Mr. Ewen told us to come by because you were looking for someone to help out with some work around your place." The boys appeared to be in their early to mid-teens, their t-shirts lazily untucked over their frayed jeans. The shirts hung loosely over their long, narrow chests and thin, tan arms, proudly displaying their allegiance to NASCAR and America.

"I'm Connor," the taller one said as he moved up the stairs and extended a hand to Dodge. "This is my brother Davis."

Dodge shook his hand and nodded. "You boys know how to take care of cattle and horses?" Dodge asked, wary about the boys' youthful appearance. He didn't have much experience with anyone younger than himself, and wasn't sure Jake had understood fully how little he knew about the land and its inhabitants.

The boys nodded their heads in unison. "Yes sir. Our mama has fifty head, and we help out our neighbors when they need it," Connor replied. He was clearly the older of the two, however even he seemed to be having trouble making direct eye contact with Dodge, his car keys nervously jingling in his hands.

"I'm sure you're more qualified than me." Dodge smiled at them, trying to put the boys more at ease. "The barn's out that way," he said pointing toward the field next to the house. "There's another one in the back with some horses in it too."

"We know sir," said Connor. "We've been here before chopping wood for Mr. Montgomery. Um, your granddaddy sir. We'll get the water troughs filled and move some more of the round bales from the barn. You got the bull out there today?"

Dodge looked out at the field. "I think so. Is that the really big gray one with the horns?"

Connor and Davis shared a quick glance with one another. "Yes sir," Connor said with a small smile. "Do you mind if we take your truck out instead of our car? The ground's still a bit soft from the rains last week. We got our car stuck out in the back fields of our place last week when we went fishing. Looks like you've got four wheel drive. We'll be real careful with it."

Dodge looked at both boys carefully. "I don't see why not," he said, although the thought of a two thousand pound bull pounding his horns into the side of it passed through his mind.

As if reading his mind Connor spoke up. "We won't let the bull near the truck, and even if he does he might just rip off a side mirror and we can fix that," he said with little concern.

"Let me get my keys." Dodge moved back inside. He glanced over at his grandfather's desk as he made his way into the kitchen, where he found them on the counter next to his pink bowtie from the night before.

As he made his way back through the front hall he could see the boys had moved onto the small circle of grass encircled by the driveway. They jumped around and at one another, wide grins on their faces as each attempted to reach the other in a mock boxing match. He watched as Connor stretched out a long arm toward Davis, who quickly stepped back and jumped sideways just before he was able to make contact with the side of Connor's head. Davis whooped and moved his right arm up next to his head as if in a fighting stance, laughing as he ducked low around Connor and landed a light kick on his brother's backside.

Dodge stood for a moment behind the screen door listening to their laughter and taunting shouts. As a child he had sometimes longed for an older brother to watch over and protect him, and as he grew older he imagined a younger brother he could do the same for in turn.

Earl and James. As he moved his hand to the latch on the screen door the words drifted into his head. He stopped and shook his head slightly. *Earl and James*, the thought came again. He looked out at the two boys, who had stopped rough-housing and were quietly showing each other their phones. *That was what they were like. Brothers.* He shook his head, puzzled as to why the thought would come to his mind. Earl had only mentioned that he knew James, that they were friends. But he didn't recall him mentioning they had been like brothers.

Dodge opened the door and threw the keys to Connor, who caught them in one hand. "Shouldn't take more than a few hours," Connor yelled back to him as they moved to the truck. "You can use our car if you need it."

Dodge glanced at the beaten up blue Toyota and shook his head. "Thanks, but that's alright. I'll be inside taking care of some things." The boys nodded and climbed into the truck, Davis back on his phone as Connor drove the truck down the drive.

In the office he began looking through the shelves of books that lined the wall between the two windows, hoping to find a photo album tucked between them. Surely somewhere in the house had to be the lost pictures of his father's family, he thought, as he pulled each one from its dusty location. With no luck he moved on to his grandfather's desk and again began searching through its contents. He opened the bottom drawer and withdrew the faded journal dated 1968, the year his grandmother had died.

He flipped through the brittle pages and stopped when a photo slipped from its pages and fell to the floor. He picked it up and sat back in the chair. A young girl and a man looked out to him from the front steps of his grandfather's house. The woman looked playfully toward the camera, her arm looped up and around the man's neck. He was tall, older than she was, his thick arm wrapped around her tightly. Her dress reached to mid-calf, and was belted at her thin waist. He squinted as he raised the picture closer to his face. The woman grinned back at him, while the man's staid demeanor didn't show even the smallest notion of a grin.

He turned the picture over. The back contained several lines of a poem written in what he recognized as his grandfather's hand. He read the words slowly:

I am forgetting you.
Like the drip of water from the faucet,
The sound, once unbearable,
Has become mundane.
Water in a cold basin,
You in my heart.

He flipped the picture over again. This was a photo of them, taken before his father was born. His grandparents. He said it again to himself; his grandparents. What had happened after she died? When his grandfather was left with a five-year-old son, to live, just the two of them, alone together in this big house. The thought made Dodge shudder.

He placed the picture on the desk and thumbed through the journal. The first pages matched those of the journals he had read earlier; livestock weights, amounts spent on supplies, hay, and grain. As it went on the entries became shorter, most consisting only of shorthand and numbers. He turned to the page dated June 29th. There was no entry at all. Just the date written carefully at the top of the page, as if that day the author had been unable to write anything more. He flipped the page back and forth. Nothing. On the next page was written June 30th and the same set of shorthand and numbers continued again. He guessed that the photo had fallen from this empty page, tucked there by the person who had nothing more to say about that day. He placed it back on the page, taking one last glance at his grandmother's smile before he shut the book.

He leaned back in the chair, and for a brief moment his own mother's smile flashed into his mind. He remembered the fear he had held onto his entire childhood, that someday she would be gone, and he would be all alone. And when she finally did leave it hurt almost as much as he thought it would, but unfortunately not more than he could bear. What was it like to lose someone, when it was almost more than you could take?

He put the journal back in the drawer and stretched his arms behind his head. He stared at the desk before him as he cupped his hands behind his head. The smooth wood top was worn away in distinct places, and the edges were softened and rounded from years of use. This worn piece of furniture was full of his grandfather's life, and before that had quite possibly been full of *his* grandfather's life before him. How many generations of Montgomery men had sat here the way he sat now? How many had sat in this very room, their breath dissipating into the air around them, their sweat cooling on their skin and dispersing out into this room where they quietly recorded what was most important in the daily moments of their lives?

For his father's ancestors, their lives had begun in this place, and ended in this place as well, with a collection of significant moments scattered between the routine of their everyday lives. Births, deaths, celebrations, accidents, miracles, milestones, and mistakes. His own mistakes were made in places he could, and would, eventually leave and never see again. What happened when you could not? When you had to stay in that very same place, living your life day in and day out, watching your loved ones leave while you sat at a desk recording the weights of animals and the numbers of hay bales? He had always questioned why his father had left his mother alone in New York, but he hadn't questioned why his father had left this place, his home. It was as if that one question having been answered necessitated a new one to step into its place. Did he even want the rest of the answers if that was the case?

He looked around at the contents of the room before him, knowing that when he left all of this would be relegated to a quick estate sale. Strangers would move through the house assessing the worth of his family's belongings. They would caress items longingly as Millie had done, not knowing or caring to whom they had once belonged. Or maybe they would know, and would understand their importance far more than he had. He suddenly felt an overwhelming desire to know what everyone else

137

knew. Wasn't it his right to at least call these things his own if only for a moment, these things his father left behind?

He began pulling the journals from the drawers. He collected them in his arms and made several trips to the large kitchen table, piling them one on top of the other. He pulled out a chair and began again with the first one, paging through each one for a glimpse of whatever it was that may have been in his grandfather's head as he wrote. He touched the pages, imagining where his hand would have lay on the page as he moved the pen across. He wondered where he had paused, perhaps looked up from the journal to hear his wife in the kitchen a few rooms away, his toddler son giggling beside her. He imagined his father running by, tugging at his father's arm before he lifted him up into his lap, grasping at the papers scattered on the desk before him. Had that happened? If it had, did it matter if no one remembered?

Outside he heard the tires of his truck crunching up the driveway. He glanced at his watch. Three hours had gone by as he had sat at the table trying to find what he didn't know he was looking for. He closed the journal in his hand and made his way back to the front porch as Connor and Davis descended from his truck, their boots muddied and a thin layer of hay dust coating their shoulders and the fronts of their shirts. The truck's tires were coated with light brown mud, but there were no tell-tale signs of bull damage from the side that he could see.

The boys climbed the porch and stood leaning against the railing. Dodge sat down in the rocking chair next to the door. They were quieter now, their t-shirts damp with sweat. "They're all set Mr. Montgomery," Connor said has he handed Dodge the keys to the truck. "The cows are all in the North pasture, and we got three round bales out for them. Should last them a week or so. We cleaned out the water troughs the best we could and refilled them. The horses will need the farrier in the next week or so I think."

"Farrier?" Dodge looked up at him from the chair.

Davis nodded. "For their hooves. He'll be by our place next week to shoe ours, we'll let him know to stop over here." It was the first time

Dodge had heard him speak, and while his voice was quiet it was also assured. "If you want," he added quickly as he looked down to inspect his muddy boot.

"Or we might see Scotty this afternoon, we can ask him to stop by if you think they need it sooner," Connor asked as he looked at Davis. Dodge watched Davis nod his head silently. The demeanor between the two boys was calm and quiet, unlike the rowdy roughhousing teens they had been a few hours earlier. He realized they were probably exhausted, and looked more like the worn cattlemen at the feed store rather than two rambunctious teenagers play fighting on the front lawn. "Davis is pretty knowledgeable about horses," Connor explained.

"Is that so," Dodge asked.

"I think they'll be fine another week," Davis said as he looped his thumbs into his jeans pocket, seemingly more comfortable talking about horses.

"I appreciate it boys," Dodge said as he stood up. "What do I owe you?"

Connor stood up. "We usually charge fifteen an hour for each of us. Was about three hours I guess." Dodge did the math in his head when he realized Connor was not going to give him a solid figure.

He pulled a hundred dollar bill from his pocket and handed it to him. "Here, can you boys split that?"

Connor nodded as he took the bill and stuffed it in his pocket. "You want us to come back next week?"

The question stopped Dodge for a moment. He looked out over the boys' heads. Would he be here next week? Or would he be back in the city? And if he was, who would be here to take care of the animals?

"I'll let you know," he said as he pulled out his phone. "Can I get your number and we'll play it by ear?"

Connor nodded. The boys made their way back to their car. "Oh," Connor shouted as he leaned in to the back seat. "I almost forgot. Here," he said, reaching in and pulling out a plate covered in foil. "Our mama made this for you. She wasn't sure if you had gotten up to the Pig yet to do your food shopping."

"The Pig?" Dodge asked as he took the plate.

Connor nodded. "The Piggly Wiggly. It's the food store in town. But you could easily just get to the Super Walmart." He shrugged. "Mama says she likes the Pig because she knows the butcher. She won't buy meat at the big stores, says they're all full of antibiotics and hormones and stuff she wouldn't feed her own cows let alone her family."

Dodge nodded. "Good to know." He wasn't sure he had ever questioned where the meat he ate had come from, nor what it had eaten before it had made its way on to his plate.

"Hey, Mr. Montgomery," Davis said as he opened the passenger side door. "What're you gonna do with the horses when you leave?" He picked at the rubber frame of the car's door absently.

Dodge stood quietly for a moment. *When you leave.*

"I don't know Davis. I haven't really had a chance to think ahead that far." He was unsure how Davis had come to the realization that he would be leaving at all.

Davis nodded his head. "Just don't take them to the auction," he said, staring out at the pasture. "Let my mama know, she'll probably buy them or she can make sure they go to a good home." He sat down inside, closing the car door quickly behind him.

"I'll do that," Dodge yelled. "I promise."

Connor gave a brief wave as he got into the car. Dodge watched as the two boys made their way down the drive. Atop the foil cover was a small white envelope containing a neatly handwritten note.

"*Welcome to the neighborhood. I was hoping to get by for a visit this week but I've got a mare about to drop a foal and you know how that is. I look forward to meeting you just as soon as I can. And don't take any nonsense from those boys. You have my permission to set them in their place if necessary. Sincerely, Nancy Vincent.*"

He peeled the foil back from the plate to find a small pound cake. His stomach rumbled at the smell of the cake's sweet scent as he made his way

140

inside and set it on the counter. Perhaps a trip to "the Pig", as Connor had called it, wasn't a bad idea. Since he would be in the house at least a few more days waiting for the return of the documents from the lawyers he could pick up a few things. He scooped up the piles of journals and moved them back to the office, setting them on the floor in front of the desk before grabbing his keys.

As he made his way down the drive he laughed at the message in Nancy's note and her permission to set her sons right if needed. He doubted any parent today would give a stranger carte blanche to discipline their child. He pulled out of the drive onto the road, thinking he wouldn't have even known how to begin doing so, considering his own behavior in his adolescence and teen years.

The sound of a police siren pierced his train of thought. He looked in his rear view mirror to see a sheriff's cruiser just behind him, lights flashing. He could not have driven more than a quarter mile out of his driveway, he thought, and was sure he had not been speeding. He pulled over to the side of the road, expecting the cruiser to race past, and was surprised when instead it pulled up behind him.

He sat patiently while he waited for the officer to approach, watching him from his side view mirror. The door to the police car opened slowly. The man that emerged was young, and what his frame lacked in height his shoulders made up for in width. He shut the door to his car and walked slowly to Dodge's window.

"Good afternoon," Dodge said with a smile that the officer did not return.

"License and registration please." The officer flipped open a long, thin pad of paper he had pulled from his pocket.

"Of course," Dodge said as he reached into his back pocket. "Can I ask why you've pulled me over?" He handed the items to the officer, who studied them silently.

"Not from around here, are you? What is someone from New York City doing all the way down here in Shelby County?" The officer continued writing, not glancing up from his notepad.

"I'm here on family business. Although I don't see how that pertains to why I've been pulled over."

The officer stopped writing and looked up at him from his pad of paper. He smiled. "Why I've been pulled over, *sir*."

Dodge gripped the steering wheel tightly with both hands. "If you would just kindly tell me why you've pulled me over," he began saying through clenched teeth. "As an American citizen I have the right to know."

The officer looked up at him matter-of-factly, clearly unappreciative of Dodge's lesson on citizen's rights. "You're driving with a broken tail light, which is illegal here in Shelby County. Maybe you should be aware that your own vehicle is not equipped properly to function on the road in Alabama," the officer paused. "Or anywhere else in *America* for that matter."

"Tail light?" Dodge said questioningly. He dropped his head against the headrest. "The boys must've knocked it out this afternoon when they were out taking care of the cattle."

"Dodge Montgomery," the officer said as he peered at the license in his hand. He looked up at Dodge with piercing eyes. "I only know one Dodge Montgomery, and you," he said as he placed the license into his front pocket, "are not Dodge Montgomery. Would you step out of the vehicle, sir."

Dodge sighed. "He's my grandfather. Was my grandfather," he added quickly.

The officer placed his hand on his belt. "Sir, I'm going to ask you one more time to step out of the vehicle." He took a step back from the truck's door, his hand hovering over his hip.

Dodge blew out an angry burst of air as he opened the truck's door. "Officer, I am Dodge James Montgomery, the grandson of Dodge William Montgomery. I'm here because I was contacted by-"

"Please step behind the vehicle, sir." The officer cut him off abruptly, his hand now firmly placed on the gun holstered in his belt.

Dodge shook his head, and as he moved toward the back of the truck he could hear the shrill sound of an all-terrain vehicle approaching from the driveway next to them. He looked up to see Earl seated behind the wheel, Miss May next to him hanging on to the vehicle's roll bar as they sped down the drive. They came to a stop in front of them in a cloud of dust.

"Clay, what on God's good earth is going on down here?" He heard Miss May yell as she gingerly pulled her large frame from the vehicle.

"Miss May, I'm gonna' need you and Earl to go on back up to your house," the officer said as he put a hand out towards her.

Miss May shook her head. "Goodness gracious, Clay, that's our neighbor, Mr. Dodge Montgomery."

"Yeah," Earl yelled from the driver's seat, "don't you recognize old Dodge?" Miss May looked back at him and they both laughed.

"This is not a laughing matter, Earl. Now I repeat, I'm going to need you to go back on up to your house."

Earl stepped from the vehicle with a wave of his hand. "Clay, do you know who you just pulled over? That there is Dodge Montgomery's grandson. *Grandson*," Earl repeated. "He's here to take care of his late granddaddy's estate. You know his granddaddy," Earl said. "The man who has contributed to Sheriff Abraham's campaign every single time he's been up for re-election. Why, his granddaddy and Sheriff Abraham are old hunting buddies if I remember correctly. Or were, to be more specific. This man here," Earl continued, "is now in charge of the monetary contributions of the Montgomery estate." Earl nodded at Dodge. "You probably don't want to be arresting him the first week he's here in town."

The officer looked at Earl carefully. "This man is driving around with a busted tail light." He pointed to Dodge's truck.

Earl moved to the back of the vehicle. "So he is. He's only been in town less than a week, and I can assure you, I saw this man a few days ago and that tail light was in fine shape. And I'm sure old Dodge here," Earl said with a snicker and a nod toward Dodge, "was just on his way to get it fixed, weren't you Dodge?"

Dodge narrowed his eyes as he looked at Earl. He glanced at the officer who was staring at him intently. "Yes, I was," he said as he glanced at the tail light. "I'm on my way into town right now."

"See there," Earl said with a laugh. "Miss May, why don't you run back up to the house and get these gentlemen some sweet tea?

"That's not necessary Earl," the officer said. He reached into his pocket and handed the license and insurance card back to Dodge. "You make sure to get that light fixed, you hear?" Dodge nodded as he placed the license back into his wallet.

"Clay, will I see you tonight over at Wade's, or are you working a double shift this evening?" Earl asked the officer as he walked him back to his car.

"I may be around," he replied as he climbed back into his vehicle. Dodge watched as Earl leaned over into the driver's side window and conversed quietly with the officer. They both looked over at Dodge for a brief moment before Earl placed a hand on the officer's shoulder. "If I don't see you tonight we'll certainly be seeing you tomorrow morning at service," Earl said with a wave of his hand.

The officer waved back and pulled out onto the road as Earl walked back toward Dodge.

"What the hell was that, Earl?" Dodge felt the adrenaline rushing through his body as he asked angrily. "I'm not even an eighth of a mile from my own driveway and I have a police officer pulling me over?"

Miss May put her hand up. "There's no need for that type of language, Dodge," she said to him with a shake of her head. "You might just be at the end of my driveway but I won't have swearing in my company regardless of where I am standing. The good Lord can hear you everywhere."

"I'm sorry, Miss May," Dodge said to her quietly. He turned back to Earl. "What would have happened if you hadn't shown up?"

"Aw nothin', Dodge," Earl said with a swat of his hand. "That man pulled you over because you're drivin' around here with New York plates on your truck, that's all. Nobody around here has New York plates and Clay knows that. He didn't care about that broken tail light."

144

Dodge sighed. "Sure, that's all it was," he said with a snort.

"That gentleman is a fine member of the Shelby County Sheriff's Department," Earl said to him sternly. "We appreciate our officers, who look out for us out here. You want to stop getting pulled over you need to get those plates changed out for Alabama plates," Earl said as he made his way back to the vehicle where Miss May had re-seated herself in the passenger seat.

"I don't know how long I'm staying, Earl," Dodge said, repeating himself for what felt like the hundredth time.

"What do you got to get back to?" Earl turned and asked him. Dodge shook his head, pushing himself off the back of his truck.

"Listen here," Earl said as he climbed back behind the wheel. "Looks to me like you need to relax, blow off a little steam. I'm going to be over at Wade's place later this evening. Why don't you come by? It's just down the road there." He pointed down the street.

"I know," Dodge said. "I spoke to Wade yesterday at the feed store."

Miss May and Earl raised their eyebrows at one another. "That so," Earl said. "Listen, Dodge, do yourself a favor and relax a little bit. Stop thinkin' everyone's out to get you. Some people still got your back, I'm sure of it. You get that tail light fixed and meet me over at Wade's later." Earl started up the vehicle. Dodge watched as he and Miss May disappeared into a cloud of dust, each waving a hand out the side in farewell.

Chapter 10

Dodge watched the afternoon sun fade silently behind the horizon as he stood over the kitchen sink and ate his dinner. He could see the horses huddled beside each other under the shade of a Bluejack tree next to the barn, rubbing their sides against its thick grooved trunk. His trip to the food store had netted him a few days' worth of food in the pantry and time to calm down after his run-in with the sheriff's deputy that afternoon.

He thought again about Earl's advice about the car tags. It shouldn't make a difference where I'm from, he thought to himself, but even as the words slipped through his mind he knew that was not true. It mattered much where he was from, and even more where he wasn't. What did it mean exactly, he wondered as he ate the last bite of his sandwich and wiped the crumbs from his hands directly into the sink. If his father was born here, and his father and grandfather before him, did that make this where he was from?

He made his way upstairs and glanced at the bags lying on the floor in the bedroom. It occurred to him that if he was staying for a few more days he could unpack and put them in one of the dressers. He chose the tall, thin dresser in the corner at the far end of the room, the least obvious choice for convenience. Opening the drawers, he found his grandfather's clothes, soft and worn flannel shirts and piles of blue jeans. He removed them carefully and replaced them with his own t-shirts and jeans, thinking that perhaps he would take the clothes to Mary's shop when he returned the borrowed tuxedo.

He lay down on the bed and closed his eyes, his head sinking deeply into the soft pillow. The room was cool, and he listened to the hollow pinging echo of water coming from the bathroom. *I am forgetting you, like the drip of water from the faucet.* He opened his eyes suddenly, staring at the ceiling as he waited for the sound of each drop.

Silence, then sound.

Silence, then sound.

Silence, then sound.

The noise was indeed now unbearable, and he shook his head, unable to understand how it had not bothered him before. He rose from the bed, grabbing his car keys and cell phone from the dresser, and made his way downstairs and out the front door.

Wade's property was not far from his own. He turned his truck onto the narrow dirt lane next to the fence lined with the small plastic black and white checkered race flags Wade had referred to at the feed store. As he slowly made his way down the dark road he could hear the sound of loud music coming from up ahead, the echoes of an electric guitar and thumping bass cutting through the still night air.

Cars and trucks had been parked haphazardly beside one another on the grass on each side of the road. From somewhere a band broke into the beginning strains of "Sweet Home Alabama", and he could hear a large crowd roar with approval. The light from a large bonfire glowed from behind the house, its thick feathery plume of smoke rising up into the black night sky.

In lieu of a well-manicured lawn, an assortment of objects cluttered the yard. Ceramic lawn ornaments shared space with whimsical metal objects of art sticking up haphazardly from the ground. Potted plants had been randomly placed across the lawn seemingly without thought or reasoning. In the center, the remains of the shell of a late-model Ford truck inexplicably sat next to a small covered wooden wagon, like the curious leftovers of an eclectic used car lot. Shiny metal pinwheels lined the stone walkway leading up to the front door where a small circle of ceramic gnomes stood huddled around a concrete bird bath, gazing up together at the night sky.

A young man and woman stood beneath the awning of the front porch smoking cigarettes. They barely looked up as Dodge nodded his head toward them in greeting. The man did the same through a haze of smoke, and Dodge got the feeling that his grandfather's name or money would not be held with as much regard here as it had at the mayor's party the night before.

He opened the door and stepped inside to the raucous noise of loud music and shrill laughter. Every inch of wall space in the cavernous room was covered in objects. He gaped up and around him at the brightly colored strands of Christmas lights that wound haphazardly around the photos, paintings, neon beer signs, stuffed dolls and animal heads that hung from every wall of the room. A pair of large wagon wheels that had been fashioned into chandeliers descended from the ceiling, their lights twinkling as they swayed slowly with the reverberating music over the revelers' heads. The floor beneath his shoes was sticky with the remnants of stale beer and liquors spilled over the years. A large sign next to the front door read "*No Smoking, Spitting in Spittoons Only*". Dozens of small cigarette burns dotted over the words.

His eyes crept over the mass of bodies filling the room. A group of older men stood next to a makeshift bar where a dignified older woman in a rattan cowboy hat and jeans poured Jack Daniels into shot glasses. Others lounged about on large overstuffed sofas and chairs. In the center of the ceiling between the makeshift chandeliers hung a large disco ball, the light from a spotlight refracting off of it and onto the mass of bodies beneath as they held onto their beer cans and danced to the music from the band before them. A small stage had been erected in the far corner of the

148

room, from which the four band members played, so close in the small room there was not much need for the tall set of speakers on each side of them. The band was breaking into the beginning notes of the next song as Dodge continued further inside. The women in the room raised their bottles of Miller Light up into the air as they moved their hips and shifted their bodies against the men standing next to them.

He made his way through the thick mass of bodies, looking for Wade or Earl. The reverberation of the noise from the band and the laughter and shouts of the partygoers melded together into one massive sound that assaulted his ears from every direction. He was all too familiar with the feeling of a bass drum beating up through a floor to meet the movement of feet and bodies, the pungent smell of beer and alcohol mixing with the heady scents of sweat and smoke.

As he moved across the room he felt himself being bumped from behind. He turned quickly to catch a young woman in shorts and a bikini top before she fell. He looked down to see that she was on roller skates, a six pack of beer in one hand. She pressed her other hand against his stomach as she tried to steady herself.

"I'm sorry," she said, laughing. "Here." She placed a bottle of cold beer into his hand. "It's on the house, handsome," she shouted as she pushed herself off using his chest and continued to make her way clumsily across the room.

Dodge shook his head. Maybe this wasn't such a good idea, he thought to himself. He remembered too many nights in loud, dark bars, and how they had sometimes tended to end for him. A blow to the face during a fight or waking up next to a stranger in a strange bed were equally distressing, if not at the time they took place then the day after. He had sworn after his mother's death that neither would happen again, and he had been careful to stay out of places and situations that were inclined to lead to one or the other.

"Dodge," he could just make out the sound of his name being called from somewhere across the room. He looked around but could only see a mass of bodies writhing around to the band's next song. The music was so loud he couldn't tell what direction the voice was coming from. As the band transitioned from '*Slow Ride*' to Steve Miller Band's '*Take the Money and Run*', the voices in the room began to rise as people tried to make themselves heard over the music and each other.

"Dodge," he heard again from far off, and turned to see Wade standing in a corner under a neon beer sign motioning him over. Dodge waved as he moved through the crowd towards him.

"Glad you could make it," Wade yelled into his ear as he slapped a hand against his back and raised his glass to Dodge's bottle of beer. "What do you think of the place?" He nodded to the room before them. "A little more exciting than that Garden Party, eh?"

Dodge nodded as he took a sip from his beer. "I'll say." Wade nodded in appreciation. "It's a bit louder too," Dodge yelled.

"Loud?" Wade shouted. "You ain't heard nothin' yet! C'mon." He waved his hand, motioning for Dodge to follow. They made their way through another dimly lit room, illuminated only by long strands of multi-colored Christmas lights that crisscrossed over and around whatever random piece of wall decor they found to precariously hold on to. In one corner a group of young partygoers gathered around a long folding table and shouted encouragement to the two teams at each end engaged in a heated battle of beer pong. He watched as the young woman at one end tossed the small white ball, cheering with her teammate as it landed in the red plastic cup across from them. The head of a large deer watched the festivities silently from the wall above, strands of colorful plastic beads hanging from its oversized antlers.

Several people shouted greetings at Wade as he made his way through the room. "When're the races starting again, Wade?" one man asked loudly as they made their way past the table.

"My racing days are over, Pratt, you know that," Wade replied. "Got the cattle out on the track now."

Wade led Dodge to a large screened-in porch. An older crowd filled the tables scattered around the room, out of the way of the music and revelers inside. The wood-paneled wall next to the entrance was lined with

150

University of Alabama football memorabilia, including a five-foot wide banner printed with a black and white team photo. The text above the players proclaimed them to be the "1961 Championship Team" and below in large maroon letters, "Crimson Tide".

Wade stopped before the picture and pointed to a young man seated in the front row. "See that there? That's me, minus fifty years and fifty pounds or so."

Dodge leaned in for a better look at the group of youthful men staring out from the photo. The fresh-faced, blond-haired man Wade had pointed out smiled back at him with a wickedly lopsided grin.

"You played ball?"

"Played ball?" Wade repeated. "I played on the nineteen sixty-one championship team. We weren't the biggest, but we were the best. Bryant said it himself."

"Bryant?" Dodge shook his head as he took a sip from the half-empty bottle of beer.

Wade looked at him incredulously. "Paul 'Bear' Bryant, the head coach of the University of Alabama football team for twenty-five years! The man is a legend, son, a legend. Three hundred and twenty-three career game winnings and six national championships. That there is his first one," Wade said pointing again to the picture. "There's a museum named after him, for crying out loud!"

Dodge smiled. "Sorry Wade, I'm not a big college football fan."

Wade's eyes widened. "Well, we are going to change that, my friend. It's never too late to come to Jesus, or become an Alabama fan," he said as he pointed his drink toward Dodge's chest. He moved to an empty table in the corner of the room.

"This here is my private area," Wade said, pointing to a '*No Trespassing*' sign hanging on the wall above the table. He reached into a small red cooler hidden away in the corner and set a bottle of bourbon and two small glasses on the table in front of them.

The smell of thick smoke from the fire outside drifted in through the open windows. Dodge looked out at a line of women moving back and

151

forth between a long table draped in shiny plastic red checkered tablecloths to the screen door behind them, a row of tiki torches lighting their way. Behind the table a group of men stood over a large pig roasting over a pit of burning coals. The table was slowly filling with food as each woman set down a large pot or bowl and made her way back through the screen door.

"What did that man mean, about starting the races?" Dodge asked as he looked over the room around him.

Wade nodded as he poured the brown liquid into the glasses and handed one to Dodge. "I used to run mud races in the back there," he said pointing a thumb out the window. "Boy, those were some good times. But it got to be too much for me. Now this is just a place where people can come and have a good time. Have a few beers, share some good food, listen to some good music. That's all."

"Where did you get all this stuff?" Dodge paused as he sniffed the contents of the glass Wade had handed him. Its scent beckoned to a buried place, the sweet aroma disguising its impending intentions. He absently took a small sip and the bourbon blazed its way down his throat. Memories of how nights ended after drinking it fumbled away as he lifted the glass again and cleared its contents.

Wade laughed. "Dunno really, just been collectin' it over the years. Started out with just a few things in one room, and then people would just bring me stuff. Didn't have anywhere to keep putting it after a while, so I started hanging it on the walls. Then the ceilings." He pointed to a group of water color paintings on the wall across from them. "Someone gave me a nice painting of some cattle once, and I hung it on the wall. So then people thought I liked paintings of cattle, and started bringing me more. I just kept hangin' 'em up, and people kept bringing me more." He shrugged his shoulders.

"So you don't live here?"

"Nah," Wade said. "This place is just for get-togethers. My place is just down the road." He looked at Dodge. "So you're from New York City," he said as he took a sip from his glass.

Dodge nodded as Wade refilled his glass. He stared down into the velvety brown liquid, tilting the glass and watching it softly incline toward the rim. "Yes," he replied.

"Born and raised there?"

Dodge nodded his head again. "Yes. My mother was born in the city, but she didn't have any family left by the time I was born. We moved around a lot, but mostly in that area." He sipped, swishing the bitter liquid until it burned his mouth.

Wade nodded. "Yep, heard that's where your daddy met her." He paused and looked at Dodge as if waiting for him to add something. Dodge sipped his drink silently. "But you know you're not really city folk, right?" Wade asked in a serious tone.

Dodge looked at him. "What do you mean by that?"

Wade shook his head. "You got Montgomery blood in you," he said, pointing a finger toward Dodge's chest. Dodge could smell the bourbon on his breath. "You can always tell a Montgomery. You have this," he waved his hand in the air, "this air about you. I thought it might be a little strange having you come down here what with your family's history and all but sheesh." He slapped the table and put a hand on Dodge's shoulder. "You, sir, are a Montgomery and you don't need to worry about any of that other stuff." He took another drink and nodded at Dodge as he refilled his glass.

"I don't know that I know what all of the 'other stuff' is exactly."

Wade batted a hand in the air. "Exactly. You know what you need?" He finished his beer. "You need to have a good time here tonight in the best darn party place in Shelby County, Alabama. Get yourself used to country living and relax a bit." He laughed and raised his glass to Dodge's. It was the second time today someone had told him to relax, and Dodge decided to do just that as he finished his glass of bourbon. As he did he heard a loud scratching noise against the screen and turned to see the outline of a large black cow standing in the window behind Wade's head.

Dodge cleared his throat. "Um, Wade, there's a very large cow behind you." Dodge nodded toward the window.

153

"Beuhla!" Wade yelled as he lifted the screen. The cow poked its head through the window toward him. "That's my girl!" Wade spoke gently to the animal as he rubbed between its eyes. Her large wet mouth moved up toward his hand, a thick pink tongue lapping about the air around it searching for food. Wade reached down again to the cooler and withdrew a bottle of beer. He twisted off the top and let a small stream of liquid fall out the window, which the cow quickly began lapping at. "My real girl is tendin' bar out there in the front room. This here's my gal." He patted the large cow on the head as she backed out the window. He took a sip from the bottle of beer as he reached down and pulled out another and handed it to Dodge.

"How much do you know about cattle?" Wade asked as he closed the window screen.

"Not much," he shrugged. "I suppose the closest I've ever been to a cow before now was at a McDonald's."

Wade smiled, nodding his head. "I figured. You got about eighty head over there at your place. Your granddaddy started selling some of 'em off in recent months. Guess he knew."

Dodge pursed his lips and nodded.

"You could have one of your cows slaughtered and fill yourself up a freezer full of meat. That's what your granddaddy used to do."

Dodge grimaced at the thought of actually slicing into one of the cows that had once gazed back at him from behind the fence.

"See that? You want to eat it, but you don't want to kill it. That is what is called irony. I think." Wade frowned.

The noise from the room behind them was growing even louder and more people were making their way to the relative quiet of the tables around them. The screen door opened and a man leaned inside. "Wade, that hog is just about ready, and the boil's about done. You better get yourself out there before there's a riot," he laughed as he pointed a finger behind him.

Wade tilted his beer bottle in the air in his direction. He pushed his chair back, steadying himself for a moment against the table before he stood.

"That would be my cue. I'm the one who decides when the hog is ready for eatin', and the crawfish are ready for peelin'. Why don't you come along and see what real food looks like?" Wade laughed again as he led Dodge across the room.

They made their way behind the house, Dodge a little less steady on his feet from the mixture of bourbon and beer. The long table outside was now completely covered in bright red crawfish and plump pink shrimp dotted between half cobs of corn and brown potatoes. Behind the table the heavy hog lay suspended over the bright red coals, its skin charred to an orange-red sheen. Next to it stood three men, each taking turns spinning the carcass tied to a long metal pole. Dodge recognized one of the men immediately as Butler. Their eyes met across the open fire, and through the haze of smoke Dodge could see Butler's forearms tense, just like his own.

Wade approached the group, pulling a knife from his back pocket. "He sure is looking good," he said as he cut into the crackling skin and placed a hunk of the pig in his mouth. "I think we are about ready, boys."

Dodge watched as two men lifted the pig from the spit and carried it to a table the women had lined in aluminum foil. Butler stood to one side, a large knife in one hand. As they set the pig down he immediately began carving into its wide belly, deftly pulling skin from muscle with the sharp blade of his knife.

The music from inside had stopped, and a steady flow of people began making their way outside. The light from the bonfire cast a crimson glow over their faces, the color not unlike that of the pig's sizzling flesh beneath Butler's gaze. To Butler's left stood a growing line of hungry people holding paper plates in one hand and cans of beer in the other. The table full of crawfish and shrimp was quickly surrounded by those who couldn't wait, and had begun digging into the heaping mass before them. The ground beneath them quickly became littered with discarded shells.

"You look like you could use a bowl of this," a voice came from behind him. Dodge turned to find an older woman offering up a plastic bowl.

Dodge took it from her extended hands. "Thank you."

The woman nodded. "There won't be much of the shrimp creole left in just a little while," she said as she smiled up at him. "I heard you were new here, and thought you should get the chance to taste it before it's all gone."

He took a bite. "That's delicious."

"It ought to be. That is full of the finest shrimp brought up from Mobile just this afternoon. It's Wade's mama's recipe. You need to get yourself some of that hog before it's all gone." She nodded at the pig in front of Butler as she walked away toward the kitchen.

Dodge grimaced. The thought of eating meat that had been touched by Butler's hands momentarily gave him a sickening sensation in his stomach.

Wade, now standing amongst the mass of bodies cracking open small crustaceans waved him over from the table. Dodge lifted his bowl in an effort to convey that he was good with what he had.

"Not one for crawfish, eh?" He turned to find Earl holding a plate overflowing with mounds of pork and various side dishes.

"Earl," Dodge exclaimed as he wiped his mouth and extended a hand. "I was looking for you."

"I like to stay outdoors where it's a little quieter. Looks like you were able to get some of Mama's shrimp creole." He nodded toward the almost empty bowl in Dodge's hand. "Someone must like you," he said with a wink. "You going to try the crawfish?"

"I don't think so." Dodge looked over at the discarded carcasses surrounding the table.

"Not for everyone," Earl said as he took a large bite of pork. "You gotta try the pig though."

Dodge glanced over again at Butler standing behind what remained of the hog. He watched as he deftly sliced the knife through the pig's hindquarters and ripped through its back legs.

Earl caught Dodge's gaze. "You're not a vegetarian, are you?"

"No, I'm just not that hungry I guess."

Earl nodded as he pointed over toward the pit of fire. "You know, Butler worked on your granddaddy's farm just about his whole life."

"Yeah, he told me," Dodge replied, recalling again Butler's vicious words.

"That boy has had a rough life. If it wasn't for your granddaddy letting him hang around his place, teaching him what he knew, who knows where he would have ended up. Started coming 'round when he was just about nine or ten years old. That was just a few years before your daddy left town."

Dodge looked at him. He could hardly feel any warmth for Butler because he had gotten the childhood experiences with his grandfather that he himself never would.

"He was always trying to hang out with the older boys. But they just shooed him away. I think that's one of the reasons he took to your granddaddy. Or why your granddaddy took to him. James wasn't much into the family farm. To him chores were something you tried to get out of. But Butler, he loved working on that farm. I think he just wanted to get away from his own life at home."

Dodge snorted. "As much as he may have liked my grandfather I can tell you he had no interest in befriending me." He jabbed his plastic spoon into the bowl.

Earl nodded. "I wouldn't expect him to. Probably just a bit of jealousy. He never got much out of life, just what he could pull out of it on his own."

Dodge could see Butler laughing with several of the men that stood around him. He turned and looked up at Dodge without a smile. Dodge watched as he leaned in toward the men around him and began speaking. One of them glanced over swiftly at Dodge, then returned to the huddled conversation.

"He was a bit jealous of your daddy too, come to think of it," Earl said, cleaning his plate.

"Really," Dodge said flatly, his eyes still locked on the group of men.

"Oh sure. Your daddy had everything he didn't. A nice big house to live in, fine clothes, an upstanding father. At first I thought he wanted to hang around your daddy, then I realized maybe he wanted to *be* your daddy." Earl laughed. "The day James left was probably one of the happiest days of Butler's life."

"I'll bet," Dodge said curtly as he finished his beer.

"C'mon, we'll go get some more of these." Earl held up his own empty can.

Dodge shook his head. "I should probably get going. I'm still getting things in order around the house."

"Oh, c'mon, Dodge. One more beer isn't going to kill your big plans." Earl motioned for Dodge to follow.

They made their way toward a row of kegs lined up beneath a tree. Next to them sat a bright colored bin of red plastic cups. Earl pulled out two and began to fill them from the keg.

"Evening, gentlemen." Dodge turned as he took the plastic cup full of beer from Earl's hand. Behind him stood Butler with the small group of men he had been speaking with. Dodge recognized the man he had met at the feed store a few days earlier, Jackson. "Nice night for a pig roast, isn't it?" Butler asked.

"Sure is." Earl finished pouring beer into his cup as he glanced up at Butler.

"Didn't see you trying any of it," Butler said as he turned to Dodge. "You ain't one of them Muslims, too?" The men around him laughed.

Dodge shook his head. "Just didn't have much of an appetite this evening." He brought the plastic cup to his lips and took a large gulp. He could feel the bourbon, compelling his muscles to tighten and flex as it fervently surged through his veins.

"You come to a pig roast and don't even try the pig?" Jackson asked with a malicious laugh. "Guess you're not used to good old southern barbecue. Not being from around here." He stared at Dodge over his own cup as he took a sip.

158

The men around him were silent. Earl took a sip from his beer. "Jackson, this young man is just trying to enjoy himself. He may not be used to our fine cuisine just yet. But he will be." Earl smiled, but his eyes carried no humor.

Jackson snorted. "Is that right?" He turned back to Dodge. "Or maybe you're just like your daddy. Too good for anyone around here."

Dodge's hand squeezed tightly around the cup and a small line of cold beer trickled onto his hand. He took a step forward. "I don't think you need to be saying anything about my father," he said evenly to Jackson. Their eyes locked on one another, and he could feel a familiar warmth moving up his arms to his neck as he held tightly to his cup.

The other men had stepped back, and Jackson and Dodge now stood facing one another, a few feet separating them. Jackson laughed. "You didn't even know your daddy. Looks to me like he left you about as fast as he left here. But he came crawling back, just like you did."

Dodge could feel the muscles tightening in his shoulders and neck. His jaw clenched as he stared at Jackson. He knew his ability to control the rising emotion that was enveloping his body was gone, the alcohol having quickened the pace of anger and adrenaline that coursed through his veins.

"Don't talk about my father."

A larger group had begun to gather around the two men, sipping their beers and murmuring quietly.

Jackson took a sip of his beer. "I'll talk about whoever I damn well please, son."

Dodge dropped his beer to the ground as Jackson did the same. Jackson came at him, swinging his right arm. The blow landed clumsily against Dodge's shoulder as he dipped his body and jerked his head away. Dodge swung and landed a clean blow against Jackson's left cheek. He returned the strike and landed a blow just under Dodge's eye.

Dodge stumbled backward for a brief moment, barely keeping himself upright as Jackson came at him again. He lunged forward, wrapping his arms around Jackson's torso and pushing against him with all of his might. The two men fell to the ground, Dodge on top. He raised his arm and landed one blow to Jackson's jaw with his right fist, and a second quick blow to the side of his head with his left. Jackson's head fell back, a thin trickle of blood forming at the corner of his mouth.

Dodge could feel heavy arms pulling him up and off the ground. Behind him Earl and Wade were yelling to Butler and his friends. They pulled Jackson up off the ground and held him as he swayed for a moment. He spat out a thick red gob of blood from his mouth. Dodge could see Butler standing behind him, a small grin forming under his hate-filled eyes as he placed a hand on Jackson's shoulder.

Dodge let Earl and Wade pull him away from the crowd. "C'mon, I'll get you home," Earl said as he led Dodge around the side of the house.

From behind the house Dodge could hear Wade's voice, loud and angry. "Why you always got to start something?" he bellowed. "That's the last time, Jackson! The last time!"

Earl helped Dodge into the passenger seat of his truck. His head fell back against the head rest as Earl lifted himself behind the wheel without a word. They remained silent as Earl backed the truck onto the dirt road.

"He shouldn't have said anything about my father," Dodge murmured, his eyelids closing.

The last thing he remembered was the band starting up again, and the words to the Eagles' 'Heartache Tonight' floating out from the house to follow them home.

Chapter 11

The next morning Dodge was awakened by a throbbing bourbon headache seemingly trying to pound its way out from inside his head. Reaching his arm out gingerly, he pulled a pillow over his face without opening his eyes. Taking special care not to move his aching head, he kicked at the covers that had balled up around his ankles and entwined themselves with the sweat-soaked sheets during the night. He listened to the gentle whoosh of air blowing from the floor vent for a moment before he begrudgingly pulled himself out of bed, steadying himself blindly with the bedpost.

He stumbled his way into the bathroom and cupped his hands beneath the running faucet, shoveling the cool water into his mouth. He splashed his face and looked in the mirror. Bloodshot eyes stared back at him. He rubbed them, remembering again why years before he had vowed never again to touch hard liquor. He winced, and peered closer at the small purple bruise that was beginning to swell beneath his left eye.

"Shit," he said aloud, remembering the fight with Jackson. His drunken blows had not landed evenly, and for that he was grateful. As he remembered the strikes he had landed he grimaced. Along with hard liquor he had also sworn off fighting, and he realized he had broken two promises to his younger self in one night.

He showered and dressed, trying to block the events from the previous night from his head. He made his way downstairs to find the front door standing open, and he vaguely remembered someone helping him up the stairs the night before. He shut the door and made his way into the kitchen. Underneath the keys to his truck sat a short note.

"Dodge, you fight like your father. Earl."

He smiled as he folded the piece of paper and tucked it into his pocket. He vaguely recalled being pulled off of Jackson, and then helped into his truck. From there the night had ended in his mind.

He picked up his keys and made his way out to his truck. While he didn't want to see anyone today he needed coffee. Strong, black coffee. He pulled out of the drive and made his way toward Main Street to the coffee shop next to Mary's store.

It was late morning and the shop was empty, most of the town's inhabitants having already come and gone before or after church. As he entered, the smell of warm donuts and coffee made his stomach growl, although he was not sure he could actually hold down anything of substance.

"Good morning," said a woman as she made her way from the back room with a tin of muffins. "What can I get ya?" she asked as she slid the muffins into the glass case and wiped her hands across the flour-coated apron covering her mid-section.

"A large coffee, black," Dodge said as lowered his head and pulled his wallet from his back pocket. "To go," he added quickly.

"You got it," she said, moving to the coffee machine. "And how about a banana praline muffin to go with that?" she asked with a wide smile as she set the coffee down on the counter.

Dodge felt his stomach rumble again. "Not this morning, thanks."

She looked up at him as she set the cup of coffee on the counter. "That's some shiner you got comin' in there," she said as she took the five-dollar bill he handed her. "My husband got one just like that last week. Kicked by a donkey while he was trimmin' hooves out in the barn." She handed Dodge his change. "You got to watch them real careful, cause they could kick you into next Tuesday if they wanted to."

Dodge nodded and thanked her for the cup of coffee. As he turned to exit the door to the shop opened and a frail old woman slowly shuffled inside. Dodge recognized her immediately from the Garden Party.

"Good morning, Mrs. Sterling. The usual?" the woman behind the counter asked as Mrs. Sterling slowly took off her thin, pink overcoat.

"Of course, Mrs. Tidmore," she replied, as she made her way unhurriedly to a table by the window. Dodge moved toward her and pulled the chair out for her.

"Thank you, young man," Mrs. Sterling said with a smile as she sat down. Mrs. Tidmore hurried over and placed a large muffin and a small china teacup on a saucer in front of Mrs. Sterling before making her way back behind the counter.

"Mrs. Sterling," Dodge said, placing a hand on the chair across from her. She glanced up at him as she gently looped the tea bag's string around her spoon. "We met the other night, at the Garden Party," he said. "Do you remember me?"

Mrs. Sterling studied his face and shook her head. "I am sorry dear, but my mind is just not what it used to be. That's what you get for the glory of living to the ripe old age of eighty-one I suppose." She continued to look at Dodge, smiling.

"I'm Dodge Montgomery's grandson. You knew my grandfather."

"Oh yes, of course. Dodge," she said with a sigh. "You said you're his grandson, is that right?"

"Yes, he didn't know I was born, or rather I didn't know he was alive, or," Dodge trailed off, realizing this was the first time he found himself having to explain his situation to someone who didn't already know all the details before he did.

"Ah yes, my son said something about that." She nodded her head gently. "Would you like to join an old lady while she enjoys her tea?" She motioned to the chair across from her. He nodded and sat down, watching as she dropped two sugar cubes into her tea and began to stir. "And please, call me Lillette. Your grandfather and I were so very close when we were younger. How much do you know about your granddaddy?" She raised the delicate china cup to her mouth shakily.

"Not much," Dodge replied. "Just what I've heard here and there over the past week that I've been here." It occurred to him then that he had slept in the man's bed for almost a week and other than a few mentions about his silence or his kindness he didn't know much more about him.

Mrs. Sterling nodded her head. "I'm sure you've heard all sorts of things." She blew gently over the top of the cup, and Dodge watched a small ripple move across the surface of the liquid. "Your granddaddy was a fine man. A fine man indeed. What you young kids would call 'old fashioned' I suppose. People around here think they know what that means, but they don't. What with all of these 'helicopter parents' and all that nonsense about treating children like they're tiny little adults..." She trailed off with a wave of her hand. "Your granddaddy wasn't raised with a mama. She died when he was just a baby, still in the cradle."

"In the tornado," Dodge offered.

"That's right," Mrs. Sterling said, setting down the cup of tea. "I was still in my mama's belly when it came through. Nineteen thirty-two. Mama used to talk about that tornado every chance she could get. Not a lot of houses had televisions back then, and there weren't any of these storm radios like we have now. People had to understand weather patterns for themselves. There wasn't some man on TV who was going to tell you that a front was coming through," she scoffed. "When a storm was approaching you had better have known what was coming."

"Of course people knew it was going to be bad, but they had no idea just how bad it could be." Mrs. Sterling took a dainty bite of her muffin. "Mama said the sky had started clouding up late that morning. Then the thunderstorms started rolling in that afternoon. And the thunder! She said it sounded like it was right up in the attic above them, just booming away."

164

"The tornado formed just southwest of town around five o'clock. They say that as it reached town its path was two hundred yards wide. Can you even imagine it? The sound it must make before it comes down right on top of you." She looked off through the shop's front window as she took another sip of tea.

"Mama and daddy went down in the cellar to wait it out. It didn't hit our house, thank goodness, but it just tore right through other parts of town, knocking the electrical plant offline so the whole county was completely dark. And the rain, oh mama said the rain just kept coming down and wouldn't stop. Daddy said he had to get out and make sure people were alright and she begged him not to go, but he told her that they were safe and sound only by the grace of the good Lord Jesus, and it was his duty to go out and help those who may not be."

Mrs. Sterling folded her napkin again in her lap. She held on tightly to its delicate edges, just as her mind held onto this brief bit of fragile memory of her mother's voice.

"Daddy took off in his truck and mama said all she could do was look out the window after him, swerving around those downed trees. There was clothing and bits of paper strewn all throughout the trees, and she said there was a rocking chair, just sitting right out there in the middle of Highway 25, rocking away silently on its own in the wind." Mrs. Sterling shuddered.

"Daddy came back that night, mama said, shaking his head. She said she never saw him look so," Mrs. Sterling stopped and again stared out the window behind Dodge's head. "She said she knew he had seen things, things no human being should ever have to see. And he told her, 'Mrs. Montgomery is dead, found her out in the field. That was all he would say." Mrs. Sterling looked at Dodge.

"Over three hundred people across the state died that day. Fourteen of them here in our town. Mama said they had so many funerals to go to that week she just about thought she would die herself from all the grief and sorrow. And your great-grandmama's was the biggest of them all. Your great-granddaddy made sure of it. The local florist had run out of flowers what with all of the funerals going on around town. So your great-granddaddy had his workers go out and pick every single wildflower in his pastures. Had them all brought into the house and placed into vases and just about any other container they could find. Mama said there must have been thousands of them all about that big old house. You could barely find a place to set a drink that wasn't overflowing with them. Seemed a bit odd, considering the stories we'd hear about him later."

"Stories?"

She waved her hand in the air. "Dodge and his daddy never got on. I think it was because Dodge looked so much like his mother maybe. And nothing at all like his father. Oily little man." She shuddered as she set down her cup. "Your grandfather was such a looker when he was young," she said, smiling wistfully. "All of the girls wanted to date him in high school, and when he went off to the University of Alabama we were all heartbroken, knowing for sure he would meet one of those university girls and marry her," she said. "But he did not. He came back to town after his graduation. And by that time most of the eligible ladies in town were married off. And for whatever reason Dodge did not find any of those remaining to be suitable for him." Her voice had a sudden bitterness to it, and Dodge imagined his grandfather rebuffing the advances of a young Mrs. Sterling.

"We thought Dodge would remain a bachelor his entire life by then. I mean, a man nearing thirty-years old and not married was almost scandalous in those days. He was becoming the talk of the town. His daddy had died just before he left for college, so he was living up there in that big house with no one to share it with. Not that Dodge cared. He had that way about him, you see, ever since we were children. All of the Montgomery's always did. Nothing could make him lose that steely exterior he always carried. He was the fastest, the smartest, the best looking, and he knew it. And believe me, he knew how to make the ladies swoon. But that was as far as he would go. Until he met her." Mrs. Sterling put down her teacup. "Your grandmother," she said, the corners of her mouth turning down as if she had just sipped something bitter from her cup.

Mrs. Sterling continued. "I, for one, never did understand what he saw in her," she said. "I mean, yes, she was pretty of course, but we were all just as pretty when we had been her age, and he could have married any girl he wanted to then. But he had to have *her*. Why, she wasn't even from here. I think she had come to town to stay with an aunt, or some other relative."

Dodge did not share the information he had learned from Mary in her shop. He surmised that anything kind he had to say about his grandmother would fall on deaf ears with Mrs. Sterling.

"Anyway," Mrs. Sterling said as she swept muffin crumbs into her hand and placed them on the saucer. "He decided to marry her, even with that dreadful age difference. Eleven years. I mean, really. And that wedding," she said, rolling her eyes. "They held it in your granddaddy's house. Brought in the finest caterers from Mobile and the best florists from Birmingham. You would have thought the Queen of England herself was getting married in that house."

Dodge could sense a long-dormant jealousy beginning to resurface and decided it might be best to skip this part in the story.

"Mrs. Sterling, the other night at the Garden Party, you said he didn't kill her. What did you mean by that?"

Mrs. Sterling peered at him, and for a moment Dodge wondered if she had forgotten who he was again. Her eyes narrowed, as if she was contemplating a box that could contain either roses or rattlesnakes, and she wasn't sure how carefully to open it, if at all.

"Your grandfather was a very good man, but he had his share of people who didn't like him. Jealousy, mostly. So when his wife died so young and so suddenly people started to say things. There were plenty of people who would have liked to have seen the great Dodge Montgomery taken down a notch, so to speak," she said. She leaned in closer across the table. "Sometimes when one person starts to say something, and then another person shares it, other people start to believe it. Knowledge is something you *know* to be true, a belief is something you *want* to be true. And some people may have wanted it to be true. But it was just a rumor. I happened to know the medical examiner and he said himself she had a weak heart to begin with, and the stress of childbirth and raising a child was just too much for her. That is what he told me personally." She took a sip from her teacup, her eyes darting back and forth across the liquid's surface.

Dodge frowned and shifted in his chair. "But, if it was just a weak heart, then why would people assume that he-"

Mrs. Sterling continued as if she hadn't heard him. "Of course, there were still all the rumors about Fiona and the," she paused, "*activities* she may have been involved in." She sniffed and added quickly, "Nothing I would know anything about. Ladies just didn't take part in that type of conversation in my day."

Dodge thought back to Mary's stories of his grandmother in Birmingham. If they had been true, what other activities could she have taken part in? And if Mrs. Sterling had known this information surely his grandfather would have known it as well. He recalled Mary's account of how his grandfather just didn't have it in him to raise a child on his own. Perhaps he didn't have it in him to raise a child that he blamed for his sickly wife's death.

"Her funeral was just as grand as their wedding had been five years earlier. I remember it all like it just happened…" Her voice trailed off, and a look of horror fell over her face. She dropped the delicate teacup onto the saucer.

"Lillette?" Dodge picked up the sideways cup and began dabbing at the tea that was now running from the saucer onto the table. "Mrs. Sterling, are you ok?"

"My Robert died just a few days after her funeral," she said very slowly, as if recalling the details of a dream she had a week before. "An automobile accident, the river…" She spoke the words sluggishly, as her brain unraveled the memories that were now suddenly flooding terribly out from the place it had hidden them. "The car with the three men inside. With my husband inside," she said, as she shook her head.

Dodge looked around, wondering if he would need to call for help.

168

Her mouth fell open and she stared at Dodge pleadingly. She grabbed his hand forcefully, pushing the teacup off the table with a loud crash. "I didn't tell him, Dodge, I swear it. I would have never told him, never."

Dodge stared back at her as her eyes searched his. She was no longer here with him, but in another place, with another Dodge.

Mrs. Tidmore rushed from the back room. "Is everything alright?" she asked as she moved to the table with a dishrag in her hand. Mrs. Sterling stared at her as she bent down to pick up the broken pieces of cup and wiped at the floor.

"Yes," Dodge said. "I'm sorry, we were just talking and it fell, and..."

"Oh, dear," said Mrs. Sterling. "I am so sorry, Mrs. Tidmore. I'll of course pay for that one as well."

Mrs. Tidmore shook her head as she stood. "No, it's no bother, Mrs. Sterling. You're the only one who drinks out of those old teacups anyhow."

Mrs. Sterling watched her move back behind the counter before turning back to Dodge. He saw a faint uncertainty cross her face for a moment. "What were we talking about, dear?" she asked him.

"My grandmother's funeral," Dodge offered, no longer sure he wanted her to remember.

"Ah, yes. After the funeral Dodge had an enormous statue erected right there in the back of the cemetery over her grave. It was nothing like our town's little cemetery had ever had before. And a little tasteless if you ask me," she said, pursing her lips. "It's a giant winged angel, made completely of marble brought in from Italy. Can you imagine, Italian marble in our little town? That's just like a Montgomery for you. It's the largest one in the cemetery and you can't miss it. You have been to the cemetery, haven't you?"

"No," he replied. In fact, before this moment it hadn't even occurred to him that there was a cemetery where the dead bodies of his relatives now lay.

"They're all buried there together. Your grandmother, your grandfather, and your father. You really should go pay your respects. Your generation just doesn't understand as much about respect for the dead as ours did. It's not your fault, of course. Everyone nowadays gets so wrapped up in life they forget about the meaning of living. And dying." Her voice broke. "The cemetery is just a few streets over from here. You just make a left after the courthouse and you'll see it just down the road on the right hand side."

Mrs. Sterling began to stand up. "I went to your grandfather's funeral. It was not as extravagant as your grandmother's, but by then there was no one left to put on a grand display." She turned to Dodge as he stood next to her. "I suppose there was, but you hadn't been found yet."

They exited the shop together, Mrs. Sterling's frail arm hooked through Dodge's. He held the door open as she looked up into the bright blue sky. "'*And He will come to us like the rain. Like the spring rain watering the earth.*' Hosea 6:3."

"Excuse me?"

"It's going to rain." She pulled a thin plastic rain cap from her pocket and placed it over her head. They gazed up together at the bright blue sky absent of any rain clouds. She tied the rain cap tightly under her chin. "When it rains, it means the dead are crying for us. Falling like tears from Dixie skies."

Dodge looked up again at the cloudless sky and nodded his head. "How are you getting home? Can I drive you?"

She pointed down Main Street and chuckled. "You don't need to worry about me. I take this walk every day, and my dear neighbors make sure they see me heading up the road to the coffee shop and safely making my way back." She laughed again. "They say they can set their clocks by me!"

Dodge smiled at her. She removed her arm from under his and patted him gently on the arm. "You're a good boy, just like your grandfather. Don't you let anyone tell you otherwise." She turned and left him, and he stood for a moment watching her make her way slowly down Main Street. A storekeeper from the shop a few doors down opened his door and stepped outside.

"Fine morning, Mrs. Sterling," the man said to her with a wave as she shuffled by.

She continued walking with a wave of her hand behind her. "It's going to rain."

Dodge smiled and looked around him. The street was as quiet as it had always been. He glanced upwards again at the clear blue sky as he made his way across the street to the florist.

Chapter 12

He exited the florist's shop with a small bouquet of hastily-bought flowers before returning to his truck. As he made his way down the street he thought about Mrs. Sterling's unexpected recollection. Her husband had died just a few days after Fiona, in a car accident with two other men, down at a river. She and his grandfather had both lost their spouses within days of one another, but oddly, all she could recall without prodding was the grandiosity of Fiona's funeral and burial. He supposed it made sense that her mind had secreted the more painful memories away, like boxes stuffed into a dusty attic, only to be unlocked by someone who didn't have the right key.

The cemetery was not difficult to find, even with Mrs. Sterling's brief directions. It was not large but appeared to be well-kept. Before each headstone sat a bouquet of brightly-colored plastic flowers. He parked his truck and began walking toward the back as Mrs. Sterling had instructed.

The statue was just as she had described, towering over the other headstones scattered haphazardly around it. As he neared he could make out the features of the angel's stoic, stone face, her eyes closed and her mouth turned down in sorrow. Large marble wings spread out around her and enveloped a stone headstone bearing the word *Hallelujah* above the name *Montgomery*. One arm rested on the top, the other reached out, palm up, as if eternally questioning why.

He set down the flowers he had purchased at the florist and bent to read the three names and dates inscribed on the front: *Fiona Elise McKay Montgomery; James William Montgomery; Dodge William Montgomery.*

He stood staring silently at the ground before him. This was where his paternal family members now rested, tucked into caskets that had been lowered into the cold earth, the only sign of their existence a melancholy angel standing guard. This was all that remained of the family members he hadn't even known existed until a few weeks ago. People whose lives had been so intertwined, and the only one left standing was him, a man who had never met any of them, through whose veins pulsed their very blood, the genetic material that had made each of them who they were, that now made him.

The grass was clipped close to the ground, and he could just barely make out where the earth had most recently been moved to make room for his grandfather's casket. He realized that this was the closest he had ever been, or would ever be, to any of them. There was no chance of meeting his grandfather, or his father. His chances to do so had faded when he hadn't even known the possibility existed. There would be no joyous meeting of father and son, or grandfather and grandson. There had been a man who had lived in the house where he now slept, who had held the key to secret stories locked away that people could only whisper about, who could have told him what had really happened. That man was here, beneath his feet, the key and he locked away forever.

He wondered how many feet of earth separated him from his father, the bones laid bare through dirt and bits of wood around a silk lined coffin. This was as close as he would ever get; the only chance life would give father and son to meet. It would not be on a playground, or in the doorway of his grandfather's house. It was here, under the wings of a sad angel

173

guarding his family's memory with a downturned gaze among a sea of vibrantly colored plastic flowers.

The thought of this brought with it a wave of emotion that made him fall to his knees. He leaned forward, his hands pressed against the ground, and began to sob silently. He pulled at the dirt beneath him, wrenching up bits of soil and grass that he gripped tightly within his closed fists. He couldn't remember the last time he had cried, and the tears came brutally, his heart seeming to compress violently within the cavity of his chest. His body shook with the total realization that there had been a place for him, that there had been people who had shared his name, a name he had not even shared with his own mother.

He cried for his father, who had left this place only to come back to die without ever meeting his own son, or knowing how badly his son had needed him. He cried for his mother, who died not knowing that the man she had loved had not left her, that he was lying here in the warm Alabama ground instead, waiting for them to find him and tell him they loved him.

He cried for his grandmother, a woman who had only wanted a child, and kindness, and who had died before she could get enough of either. He cried for his grandfather, who loved her so much he had no love left to give to his own son, and because of that had died never knowing he had a grandson who walked the earth carrying his own name.

He wanted to go back and save each of them, to reach back in time and pull them all forward to tell them what he had learned, and how he could have helped them. That he was proud of each of them, and hoped that they were of him as well. That he didn't care about the big house or the acres of land, or the money that now sat in a bank account. That he just wanted them to know what he knew, that he loved them.

Dodge placed his forehead to the ground. His sobs began to subside, and he listened to the quiet stillness around him. As he tilted his head slightly he felt a drop of water splash lightly against his cheek. He lifted his head up as another fell silently on his nose. He had not noticed the small gray wisps of clouds that had moved overhead as he had lain on the ground. He lifted his face to them as they lightly scattered their weight of water to the earth and him, then silently moved on.

He stood and wiped his face with the back of his hand. He picked up the flowers he had brought from the florist and laid them gently against the headstone.

"Hello there," a voice called out from behind. He turned to see a man in jeans and work boots standing behind him, a rake in one hand. He approached Dodge with a slow wave.

"I didn't want to interrupt you." The man extended his hand. Dodge shook it hastily and wiped his eyes again with the back of his hand.

The man pointed to the grave marker. "Montgomery, eh?"

"Yes," Dodge glanced back at the headstone behind him. "My family."

The man nodded again. "Name's Marshall. I come back every now and then to take care of my family's plot too," he motioned toward the front of the cemetery. "The caretaker here does a fine job, but, I don't know…" he trailed off. "Just seems right to visit and take a little more care with the graves. Gives me something to do I guess." His voice trailed off. "I heard about old man Montgomery's funeral a few weeks ago." He looked at Dodge suddenly. "I don't mean any disrespect. That's what James used to call him," he said with a small, sad laugh. "The old man."

"You knew my father, then," Dodge asked wearily, staring at the name etched into the headstone before him.

"Oh. Yes. He was quite a rascal." He shook his head at the gravestone. "Was a shame him dying so suddenly like that."

Dodge nodded grimly.

Marshall nodded. "Boy, could I tell you some stories though. Your daddy wasn't afraid of nothing, not even old man Montgomery. Not that he was a scary man. He was just," Marshall shrugged. "Tough, you know?" He continued before Dodge could answer. "I remember, one time James decided he was going to race the bull, you know what that is? When you get into the pasture and see if you can make it across before the bull catches up with you. Let me tell you, that bull caught up with him all right,

175

just before he made it to the fence. Picked him up off the ground and threw him clean over the fence. Had to have thrown him eight or ten feet at least. James had a nice gash in his leg from that one, yes he did. When the old man saw us walking him back up to the house, James limping with a bright red blood stain on his jeans and a big smile on his face, from the look on his face we thought James would've been better off letting the bull get him. Old man Montgomery just nodded at us and threw me the keys to his truck, and said, 'Don't get any of that blood on the seat,' and went back in the house." Marshall shook his head. "He was funny like that, you know?"

Dodge nodded. "Did you see my father when he came back to town? The last time. Do you know why he came back here?"

Marshall shook his head. "No, I wasn't here then, was off at Auburn. James was supposed to go to Auburn too," he said. "We both got our acceptance letters on the same day. We played football together in high school. I think he even had a scholarship. But he decided to go to New York instead. Said he wasn't going to college and that was that. I was second string then. James was first, and he was a damn fine football player. I'll bet the old man wasn't too happy about that either."

"I'll bet," Dodge repeated absently, thinking again of what Mary had said. *Just two men who were too much and not enough alike.* "I guess there are a lot of things I'll never know about them."

"Yes, I suppose," Marshall said, staring at the headstone. "Earl would probably know though," he added off-handedly.

"Would know what?" Dodge's eyes narrowed quizzically at the mention of Earl's name.

"Why your daddy came back to town. Those two were inseparable. Best friends since grammar school. I'm sure your daddy wouldn't have come back to town without seeing Earl."

He tried to recall his conversations with Earl at his house and the party the night before. He didn't recall Earl ever telling him he and his father were best friends, or that he had even seen James when he had returned to town.

"You'd have to ask him straight," Marshall offered. "Earl's not one for long conversations, but he'll always tell you the truth. Anyway, I've got to get back on the road. It was nice to meet you."

Dodge's brow furrowed. If Earl had seen his father when he came back to town wouldn't he have told Dodge? And if they were such good friends why hadn't he said more to Dodge about him? He stared at the gravestone again. How much more was there for him to learn?

"Nice meeting you too," Dodge said absently as he watched him turn and head back to his car. Marshall put the rake in his trunk and got in, waving as he slowly drove off.

Dodge looked back at the stone angel, her face apologetically turned to the ground, as if even she could not have fought against the inevitable sorrow of lives lost and returned to the ground before her. It was not her fault, but she would take the blame, forever spreading her wings to stop the tears from the sky above her from reaching the lonely trio of bodies resting beneath her.

Chapter 13

On his way home from the cemetery Dodge pulled into Earl's dusty drive, the dogs yelping and howling their reception. There was no answer at the door, and he remembered Earl's statement at their first meeting. *"One of us is most always home, 'cept Sunday for church, of course."* Pulling a crumpled receipt from beneath his front seat, he composed a brief note that he slipped behind the battered screen door. "Earl, come see me," he wrote, and signed it with his name.

That night he lay in bed with the bedside lamp glowing, the figure of the angel from the cemetery burned into his head. He could be buried there, he imagined, with those people he had never met, and she would watch over him too, her silent sadness keeping guard. He wondered if, as they lowered his body into the ground, it might perhaps rain, the dead crying for him as well, and imagined a small drop of rain falling from her eye onto his dark, cold casket before it was lowered into the ground next to the rest of them.

In the morning, he awoke to a gentle, muted grayness in the room around him. It was daybreak, and the thin, faint white sheath of curtain could not keep out the light as it pressed its way through the velvety, gray clouds that hung over the house. Overhead he could hear a light rain falling against the roof.

He showered and made his way downstairs. He entered the kitchen to find Earl sitting at the table, a tin of rolls before him and one set out on the plate before him untouched. He held a cup of coffee in a paper cup in one hand. Another sat on the table in the cardboard take away tray.

Dodge stopped short in the doorway of the kitchen as Earl looked up at him.

"Morning." Earl looked up at him as he took a sip from the coffee.

"Morning," Dodge replied. Earl lifted the second cup of coffee from the tray. "I brought you some coffee." He nodded at the metal tin of rolls. "Miss May made you some yeast rolls. They're nothing special, but they're nice with some strawberry jam and butter. She worries about you up in this big house by yourself." His voice trailed off as he looked at the roll sitting untouched in front of him.

"Thank you." Dodge picked up the cup of coffee and took a sip.

"You told me to come by and see you."

"I didn't mean to bother you. I mean," Dodge said uneasily. "I didn't mean you had to come by first thing this morning."

Earl gave a thin chuckle. "When a man tells you he wants to see you, you make it a point to do it as soon as you can. Like when you got an animal down and you think it's time. You do it right then. Ain't no use waiting on the inevitable."

Dodge stood stiffly at the table next to him.

"I heard you were by the cemetery yesterday."

Dodge nodded. "Yes. Mrs. Sterling told me where it was."

Earl laughed. "Ol' lady Sterling, always got something to say, doesn't she." He sipped his coffee and nodded. "She's harmless. Now."

Earl picked up the roll from the plate before him. "Lots of people don't like cemeteries." He studied the roll in his hand. "They don't want to be that close to somewhere they know they're going to end up anyway. When I die, I'll know I'm going back to where I came from. You see I

179

believe people aren't afraid of dying. They're just afraid of not existing."
He set the roll down on the napkin in front of him untouched. "But we all
already didn't exist, before we got her. Do you know what I mean?"

Dodge sat down in the chair across from Earl. Before yesterday's trip
to the cemetery he hadn't thought at all about death since his mother's
passing. And he had grappled with the overwhelming sadness he had felt
when she passed by drinking himself into a stupor until he had no longer
cared about his own life or death. By the time he lifted himself out of the
fog of alcohol a year later, he found that he didn't want to think of death
anymore.

Earl continued. "When I die, Miss May is going to throw a party."

Dodge smiled weakly. "To celebrate your life?"

"Hell, no," Earl said loudly. "To celebrate me going back to where I
came from."

"Ah, to be with God, you mean?"

Earl shook his head. "I don't know what we all go back to, whether
it's God or heaven or Jesus or whatever. I just know that I've been there
before. We all have." He took a sip from his coffee. Dodge watched his
face, etched with lines from years of laughter and hard work and he wasn't
sure what else. There was always something soft and serene about Earl, but
also something just underneath his silence.

"You know what I tell people when they ask me if I've found Jesus?"

Dodge shook his head.

"I tell 'em, I ain't never lost him." He sat back in his chair with a
sharp laugh. "And that's the truth. You can't be looking for something you
already had all along."

Dodge nodded. "Earl, you knew my father pretty well, didn't you?"
You'd have to ask him straight.

Earl twisted the coffee cup in his hands. "Yes, I did."

"What was he like?" He shifted in his chair. "I mean, I know he hated
his father and he wanted to leave here, but what was he *really* like?" The
words came out quickly, his heart rushing out what it sought to know
before his brain could stop his mouth from seeking it.

Earl looked at him for a long moment. He took his hand and cupped it over his mouth, as if his body was physically trying to keep his mouth from letting out something it needed to say. He looked at Dodge without a smile, and let out a deep breath.

"He was my best friend," Earl's shoulders stooped forward as his body lost the battle against the words his soul needed to say. "We grew up here right next door to each other, and spent our days out there in those woods behind us." He smiled sadly. "He was such a good friend. Someone you could count on, who would do the right thing, every time." His voice trailed off as he stared at the window above the sink. "And he didn't hate your granddaddy, at least not as much as he said he did. Your granddaddy never laid a hand on him, not in anger," he shook his head, "but not in any loving way, either. Guess that's what comes of two men who each grow up without a mother. Both of them knowing what they need, but neither of them able to tell the other." They sat in silence for a moment, Dodge sipping his coffee as he waited for Earl to continue.

Earl pushed the plate away from him with a sigh. "I knew about you, Dodge," he said slowly.

The words reverberated through the thickened silence they created. Dodge's coffee cup froze in mid-air as he stared at Earl. "What did you say?" he asked, processing words that for some reason could not have the meaning he thought they did.

"I knew that James had gotten your mama pregnant."

The air around him suddenly felt colder. Dodge placed the cup of coffee on the table and pushed it away from him, as if its contents had suddenly soured. He could feel his hands clenching into fists, his knuckles pressing into his ribs sharply.

"How could you have known?" Dodge wasn't sure he was phrasing the question correctly. *How could you have known*, or, *how could you not have told?*

Earl's eyes lowered and he stared at Dodge's cup. "James came to see me when he came back to town." He looked up at him. "The last time." Earl whispered, as if the words were a physical ache to say. "Of course he came to see me. He was my best friend, closest thing to a brother I ever had. We grew up together out there, in those woods, on those roads."

The voice came into his head again, as it had before when he had watched Connor and Davis on the front lawn. *"Earl and James. That was what they were like. Brothers."*

Earl continued. "He came to see me after he saw his daddy. We sat over at my place on the front porch and drank some beers." Earl paused. "He didn't want to go home. He never did." He turned the coffee cup in his hand on the table. "He and I would sit out in those woods back there." He nodded his head toward the window. "Your granddaddy built him that hunting blind out there. We would sit up there nights, just the two of us, talking about our big dreams for the world. Guess your daddy's were just bigger than the rest of ours."

Earl looked at Dodge. "He told me he had met the love of his life in New York, and that he had a baby on the way. He was so happy. Just elated that he was going to have a family of his own. He had left here just a broken boy," Earl said. "And when he returned he was different, like she had maybe taken all the broken parts and put them together where they belonged."

"He said she was the woman he knew he would find. That leaving here was the best decision he ever made, if the only other thing that happened from it was that he had met her. Your daddy," he said, looking at Dodge, "Your father, he was always a happy fellow, even with all the sorrow in his life. He just always made the best of things, you know? But here, he knew he wasn't going to find that someone who was going to make him happy. Said his daddy told him he waited years to find the love of his life. Then she left almost as soon as he found her." Earl looked down sadly at the coffee in his hand.

Dodge's mind raced as it tried to grasp that the man sitting in front of him had not just known his father, he had seen him when he had come back. He had known all along that Dodge was alive, that his mother was waiting for his father to return. And he hadn't said anything.

"Why didn't you tell my grandfather about me? Or about her?" Dodge questioned, his hands still clenched tightly against his torso. "After he died, you could have…" His voice trailed off.

"Your father swore me to secrecy that night," Earl said, shifting uneasily in his chair. "Said he didn't want his child having anything to do with his father. That he was just in town to get the money from a trust that had been set up for him when his mama died. It was rightfully his, and he was entitled to it when he turned eighteen. When he had left he didn't even want that money. Told me that he wasn't going to come crawling back here just to get it. And yet here he was."

Dodge sat in stunned silence. His father had returned to get money for him and his mother. And then he had died, here, and Earl had not told anyone about Dodge or his mother.

"I don't understand, Earl. We had nothing when I was growing up. My mother had to work so hard just to support both of us. If she had had that money…" he trailed off. "If my grandfather had known I was alive—"

"There was no way your granddaddy was going to give her that money," Earl said forcefully. "You and I both know that." He looked Dodge in the eye. "You think your life would have been much better if you had your granddaddy's money? Your daddy hated the money he grew up with, hated living in this big house around all this fancy furniture in a bunch of big rooms that no one ever wanted to go into 'cept some folks once a year for a tour. The only reason your daddy wanted any of that money was because he had a baby on the way and he knew he needed it. You might think your life would have been better if you had had more money, but let me tell you from watching your daddy, that would not have been the case."

"You can't have known that!" Dodge roared. He could feel his face growing hot, his clenched hands beginning to shake against his ribs. "It wasn't your right to keep that from him!" Dodge banged his hand against the table in front of him. "He was *my* grandfather, not just James' father," he said bitterly.

183

Earl let out a long breath and lowered his head. The air in the room around them was heavy, the dark wooden table a long distance between them. "Your daddy made me swear that I would never tell your granddaddy about your mother or you, and I don't break my word." Earl paused. "I would never break my word to James. I just didn't know," Earl stopped, wiping his hand beneath his nose. "Then when he died a few days later, I had just lost my best friend. He had just come back and now he was gone again, for good." He rubbed at his eye with the back of his hand.

"Your daddy didn't leave your mother, and he sure as hell wouldn't have left you if he could've helped it. It was an unfortunate accident the way your father died, but you need to understand that he would have never left you if he could have helped it."

Dodge looked up, remembering the death certificate he had read in the lawyer's office. "He fell? Where? How?" Again the questions came, questions he had never wanted to have to ask but knew he wanted to have answered.

Earl nodded. "Right here in the back of this farm. From the top floor of the barn."

Dodge's eyes widened. The barn he had walked through was the place where his father had died. For a brief moment he imagined his father's crumpled body on the dirt floor that he had casually passed over as he had entered.

Earl spoke again. "He was working up there, I guess. Throwing down bales of hay. He must've slipped and fallen as he was working. Your granddaddy found him," he said softly.

"He just fell from the top of a barn and that was it? That was it?" Dodge shook his head. To him death was something that crept up sluggishly from an unhurried disease, or too quickly in the split second of a horrifying moment you couldn't control. It was not something that dropped in during a placid visit to the country, in a place you called home where you were supposed to be safe.

Earl nodded. "It happens. Those types of accidents just occur out here while people are working alone." He stated it matter-of-factly, but Dodge could hear an unrest in his voice.

His stomach turned at the awareness of his father dying alone in this place he had fled from. He had lived his life hating a man he had believed had abandoned him, a faceless ghost who couldn't take form to haunt his dreams. And here he had fallen and now lay, lifeless beneath a sky he could never escape.

"Don't you feel sad for your father," Earl said, looking at his face carefully. "He was the happiest I ever seen him when he came back here."

"Fat lot of good that did him," Dodge sniffed as he pushed the coffee cup farther away from him forcefully. "Or us." He thought again of his mother, sitting at a kitchen table, a jazz song playing from the radio on top of the refrigerator, staring off blankly at a memory on the wall that wasn't there.

"I knew you'd get your money, Dodge. Maybe not right then, but I knew you'd get it."

Dodge exploded from the table. "I don't care about the damn money!" His voice roared as he threw the coffee cup against the wall next to him. Earl sat silently. Dodge paced the kitchen, holding his head in his hands. "I don't care that my grandfather was such a bastard that his son, his own son, didn't want him to even know I was alive. I don't care that I live in this house, next to," he sputtered as he pointed out the kitchen window, "next to the barn where my father died when he came back here to get money because of me." He pounded his fist against his chest. "*Because of me.*"

He stopped pacing and looked at Earl. "What I care about is that there are all of these things that no one ever wanted to talk about, but everyone wants to tell me. That I have lived my entire life believing something that wasn't true. That I couldn't do anything to save them." He stopped and looked up at the ceiling. "That I was the reason he came here, and I was the reason he died when he left her to come here." He stood in the middle of the kitchen. He rubbed his eyes and turned away from Earl and stared out the window.

"I could burn this place down," he continued. "I should burn this whole place down with everything in it. All of this," he waved his hands around him, "all of this that no one even wants, that none of them ever wanted, that never helped any of them in the end."

Earl waited for a moment and then spoke softly. "Sit down, Dodge."

Dodge did not move, continuing to stare out the window. He was breathing heavily. "I can't believe I spent my entire life wishing I lived in a big house like this," he said, waving his arms around him. "I would have given anything to live here, to have a family name that meant something to anyone, to have enough money so my mother didn't have to worry all the time and just muddle through life from one job to the next," he said. "And now, I can't stand the thought of this place, these people, all of these stories," he said. He laughed bitterly. "I guess I have been given what is rightfully mine, wouldn't you say, Earl?" He looked at him. "I get all of what my father didn't want, and what my own grandfather would have never have given me had some law firm not found me."

Earl sat back in his chair. "I told Henry Wallace about you."

"You what?" Dodge spit the words out of his mouth, staring at the man sitting before him who was supposed to have been his father's friend.

Earl nodded. "Right after your granddaddy died, I went to Henry's office. Told him that James had a child somewhere up in New York. That he had had a girlfriend in New York who was pregnant when he died, and that they needed to find that child." He sipped his coffee again and looked at Dodge. "And that if they didn't at least do their due diligence in finding Dodge Montgomery's grandson and rightful heir that I would tell the damn whole town."

Earl continued. "Once your granddaddy was dead, I figured I had kept my promise to James. I had kept my word, and not told your granddaddy that he had a grandchild somewhere out in the world. Maybe it wasn't the right thing to do, to keep my word to your father all those years. I don't know. But I was damned if I was going to see what was rightfully yours pissed away by a bunch of lawyers."

186

"You might not think it's much, Dodge." His words came more forcefully. "Or maybe you think it's too much. You might think this is all just a burden for you. The lies, the secrets, the sadness. But it is rightfully yours. Your daddy might not have wanted you to grow up here, or live in this house, or know your grandfather. And your grandfather might not have wanted a son or a grandson to carry on his name. But this is yours, just like it has always been. You are a Montgomery." He pointed a finger at him. "And you are James' son."

Dodge laid a hand against the counter as he felt his legs give way beneath him. His body slid slowly down against the counter as his hands grasped for the ground below him. He was falling, slowly, his brain knew that, but his body couldn't stop itself. He was crumbling in beneath himself, his body curling up upon itself as it had as a child. He shook his head slowly as he stared at the floor.

"Why didn't you just tell him I was alive? Why, Earl?" He pleaded as his eyes welled up with tears. It was his last time to ask this question, and the last time to get the answer. "Just to keep a promise to a friend? Just to keep your word?" The words didn't mean anything to him, as he had never stayed anywhere long enough to have a friend to whom a word meant keeping. Because he had never had a brother, or anyone who even remotely resembled one to him in his own life.

Earl shook his head, but as he did his shoulders tightened and his hand curled tightly around the coffee cup in his hand. He stood up from the chair, toppling it over behind him. "For what, Dodge, so you could come live with a man who didn't even want to live with his own son?" he yelled at Dodge as he towered over him.

The cup in his hand crumpled within his tightening fist. His chest heaved as he stood over Dodge staring up at him. Slowly he began to shake the coffee from his hand and sat back down. "I didn't mean that."

Dodge nodded slowly. "Yes, you did."

Earl sighed. "No, I didn't mean that. Your father made me promise him I wouldn't say anything. I was the only person he told in the world. He loved your mama, and he didn't want her coming down here and living this life. He didn't want you to live this life. I see that he was wrong. But I can't change that. Couldn't change it then. This is yours, Dodge, just as much as it was your daddy's, and your granddaddy's, and his granddaddy before him. Your daddy was wrong Dodge. If it was going to be bad, then at least it was going to be yours."

He could see Earl's eyes reddening, the skin around them softening beneath tears that would not fall.

"He was scared, Dodge. More scared of what he could give you than what he couldn't. Do you understand that?"

Dodge shook his head. "No." He didn't understand any of it, the jumble of stories of people he didn't know, but whom he shared a history with. These people who lived here, safe and content in their big house with land and money, who loved each other and hated each other and left it all for him, whether they knew it or not. Here he was, all alone on a kitchen floor, with all of everything they never wanted to give him.

Earl nodded his head. "All of this isn't just land and a big house and a bunch of journals and boxes in an attic. It's secrets. Things people tuck away that they don't want anyone else to see but that they can't leave themselves. It's a life that you don't ask for, that you might not even want, but that you can't walk away from. James walked away. He knew your granddaddy couldn't do that. And he didn't want you to be saddled with the life he couldn't even stand to live himself."

"That's why I didn't tell your granddaddy. If my best friend that I loved like a brother ran from it and made me swear I would never tell anyone about the new life he was building so far away, how could I do that to him if he was alive, let alone once he was dead? If he couldn't get away from it in the end, what good was I going to do by giving it to you?" Earl's voice broke as he reached his hands out pleadingly toward Dodge. "What would I have given to you?"

The room was silent for a few minutes. Dodge continued to sit on the floor, his hands planted solidly on the worn wooden kitchen floor beneath him. The floor his ancestors had built, away from the rest of the house in case it caught fire. That was what you did when something was dangerous, when you needed it but you didn't want to take the chance that it could be consumed by fire and destroy everything else around you. You separated it, put it in a different place and left it there.

Earl wiped at his eyes. "I don't know if what I did was right, not telling your granddaddy. Not finding you before he died. I still don't know if it was wrong, either. But you're here. This is yours. Not just this house or that pasture or those cattle out there. This is yours, everything that comes with it. And you no longer have an option to walk away. Because even if you leave," he said firmly, "Even if you leave, it goes with you. That's what you give someone when you tell them something they might not want to know. You give it to them, whether they like it or not, and you can't take it away."

Dodge wiped at his own eyes and stood up, uncrossing his arms. "Thank you, Earl, for telling me." He looked at him, this old man sitting in front of the child of his best friend, a man he loved so much he would keep his word to him, regardless of life or death.

Earl waved his hands and Dodge cut him off. "No, Earl, thank you for being his best friend, for keeping your word, and for finding me." He shook his head. "I don't think that what you did was wrong. You did the best you could, and that's all anyone can ask from anyone."

Earl nodded and stood up. "You're a good man, Dodge. Your daddy and your granddaddy would have been real proud of you, I know that much. And you would have been real proud of them." Earl stood and Dodge followed him through the hallway into the center hall.

"You gotta keep that door open," he said, as he moved toward the front door. "That's how your neighbors know you're home, if your door is open. Then they don't have to leave a note."

He smiled as he opened the screen door and exited. Dodge moved to the door and watched him walk slowly down the steps to the drive. Earl turned and made his way across the side lawn toward his own house, and it occurred to Dodge then that he had not driven over but had walked through the woods. As he watched, he imagined Earl traveling the route as a young man, waving behind him at James as he crossed the pasture into the woods.

Dodge lifted his hand in goodbye, though Earl did not turn to see him do so.

Chapter 14

He awoke the next morning to the vibrating hum of his cell phone. He fumbled from beneath the covers and reached for the phone on the nightstand next to the bed. Rubbing his eyes he glanced at the clock. Eight fourteen a.m.

The number from the New York area code flashed on the screen. "Hello," he said groggily into the phone.

"Mr. Montgomery, I just wanted to let you know that we received the paperwork you sent to us. I took a preliminary look at it this weekend and it all appears to be on the up and up. What would be best is if you go ahead and sign the necessary documents with the attorneys down there in…" The attorney paused and Dodge could hear papers rustling in the background. "Shelby County, Alabama? Yes, if you just sign the paperwork there and have the attorneys fax it to us, we'll handle the rest from there. You will be back in the city this week?"

Dodge sat up in bed, staring out at the room before him. Sunlight filtered through the tall windows at the far end, the dark shadows of their panes reaching out toward him in the bed from across the room. The air conditioning hummed lightly, unable to drown out the incessant dripping sound from the bathroom.

"Mr. Montgomery?" The attorney's voice broke into his thoughts.

"Yes, I plan on being back in New York very soon. Perhaps tomorrow night."

"That's fine then. You can give the attorneys down there our information and we can take care of the rest of it. Oh, and congratulations, Mr. Montgomery. Sounds like you are now a very wealthy man."

Dodge stared vacantly at the room around him. "Yeah. Lucky me."

He ended the call and immediately dialed Henry's law office. The receptionist put him through with a cheerful note to have a blessed day.

"Dodge, my old friend," Henry yelled into the phone. "You recovered from that party yet?"

Dodge paused. Had Henry heard about Saturday night already?

"I know those fancy pants parties may not be your style. But you sure looked fine in your pink ensemble like the rest of us." Henry laughed, and Dodge could envision him leaning back in his big leather chair.

Dodge grinned despite himself. "It was really nice, Henry, thank you again for inviting me. Listen, I just got a call from the law firm in New York. They said to go ahead and sign the paperwork, and then have you send it up to them. And then," he paused. "And then I'll just head up there and finalize everything from the city."

There was silence on the other end of the phone.

"Henry?"

"Yes, I'm here. That will be fine. When are you looking to come by, tomorrow maybe?"

"Today, Henry. This morning, if possible."

"Oh. Alright." Henry's voice no longer held the same cheerful tone. "We'll be here, whenever you want to come by."

"I'll be by within the hour." Dodge hung up the phone.

He moved out of bed to the bathroom to brush his teeth. He looked in the mirror. The bruise under his eye from Saturday evening's fight had turned from bright purple to a muted blue, just barely perceptible beneath his skin. He looked into the basin one last time, then knelt down and reached under the sink and turned off the water, the drip ceasing.

He dressed and grabbed the tuxedo that still hung from the back of the bedroom door before making his way downstairs and moving quickly through the front foyer and out the front door. He drove to town in silence, the radio off and the windows rolled up, the blast of cold air from the vents chilling his skin. He eased his truck into a parking spot in front of the drugstore and stopped to look out over the quiet stretch of street ahead of him before he exited the truck, shutting the door behind him with a slam.

Henry's receptionist greeted him brightly before showing him into his office. As Dodge entered Henry looked up from the paperwork he was hunched over, his large frame almost enveloping half the desk.

"Thank you, Gladys." He nodded to the receptionist as Dodge took a seat and she shut the door.

"So," Henry began with the faintest trace of an awkward smile. "This is it then, eh?" He opened the file folder before him and pulled out a set of tabbed papers, pausing before handing Dodge a pen.

"I suppose so," Dodge replied as he looked down at the paperwork, unable to meet Henry's gaze. Henry began handing him pieces of paper, each marked with a brightly colored tab showing where his signature was needed. Dodge signed them swiftly, handing each one back to Henry, who slowly set them face down in a pile next to him.

Henry paused at the last piece of paper in his hand. "That should do it." He handed it to Dodge, who hurriedly signed it. "We'll get copies of these signed documents off to your law firm in New York this afternoon."

"I appreciate all of your help, Henry," Dodge said as he watched him fold the papers up into the file. "I'm wondering if you can recommend a good realtor, to list the property."

Henry pursed his lips together as he sat back in his chair. "You're sure that's what you want to do?"

Dodge looked away from Henry's gaze. "Yes. It's just not somewhere I want to be."

Henry removed his reading glasses, folding them up and turning them over in his hand. "I suppose Freddy Highland would be the best person for the job. His office is just around the corner from here. You can probably stop over this morning, or better yet after lunch-"

"No, that's alright," Dodge interrupted him. "Maybe I'll just give him a call or send him an email when I'm back in the city tomorrow night."

"Tomorrow night?" Henry sounded surprised. "You're high-tailing it out of here then, aren't you?"

"There's no reason for me to stay any longer," Dodge replied. "I'll probably head out tomorrow morning, get an early start." He rose from the chair and extended his hand across Henry's desk. "Again, I appreciate your help. I'm sure you and the law firm in New York can handle things from here."

Henry reached up and took his hand lightly, barely moving it up and down in a shake. Dodge moved toward the door, Henry still seated behind the desk, a solemn look covering his face.

"Say, what about dinner tonight?"

Dodge turned in the doorway. "I don't think so, Henry."

"Aw, c'mon Dodge. It'll be your last night here, and from the sound of it, you don't plan on coming back, do you?"

"No, I don't."

"So one last dinner here in town isn't going to kill you, is it?" Henry rose from his chair and moved from behind the desk. "You haven't even had a chance to try the best restaurant in town, Barney's. It's just on the corner across from the old courthouse, and they serve the finest –"

"Really, Henry, I just want to get a good night's sleep and head out in the morning. I'm not really up for any more socializing."

Henry nodded his head and sat back down in his chair. "If you change your mind, you know where it is." He placed his reading glasses back on and picked up a piece of paper from his desk and began to peer at it intently.

"Goodbye, Henry." Dodge gave a small, feeble wave.

He made his way out the door of the office and back to his truck where he pulled out the tuxedo. The sign on the door to Mary's shop was turned to Open, and as he pulled it open two women stepped out, smiling up at him. He did not return their smile as he held the door for them to exit. Inside, Mary stood behind the counter, holding up a long strand of pearls before the woman in front of her. Dodge made his way in quietly, moving to the corner of the store behind a tall rack of clothes.

"These just came in yesterday," Mary was telling the woman. "Absolutely gorgeous, aren't they?"

"Why, yes, they are. Who did they belong to?" Dodge could hear the woman ask in a hushed tone.

"None other than Mrs. Kathleen Fullerton."

"You don't say!" The woman took the strand of pearls in her hands. "Sellin' off her grandmamma's pearls?"

"Mmm-hmm," Mary replied with a slow nod of her head. "Seems that girl developed a terrible internet shopping habit, and she's been hiding the bills from her husband."

"Oh, dear."

"You didn't hear it from me, but apparently she's run up all of her credit cards 'til they're just about maxed out."

"Oh, that poor girl," the woman said with a shake of her head.

"Poor girl?" Mary scoffed. "Why on earth is she purchasing all those things on the internet?" She looked about at the store around her. "When she could be buying them here?"

Dodge smiled and shook his head.

"I will think about it," the woman said as she handed the necklace back to Mary and stood up from the stool. "Lord knows I don't really need another pearl necklace. But it certainly is beautiful."

"It won't last long, either," Mary said as she tucked the necklace back into the case. "You might come back tomorrow and it will be gone," she warned her.

"I'll take my chances. Will I see you at Bridge on Thursday?" the woman asked as she made her way to the door.

"Of course," Mary replied with a wave.

Dodge stepped out from behind the rack of clothing. Mary looked up with a gasp, placing her hand against her chest.

"Good Lord above, Dodge Montgomery. When did you sneak in? You just about scared me half to death!"

"Sorry, Mary, I didn't want to interrupt." He moved toward the counter. "Just bringing back the tuxedo I borrowed. I don't have time to have it dry cleaned." He set the garment bag on the counter and reached for his wallet, pulling out a twenty-dollar bill and placing it on top. "This is for the cleaning."

Mary peered at him suspiciously. "What do you mean you don't have time?"

"I'm going back to New York tomorrow. I'll be heading out in the morning."

Mary picked up the garment bag, setting the money back down on the counter. "Don't you worry about it, darling. When you get back we can settle up on the dry cleaning." She picked up the bill and began to hand it to Dodge.

Dodge looked at her hand and shook his head. "I'm not coming back," he said, his eyes unable to meet hers.

"Not comin' back? Not comin' back soon, or ever?"

"Probably not ever." Dodge rubbed the back of his neck and looked around him.

"Who will take care of your granddaddy's land?"

"I'm selling it."

Mary drew in a deep breath and turned her head slightly. "You're going to sell- your granddaddy's farm," she said slowly, pausing between the words as if hoping it would sink in to both her and him.

"Yes, actually I was hoping you could possibly go over there and go through all of the belongings to sell whatever you can, and the rest can just be donated."

Mary's eyes widened. "Sell their belongings?"

"That's what you do, isn't it?" Dodge laughed. "Sell off people's belongings?"

"Darlin' I sell things that people no longer want, or can no longer afford to have. I can't believe either is the case for your belongings."

Dodge shook his head. "They're not my belongings. They belonged to someone else and I don't need or want them. If it's too much, I can see if there's someone in Birmingham who can set up an estate sale."

Mary's mouth dropped open and she moved her hand to her face. She pursed her lips together and stood up straighter. "Dodge Montgomery, you listen to me." Her tone was stern but her voice shook slightly. "You have only been in this town one week, that's hardly enough time for you to decide to sell off all of your family's possessions to the highest bidder. And if you think-" She stopped and shook her head. "If you think for one second about having one of those Birmingham people just come down here and put a price tag on the contents of that house to sell to the highest bidder, then you are worse than they are."

"Mary, I didn't come here to start living in an old farmhouse out in the sticks," Dodge replied exhaustedly.

"You just came for your money. That was it all along wasn't it?" Her face fell, as if it was a sudden realization, not the truth the whole time.

"That's right." Dodge nodded. "I appreciate your sharing your stories about my grandmother with me, and being so kind to me while I was here. But I have to go."

Mary nodded. "So like your father," she said with a small, sad smile. "And he like your grandmother. Never able to stay in one place and just be happy with it. History can't help but repeat itself."

Dodge looked away from her, unable to bear the thought that his leaving was somehow letting her down.

"What if we have dinner tonight, Mary? I hear there's a great restaurant right down the street, across from the courthouse. It can be a farewell dinner."

She looked down at her hands.

"Please, Mary." He placed a hand over hers. "I don't want to leave knowing you're angry with me."

Mary smiled and placed her hand over his. "I'm not angry with you, Dodge. I just thought the story would have a different ending is all." She picked up the garment bag and moved slowly away from him toward the back of the store. "Barney's opens at five and I close up shop at six."

"I'll meet you there at six," Dodge shouted to her as he watched her move into the back room. He made his way out of the store hurriedly, leaving the twenty dollar bill on the counter, knowing he had one more stop to make before he left.

"Mr. Montgomery," Jake said from behind the counter of the feed store as he entered. "What can I do for you this fine day?"

"I'm heading back to New York. Tomorrow."

"You lookin' for someone to take care of the animals for a few days?"

"Actually, I'm not going to be returning. I was wondering if you knew how I would go about selling the livestock. Not the horses," he added, remembering Davis' request. "I think I have someone to take the horses."

Jake pressed his hand against his chin. "I'm sure Butler can take the cattle to auction. I can have him go by your place this week and get things started."

"Is there anyone else who can do it? I mean, besides Butler?"

Jake's eyes narrowed. "Butler would be the wisest choice, seeing as how he knows those cattle and the farm better than anybody else. Doesn't seem to make much sense havin' someone else do it."

"That's fine," Dodge replied, confident that he would be long gone before Butler stepped foot back on the property.

"So you're sellin' the place then."

"Yes, I'll be putting it on the market as soon as possible."

"Not too many people looking for a house that's more than a hundred years old nowadays. Might find someone who wants the land."

"It doesn't matter. Whoever wants to buy it can have it." Dodge turned back toward the door. "You'll speak to Butler then?"

"Yup," Jake replied. "Don't you worry about a thing. I'm sure Butler will take care of it."

Dodge nodded his head as he exited the store.

He spent the rest of the afternoon packing up his things and moving through the house ensuring the windows were locked and no lights were left on in any of the rooms, leaving it just as he had found it a week before. At last he came to the closed door on the second floor. He opened it again, and stepped inside the blank room, moving to the two tall windows at the end. He lifted up against them, ensuring they too were still locked tight. As he pushed up a small screw fell from one of the locks and tumbled to the floor. He had to leave it just as he found it, he thought to himself as he bent to retrieve it. As he did his eye caught something on the bottom of the window sill. There, carved into the wood was his father's name. James. He gently traced his finger against each letter. How old had his father been when he had left them there? Had he carved each letter into the soft wood for his own amusement, or for someone to find, years later, hidden in a secret spot beneath the ledge where no one would care to look?

He let out a sigh and stood up, staring out the window in front of him. *Stay*, he heard her voice in his head. *I can't*, he silently replied. *I have to go. Mama, I have to go.*

He turned from the room, closing the door behind him and listening for the click ensuring it was shut tight. He made his way to his grandfather's room, laying out his clothes for the next morning and then zipping up the duffel bags stuffed again with his belongings. He wanted to be ready to take off before dawn the next day, sure that there was nothing he would leave behind or take with him.

He sat down on the bed and looked around the room. Whatever casual familiarity he had gained was gone. He made it again just a place, somewhere he had laid his head as he waited for the next place to go. He rose and made his way downstairs, to head into town and wait for Mary at the restaurant.

Barney's was easy to find, at the end of Main Street in front of the old courthouse as Henry had described. He felt a tinge of guilt that he had turned down Henry's invitation to have dinner here tonight, but was now here meeting Mary. He chuckled as he thought of Henry's face tomorrow when he undoubtedly would hear of it from someone in the small town. *"Why Dodge Montgomery's grandson was dining at Barney's last night with Mary. You don't say?"*

Dodge made his way inside and directly to the bar that lined the wall across from the entrance. Even though the restaurant had just opened most of the tables were already filled with the early bird diners while the bar stools sat empty. He took a seat on the one farthest from the door to the kitchen as the bartender made his way over.

"What're you havin' this evening?"

"A bottle of light beer is fine," Dodge replied.

The bartender reached into the cooler beneath the counter and pulled out the cold bottle, opening it and setting it on the counter in front of Dodge. "Menu?"

Dodge shook his head. "I'm waiting on someone for dinner."

The bartender nodded and turned to the television on the wall above his head. Dodge looked around at the tables behind him. Most of the patrons appeared to be at least twice his age, couples sitting together at tables in groups of twos and fours. He was the only single patron in the restaurant, sitting alone at the bar with his bottle of beer. This was what he had to look forward to again in New York, he thought as he swallowed a gulp of beer. He watched the door to the kitchen open every few minutes to a waitress carrying out trays of food. None of them made their way to the bar to pick up drinks.

"Looks like a slow evening for you," Dodge commented as the bartender set down his second bottle of beer.

The bartender laughed. "This crowd? They wouldn't order a drink from the bar if someone put a gun to their head," he laughed. "You know if you want to have a good night of drinking you invite one Baptist. If you want to have a cheap night of drinking you invite two."

Dodge laughed as he took a sip from the bottle.

200

"You got a hot date tonight, my friend?" the bartender asked as he absently wiped the counter.

"Oh, yes," Dodge replied. The bartender raised his eyebrows and continued wiping the counter. Behind him Dodge could hear Mary's voice coming from the front door.

"Oh, Ora, the place just looks fabulous. I know, I should get here more often, but you know the hours you have to keep as a business owner. Why yes, you should come by more often. In fact, I have just gotten in an absolutely gorgeous pearl necklace that would look absolutely fantastic with that outfit, or just about any outfit. Why, there is my date now." He turned to see her wave at him.

Dodge rose from his stool as Mary approached the bar. "Good evening, ma'am. Should we get a table?"

"Let's just eat here at the bar." Mary slid onto the stool next to him. "You seem to be settled in here nicely and it's been so long since I've dined at the bar, it'll be kind of fun." She waved to the bartender. "Michael, I'm feeling good this evening. Why don't you fix me up a Tom Collins?" she asked as she set her large purse on the counter beside her.

"A Tom Collins?" Dodge asked.

"Why, yes darlin', have you never had one? It's just lemonade and a bit of liquor – Michael, fix my friend up here with one as well," she shouted as the bartender nodded.

Dodge put out his hand. "I don't need any liquor tonight, Mary. I'm sticking to the light stuff." He lifted his bottle of beer toward her. "I've got an early start ahead of me tomorrow morning."

"Nonsense," Mary scoffed. "You can join an old lady for one drink before dinner, can't you?"

Dodge nodded, realizing that arguing with Mary would be futile.

The bartender set the two tall glasses before them, dropping a cherry into each. Mary picked hers up and held it before her, as Dodge did the same.

"Cheers, Dodge," she said as their glasses clinked. "Here's to hoping you find what you're looking for in life, no matter where that may be."

"Thank you, Mary." Dodge set the glass down in front of him without taking a sip.

"My husband and I used to drink these on special occasions. Just the taste of one of them brings back so many memories." She gazed at the glass in her hand. "You just never know when something as simple as this, a shared drink with someone, will just become one of the things you have left to remind yourself of them after they're gone."

Mary motioned to the bartender. "Michael, we're gonna need some menus. Dodge here has never been here before. And it's his last night in here so we have to make sure he gets something good."

Michael nodded and brought over two menus. "The grits are excellent, as usual."

Dodge looked over the entrees listed on the menu, unsure even how to pronounce the unfamiliar dishes like *etouffee* and *mufalettas*. "What are you having, Mary?"

"Hmmm, I don't know. It's been so long since I've had some good Cajun food." She perused the menu before her. "I think I will just go with whatever the chef's special is this evening. That always works out for me." She closed the menu, setting it down on the bar before her. "I don't get out all that often for dinner anymore, so I'll just leave it up to him."

"Then I will do the same," Dodge said as he gratefully closed the menu.

The dining room was slowly filling with people and the sound of their conversations reverberated off the walls around them. The bartender set a fresh bottle of beer down, spilling out half the Tom Collins from Dodge's glass when Mary leaned down to reach into her purse.

"Oh look, there's Dodge." A woman's voice floated over the noise around them and he turned to see Anne and Martin standing side by side at the hostess station. Anne gave a small wave, and Dodge motioned them over.

"I can't believe I am seeing you for a third time in one week." Anne placed her hand on his shoulder with a wide smile. "That's small town living, I suppose."

Dodge shook Martin's hand. "Dodge, my old friend."

"Anne, Martin, this is my friend Mary." He nodded as Mary set down her drink and reached out a hand to both of them.

"Mr. Montgomery and I are enjoying a farewell dinner here at the bar." Mary patted the seat next to her. "Y'all are welcome to join us."

"A farewell dinner? Already?" Anne's face fell. "You're coming back, aren't you?"

"Yes, who will help me wrangle large animals on the side of the road?" Martin chuckled.

Dodge shook his head, picking up his bottle of beer and staring at it intently. "I'm afraid I have decided to leave. The house is too much for me, and I just don't have the desire to take care of that much land. It's too much. All of it."

Mary raised an eyebrow and silently took another long sip of her drink.

"Well, then," Martin said, "We'll have to join you for your last dinner, if that's alright." He pulled out the stool next to Dodge and motioned for Anne to sit.

"Tom Collins for everyone!" Mary shouted as she emptied her glass.

"Oh, Mrs. Harris," a voice came from behind the bar. "Are you causing trouble again?" They looked to find a man standing behind the bar filling a large plastic pitcher. He wore a long white apron, and looked over at Mary with a mischievous grin.

"If it's none other than the chef himself," Mary said as she pushed her drink away from her. "Michael, a few more Tom Collins for me and my friends," she said as she tapped the empty glass.

The chef made his way over to the group. "Are you finally dining again in my fine establishment, Mary?"

"Oh, you know I would eat here every night if I could," Mary replied, clinking the ice cubes around in her empty glass. "But a woman of my stature has many social obligations," she said with a smile.

He smiled at her. "And what are y'all havin' this evening?"

"We were hoping to leave it up to you," Mary replied as the bartender set a fresh batch of drinks before them. "I doubt my friend Dodge here has had time to try any of your delicious dishes, considering how little time he has decided to spend here." She threw Dodge a glance over her glass and he gave her an exasperated look.

"Whatever you recommend is fine," Dodge said to him, hoping it whatever it was would be quick.

Anne and Martin sipped their Tom Collins and nodded their heads.

"These Tom Collins are enough to make a grown man's head swim. Don't you agree, Dodge?" Mary looked down at the drink before him.

"I'm sorry, Mary, but I don't usually drink liquor and lately it appears that is a wise choice for me."

"Don't you worry about it, sugar." She pulled his drink closer to her. "I will help you out with that."

A waitress appeared with a large tray full of food and set four steaming plates before them.

Dodge ate silently as they laughed at the story Mary was telling. Mary reached her hands high above her head, and Dodge smiled as he wiped his mouth and caught his reflection in the mirror behind the bar. Here he was, amongst friends, laughing and enjoying this moment. How long had it been since this had happened, since he had sat with people whose company he enjoyed just before leaving them?

The memory floated into his head, drowning out the voices around him until he again only heard hers.

"You what?" She stood in the entryway of the apartment. The worn fixture above her head cast a dull, yellow light onto the walls around her. Her coat, the one she wore every winter, orange and thin with the fraying edges, hung limply on her thin frame. The rest of the apartment was dark except for the fluorescent light on the ceiling of the kitchen above him. She had not even had a chance to turn on the lights before he had accosted her with his news. "What did you say?"

"Ma, you heard me," Dodge said, leaning against the counter of the kitchen in the small apartment. This was not his apartment, it was where

204

they had last unpacked their things, temporary and uncomfortable, just like the others before it.

"Say it again," she said, raising her hand to her collar, the large bag of random items she had brought home dropping to the floor beside her. "Say it again," she said to him almost pleadingly.

"Ma, I enlisted in the army," he answered, tracing his finger along the long, deep crack in the tile of the kitchen counter. He had decided earlier that he would tell her tonight, after dinner, but his nerve, or lack thereof, had gotten the best of him, and he had blurted it out as soon as she had closed the front door behind her. In the last moments, his mind must have decided it would be best to do it quickly, to rip the bandage from the delicate skin of a wound that would not heal regardless.

She heaved the bag up suddenly from the floor and threw it against the wall beside him. "You're all I have, Dodge, you're all I have!" she screamed at him as the contents fell to the floor next to him. "You're only eighteen years old, what do you know?"

"I know I've been hearing that I'm all that you have for the last eighteen years. I've been hearing it my whole life." He pushed himself up off the counter and crossed his arms against his chest.

"Because it's true," she said as she slowly moved forward and fell into the worn sofa in front of her. She looked so small, so frail. So unlike the woman he had envisioned her to be his whole childhood.

"I don't want it to be true anymore!" He slammed his fist against the counter. "I can't be everything you have in this world. It's too much for me. And it's not enough for you."

"You're going to leave me," she said sadly as she placed her head into her closed fist. "You're going to leave me just like he did, and I'll never be able to stand it."

"Ma, stop, please. I'm just going-"

"It's dangerous, Dodge. The world is a dangerous place. Do you even know what that means?" She screamed the words at him, hurling them across the room as forcefully as she had thrown the bag.

Dodge sighed. *"Yes, mom. But I need something more!"* His voice broke and he looked down again in silence.

"Something more than this," she said as she looked around the dark, shabbily furnished apartment around her. *"Please, Dodge. Stay."*

"I can't," he replied. *"I have to go. Mama, I have to go."*

It had always been the same for her, picking him up like a piece of furniture to move about from one place to the next. But for him it had always been something different to become accustomed to. A new school with the same cast of characters with different faces. A new address and phone number to memorize. A strange bed to lay in before the next one. The anger came in that moment, anger that she would even ask him to stay here with her, when she had never let him stay in one place long enough to make it matter. *"There's nothing here for me to stay for,"* he stood up and yelled, instantly regretting the truth that came rushing out of his mouth.

She looked at him for a long time. He dropped his head again and stared at the counter before him. *"I didn't give you enough,"* she said wearily. *"I never created something for you to stay for."*

"No, that's not it," he said, moving forward into the room and kneeling down next to her. He took her hands in his as her head dropped against his.

"It is, Dodge. I never wanted you to have something that someone could take away from you." She paused. *"No, I never wanted anything someone could take away from me."* She picked up his head and looked into his eyes. *"Because I already had that with you."*

He sat on the floor beside her and laid his head in her lap. *"Please, Mama,"* he said as he stared at the worn fabric of the couch's arm. *"I just need something else. I don't know what it is."*

She leaned down and kissed the top of his head gently, and he felt the moist tears from her cheek.

"I know, Dodge. You're the best thing I ever got in my life," she said, cradling his head in her arms. *"It was never about where you'd go. Just when you'd leave."*

The bar around him came back into focus. Voices were beginning to raise and people laughed. Someone touched his shoulder and he raised his bottle of beer to their drink with a smile. He stared at the mirror behind the bar in front of him, trying to adjust his vision. For a moment he stared at himself, his green eyes staring back from a face he didn't recognize.

"Ora," he heard Mary yell as small drops of her Tom Collins fell to the bar. "Have you met my friend Dodge Montgomery?" She turned to Dodge. "Ora owns this place."

Dodge looked up at the woman standing behind the bar in front of him. "Oh my word," she said as she reached over and clasped his hands in hers. "You are James' son, aren't you?" Her soft eyes looked into his without a trace of questioning.

"I am."

"I may have something to show you, if I can find it." She bent over and peered under the bar as Dodge looked at her questioningly.

Mary leaned in closer to him. "Ora," she whispered, "fancies herself a bit of a historian. Most folks would just call her a hoarder, but we like to let her think she is doing something important for the community by holding onto a bunch of old junk that should really just go in the garbage." She took another sip from her drink as she raised her eyebrows.

"Here it is," Mrs. Shriver's voice called, bringing him back into focus. She had put on a pair of reading glasses, and pulled a faded yellow newspaper clipping from a large maroon binder before her. "Your daddy's obituary," she said proudly, handing Dodge the slip of paper.

Dodge set his bottle of beer down and held the piece of paper in front of him with both hands. The young man stared back at him, his closely shaved head unable to conceal his blond-white hair. His lips turned up into a faint smile as he stared assuredly at the camera before him. Dodge could feel his hands beginning to shake as he read the obituary carefully.

"James William Montgomery died August 15th, 1984 from injuries sustained from a fall on his family's property. Beloved son of Dodge William Montgomery and the late Fiona McKay Montgomery, James William was pronounced dead at Shelby Memorial Hospital. He graduated

from Shelby County High School, where he was the first string quarterback of the varsity football team. James had been awarded a football scholarship to Auburn University. He is remembered as a warm and loving son, and a good friend to many in the community."

Here it was. The face of the father he had never seen, the man who had loved his mother, so much so that she had never loved another man again, even after she had thought he had left her. So much so that she had held onto Dodge, afraid that he too would leave her like the only man she ever loved. And in the end he had.

He imagined the two of them, this young, blond, rich, willful boy, and her, the woman he had loved beyond any other. What would have become of all three of them had fate not stepped in to tear it away from them? What would have happened if he had stayed? Would things have worked out differently, or just the same with an extra character to bear the pain?

"Dodge Montgomery," the voice called out from the front of the room. He sat up in his cot, his t-shirt stuck to his damp, warm body. "Private Dodge Montgomery," it yelled again from the long rows of cots in front of him. He hurled his body out of bed. "Sir, yes, sir," he said as he stood at attention.

"A phone call for Montgomery," the voice came again, and the soldier moved out of the doorway. Dodge made his way down the long row of soldiers staring at him in silence. He moved from the tent out into the bright sunshine of the desert before him. The soldier standing before him was not at ease. "You have a phone call, Montgomery, at the front desk."

He followed behind as the soldier turned on his heel. They made their way across the thin path between sand colored tents to the sergeant's office. Entering, the soldier behind the desk looked up at him quickly and then looked away. He approached the counter. "Private First Class Montgomery," he said, "I have a phone call."

The clerk picked up the phone that had been placed carefully on the desk beside him, handed it to Dodge, and walked away. "Montgomery," he said into the phone, his jaw tightening.

208

"Mr. Montgomery, this is Dr. Freer. I'm calling from Mount Sinai hospital in New York. Your mother was admitted here a few days ago," he said. Dodge held the phone against his cheek and stared off at the drab tent wall before him. *"I'm sorry, Mr. Montgomery, but your mother passed away this morning. I'm sure you're aware that by the time the cancer was detected it had already spread beyond what was treatable."* Dodge did not hear the rest of what the doctor said, even as he continued speaking through the receiver into his ear. He dropped it to the counter before him and made his way out of the tent.

"Montgomery," the sergeant called to him from the doorway. Dodge stopped and turned. *"Are you going to need a few days of leave, soldier?"*

Dodge straightened his back. *"No sir. There's nothing for me there."*

The sergeant frowned as he stepped toward him. *"Your mother's funeral."*

Dodge stared at him. He shook his head. *"There's no one to attend a funeral, sir, except me,"* he said, and turned on his heel.

Dodge's eyes came back into focus and he stared at Ora, his eyes glasslike, the yellowed piece of paper hanging limply between his fingers.

"Are you alright, Dodge?" Ora asked, gently taking the clipping from his hand and pushing it back into the binder.

"He left," he said absently. "He left because he wanted to get more for us. He came back here for us. And then he just fell," Dodge's eyes stared unfocused into Ora's.

Mary looked over at him carefully. "Dodge?"

He looked at Mary and smiled. "He just fell, Mary, just like that." He snapped his fingers together. "He left this place, and then he came back, and then he fell." He was sure the words made sense somehow as they tumbled out of his mouth. The boy in the picture, smiling up at him, had smiled at his mother, had made her love him with all her heart, and would have possibly loved him as well. But now Dodge was here, and she was not and he was not. No one from his family was here with him, and all he was left with was a big house and a piece of land and money he had no use for.

"I'm sorry." Ora closed the binder and slid it beneath the counter. She looked at Mary pleadingly. "I'm sorry, Mary. I thought he would want to see it."

Dodge stood up from the barstool. "He fell, Mary, did you know that?" His eyes stared blankly at the bottle of beer on the counter. "Did you know that all of these years? Because I didn't. I didn't know until I got here a few days ago."

"Yes, I did know that, Dodge." She placed her hand on his shoulder.

"Right out back, behind that big house," he continued. "He fell from the barn. The barn that I walked through. I didn't even know," he said, his eyes trying to bring the room around him back into focus. This overwhelming feeling was much deeper and sadder than anything any bottle had ever given him. "My father died here, when he came back to get money for me and my mother. And no one ever told us." He placed his hand on the chair next to him. He could see Martin place his hand on Anne's shoulder protectively.

"I was waiting for him. I was waiting for something and then it turns out there was nothing to be waiting for. All of those years she waited for him, and he never came because he was here. Buried in a cemetery a few streets over," he said as he pointed out the window. They looked at him silently, each of their faces reflecting the sorrow and regret his words conveyed. "I thought when I came here." He lowered his head with a gust of air. "I thought when I came here that someone would tell me it was a mistake. That it couldn't possibly be my family here, here in this place all along while I was somewhere else. I really thought that it would all be clarified and rationalized to me when I got here and it hasn't been clarified at all."

He paused and looked at Mary, who tilted her head and starred at him sorrowfully. "It's just a bunch of stories, Mary. It's just a bunch of stories that I didn't ask to be told. I didn't ask to come here, and my mother wasn't asked to come here, and all of them are dead, and I don't want to be the only one left here. To take on the burden of what they lost. My father didn't want to be a Montgomery, and apparently his father didn't want to

210

be a Montgomery. And I don't want to be a Montgomery. Do you understand that? I need you to understand that, Mary."

She took his hand in hers. "We'll get you home, Dodge," she said as she motioned to Michael to come around and help her.

"No, I'm fine. I can make it on my own." He opened his wallet and placed a few bills on the counter. He leaned in and kissed her cheek. "I have to go. I have to go home." He turned and left them, and they watched silently as he opened the door and walked out into the quiet night.

Chapter 15

There was no sunlight to wake him at dawn the next morning. He did not stir as dark clouds kept the sun at bay, no warm shaft of light to fall silently over him in bed. The house stood in all its soundless glory around him as the rain began to fall against it. He breathed its air in and out, unaware that time was going forward while he slept, calm and serene like a baby wrapped in a warm bassinet tucked into a shadowy corner.

He opened his eyes to the beating sound of rain, hard against the roof and the thick panes of the windows. He reached for his phone from the nightstand, his eyes adjusting slowly to the illuminated screen. Ten-eighteen a.m. He had missed his own deadline to creep from the house under cover of darkness and start his journey back. He lifted himself from the bed with a deep sigh of disapproval, glancing out through the wet pane of glass, droplets of water etching themselves silently downward to block his view of the woods beyond.

After showering he packed up his remaining toiletries from the shelf, leaving those he had found when he had first arrived. He made the bed and closed the bedroom door behind him as he exited the room with his bags.

Downstairs the house was still, as quiet and composed as it had been when he had found it. The souls that had clamored through its doors were silent, the echoes of lost voices tucked deep again into its wood and walls, the only sound the drumming of water outside beating against it to be let in.

As he passed the doorway to his grandfather's office the pile of journals he had removed from the desk caught his eye. He had to move them back to the drawer, he decided as he resignedly set his bags down on the floor. Everything had to be as he had found it, everything the same when he left as when he had arrived. The newness was gone, replaced with the tired weight of somewhere one no longer wanted to be.

He made his way slowly into the room and knelt to begin placing the journals back in the drawer. He did not look at the bindings as he stuffed them back in, like a surgeon whose job is not to save the limb but to stop the bleeding. At the last one he stopped, holding it tightly in his hand. It was the year prior to his grandfather's death. He had not found anything of interest in any of them so far, and as he flipped it over in his hand he doubted that this one would be any different. This was the last thing he would hold that belonged to them. He broke it open, one last memory of the place he owned but did not hold. He flipped absently through its pages, pausing as his eye caught one page unlike the others. There was little writing on the page, just a few sentences, and nothing at all about the cattle or the land. Dodge read slowly in his grandfather's hand:

"He told me today that he was in the barn when James fell. An accident he can't explain. He has been as much like a son to me as James was, at times maybe more. It was so long ago. I don't know that there is any usefulness in bringing up the past at an expense I have never myself paid."

Dodge sat back on the floor, holding the journal in his hand. *Justice in bringing up the past? Like a son to him.* The words circled through Dodge's head. *"Accidents happen out here while people are alone."* Earl's words slipped into his head quietly. My father was not alone, he thought. Someone was here with him the day he died. Someone who was also like a son to my grandfather. Someone who had said nothing about it until just before his death. He slipped the journal into his back pocket, picking himself up and moving hurriedly from the room.

He shut the front door tightly, locking it behind him. He glanced up as a rumble of thunder boomed overhead, and watched as a steak of lighting made its way across the sky. Before him, parked nose to nose with his own, sat the bright yellow truck. As he threw his bags into the back seat he glanced over at the barn, its big, heavy doors standing wide open. He stared up at the window above them, the spot where his father would have taken his last breath before plummeting to his death on the dirt floor below. He shuddered and shook his head as he made his way toward it.

As he neared he could hear a sharp, ringing noise from inside, the same heavy metal pinging as when he first arrived. *Butler.* His body tensed, and he stopped in mid-stride. He glanced at the barren field next to him, staring at the deep woods just beyond. He took a deep breath, continuing on through the doors into the dark coolness of the barn's interior, not glancing up at the empty window above it or the dirt floor beneath it.

Butler stood at the far end of the breezeway. As his eyes adjusted, Dodge could see his large bag of tools on the floor beside him, the scene just as he had happened upon it when he had first arrived. It appeared that Butler had again made himself at home here, even before Dodge had a chance to leave.

Butler glanced up from the worktable as Dodge approached. The two men stared at one another in silence, their revulsion for each other hanging thickly between them like the heavy, dampened air.

"Thought you would be gone already," Butler said curtly, bringing down the heavy mallet against the shiny sheet of metal laid out before him.

Dodge nodded as he slowly walked forward. "You're parked in front of my truck. So I guess you knew I was still here." He stiffened as he said the words, and he could hear a slight snap in his back as his muscles became taut around his spine. Thunder rumbled through the open doors from behind each of them, and a pelting rain began to drum thickly against the roof of the barn.

"Don't worry about your granddaddy's animals. I'll take care of them, and his property. Just like I always have." He made his way around the table toward Dodge, who took a slight step backward as his body tensed further.

"Figured you wouldn't be staying long," Butler continued as he glanced down at the heavy mallet in his hand, gently rubbing the worn, wooden handle. "Gotta hurry up and get back to that big city, don't ya?"

A thin grin turned up the corners of his mouth but did not deliver a smile. Dodge could see that he was more relaxed than he had been in their prior encounters. The bitter edge in his words was now a calm sureness, as if they had been spoken before.

"You won't be needed here for long," Dodge said dryly. "I'll be putting the place up for sale as soon as I'm back in New York."

Butler continued to grin at him, nodding his head slowly. "I should've known you'd turn out just like your daddy. He always wanted to just be rid of this place." He leaned back against the table, crossing his arms and staring at Dodge across the long expanse of the barn. "And instead it got rid of him."

Dodge's eyes widened at Butler's words. "And just what would you know about that?"

Butler continued to grin, his eyes narrowing. Dodge took a step forward as a bolt of lightning lit up the dim interior. The smell of wet rain mixing with dirt wafted to his nostrils as a small line of water began to push its way in through the open barn door like a fat, black rat snake quietly stalking a mouse. He watched it uncoil its way past bits of debris, settling itself right at Butler's boot. The words from the page of the journal filled his mind. *"He was in the barn when James fell."*

Butler shrugged. "Places like these," he said as he looked up at the high beams of the barn above him, "they have a soul. They're alive, see, from all the energy of everyone around them." He twirled his heavy fingers around in the clammy air. "They keep secrets, and when you become a part of their secrets, you become a part of them."

215

"What kind of secret do you have, Butler? Maybe something you haven't ever told anyone. Except." He reached into his back pocket for the journal. "Except my grandfather." He dangled it languidly in the air, knowing Butler would recognize it immediately.

The grin slowly faded from Butler's face and Dodge felt a small bit of satisfaction. "What are you going on about?" Butler nodded at the leather in his hand.

"You could never have what my father had. In fact," Dodge continued as he took another step forward. "I'm guessing that's why my grandfather left you out of his will altogether. I bet you thought you were going to get all of this." He waved his arms around him. "I'll bet you thought this place was rightfully yours, but instead, you could never take what rightfully belonged to my father, and is therefore mine."

Butler looked at him. "How would you know what's yours and what's supposed to be mine?"

He was breathing more heavily, and Dodge could see the rage building inside him and seeping out slowly like a cold sweat he couldn't control. They both paused, staring at one another, as the rain cascaded down violently against the walls of the barn, the thunder above them rumbling against the backdrop of the cracks of lighting that lit each of their faces.

"I know," Dodge said calmly. "I know you were here in this barn the day my father died."

Butler was suddenly still, his thick body leaning against the table without movement. He smiled and picked up the mallet from the table where he had set it down. His grip on it tightened as he stood up from the table with a smile.

"I don't know what you're talkin' about," he said, shrugging his shoulder. To anyone else the small movement of his shoulder seemed to say, maybe I did, but to Dodge it conveyed that he had, and that it didn't matter.

"My grandfather wrote in his journal that you told him you were here the day my father died," Dodge said, leaving out that the entry didn't

216

specify a name. "My grandfather wrote your confession, in his own hand." He held up the journal before him, thrusting it in the air toward Butler.

The color drained from Butler's face as he stood up straighter. "That's not true," he said in a low voice. "Mr. Montgomery would never have..." He trailed off as his eyes searched the air around him. "That's none of your damn business what's in any of those journals."

"None of my business?" Dodge could feel his hand gripping tighter on the journal, his fingertips turning white as the blood drained away as he pressed them against it. "None of my business? It was my father. It was my grandfather. It was mine, and you were here when he died."

He watched Butler's face carefully. "What happened, Butler? What were you doing here the day he died? Why were you here on my grandfather's land, on my father's land, and why did my grandfather write about it in his journal?" It took every ounce of his being not to throw the journal at him before he lunged on top of him, to find the truth in this man who had been here when he had not been given the chance to be.

Seeing the anger in Dodge's face, he smiled. He leaned back, spitting on the floor. "Let me tell you something that you don't know." He stood, very still, and stared at Dodge coldly. His body shook with a silent laugh, and his eyes almost gleamed as he said the words slowly and deliberately, "Your daddy going out that window?" He pointed upward behind Dodge's head. "It wasn't no accident either."

Dodge felt the familiar tingle of energy shifting downward, making its way slowly from his head to his torso, through his arms and legs. He was standing not just before the man who had inexplicably been here the day his father had died, the man who hadn't told anyone up until a year ago that he was in this very spot on that day. He was standing in front of the man who had murdered his father, the man who had taken him from him, from her.

Butler slowly eased himself up off the workbench. "Your granddaddy was the finest man I ever met. He was smart, and patient, and kind. And your daddy did nothin' but give him grief his whole life. Like that man wasn't good enough for *him*?" He spat the last word. "From the time I got

217

here, your granddaddy taught me things - how to take care of them cattle, how to hunt, how to fish. And your daddy wanted nothing to do with any of it. That snotty, little rich brat. He didn't even know what he had. All this, all of this, and he thought he had nuthin' to stay for?" Butler voice rose as his arms stretched out to the barn around him.

"You know what my daddy ever gave me? Nuthin' but a good beating every once in a while. I got nuthin' from mine, because that's where I was born. But your daddy? He was born here. And his daddy never laid a hand on him. Not once, not ever. Do you think he even knew what that meant?" Butler's voice roared, echoing through the hollow air. "The only person who ever treated me like I was anything, like I was a son, was your granddaddy, and his own good for nuthin' son gave him nuthin' in return."

"Your daddy," he spit out, "Your daddy left here, sayin' he didn't want nuthin' to do with this place." His eyes were wild, his motions jerky and hard. "Your granddaddy did everything for that ungrateful son-of-a-bitch and he left him. Just left all this." Butler again waved his hands around him.

"Then," Butler said calmly, "he comes back to town looking for money. That's the only reason he came back here, to get money that he didn't ever do a damn thing to deserve, except be born." He said the last three words slowly and purposefully. "Just like you."

The curtain of rain beating against the barn's walls had turned to hail. Solid orbs of ice broke into tiny shards of glass against the ground, their sound like a thousand snare drums palpitating to a final crescendo.

Butler's eyes were two small slits full of rage. "And do you know what that money was for?" He looked at Dodge coolly. "For some black girlfriend and his soon-to-be-born black child."

Dodge froze at the words that hurled from Butler's mouth like a blade tearing into his chest. There it was. Dodge had prepared himself to hear it before he had even arrived in the sleepy southern town. It had been said to him before, and he expected it here, but now it felt like a physical blow, gathering up a rage inside that made his body shake.

218

"Don't worry about people not being accepting of you", *"There was a time when a black man couldn't sit at this counter"*, *"You don't look nuthin' like your granddaddy, but I guess you already knew that"*, *"There wasn't no way your granddaddy was going to give her that money. You and I both know that."*

He recalled the sideways glances and whispers of the people who didn't just want to see the new Dodge Montgomery. They wanted to see the new *black* Dodge Montgomery, the one who would carry on the Montgomery family name.

He stood, too stunned for a moment to speak. He stared at Butler with a heated rage that even the anger of every fight he had ever been in combined could not compare to.

"That's right," Butler said with a laugh. "Oh, he told me all about your mama. He was pleased as punch, in fact, that day here in the barn." Butler snorted. "He never even came out here to this barn, this was my place." He punched his index finger into his chest. "That day, he came in here, lookin' around, starting trouble with me as usual." Dodge could see Butler's eyes moving to a far-off place. "I told him, too, how glad I was he had left, and how happy I would be if he never came back."

Butler stepped toward Dodge, his body heaving as he spit the words from his mouth. "But he couldn't leave it at that, could he?" he said, taking another step closer to Dodge. "He always had to show me up, always had to show me what he had that was better than mine. I was up there." He looked to the loft above them. "Doing work he wasn't ever going to do. And he had to climb up there and start with me, showing me a picture of his new girl up in New York. Like he was pleased about it. And then he told me he was going to be a daddy, that maybe he would just bring his little family back down here, to live here on this land. And his child would be the heir to this place. His damn child. With *her*."

His face contorted into an uglier grin. "He didn't even want it! He didn't even want it and then he was just going to come back one day and take it all? And then what? Can you even imagine? A black man owning

Montgomery farm? That was all he could give his daddy?" Butler's face contorted with hatred.

"He was standing there. Laughing at me." Butler was still looking upward, the mallet hitting his palm harder now. "And he moved over to the opening above the door, looking out at that land that he always hated and had run away from, and I knew, I just knew, the right thing to do."

The crumpled body of the blond-haired boy from the newspaper clipping flashed through Dodge's mind. "He wasn't coming back, Butler," he said flatly. "He was never coming back." He bit his bottom lip, tasting blood, and pressed his hands against his thighs to keep them still, so his legs did not hurl his body at the man before him. "It wasn't yours, and you took it all. You took everything and you didn't even have to do it."

"Oh, it was going to be mine. With James gone, Mr. Montgomery had no one else to give it to. Until you came along." He grimaced. "This farm, this land —"

"You think that's what you took?" Dodge exploded. "Some land, and a house, and some cattle? That's all you think you took?" His arms reached out at the air before him, his hands clenched into fists. "You took my father. You took the only person she ever loved. You took," Dodge drew in a deep breath. "You took something that couldn't be replaced. That couldn't be given back. Beyond all of this," he waved his hands out at the barn around him. "None of this means anything. He understood that, but do you understand? This means nothing because it was never about things that you can hold in your hand. Physical things that you can possess and keep. You never understood that. That was your problem. You wanted something physical that you could never have, and you took away something so much better."

Dodge breathed in and out forcefully. Butler had been given something by his grandfather, kindness, and he had thanked him by killing his own son.

Dodge let out a long breath and shook his head. He stared at the journal in his hand, and looked up at Butler again. "I guess you didn't get your wish after all then, since a black man does own Montgomery land after all."

He glanced at the heavy mallet in Butler's hands, the only thing stopping him from lunging on top of him. Here he stood, in the same place his father had died, from this man's hands. It took every ounce of everything in his body to keep himself still, even as his body shook from the blood rushing through his veins.

"You just don't get it, do you?" Butler shook his head. "When I pushed your daddy out that door it wasn't for me. It was for your granddaddy. I understood then that I was doing something your granddaddy couldn't, or wouldn't do. I was doing him a favor. Letting it all die with your daddy. And if it wasn't for Earl, you wouldn't even be here at all. And now, you think you're gonna come in here and take it and sell it off to the highest bidder? You don't give a damn about this place, just like your daddy."

Dodge could not get any more words out of his mouth, his body shuddering with uncontrollable hatred for the man before him.

Butler smiled. "And when I kill you, it won't just be for your granddaddy. It will be for this land, for everything any Montgomery ever stood for that you and your good-for-nuthin', ungrateful daddy never understood." He swung the head of the mallet lightly into his palm, and Dodge could hear the sound of the cold metal hitting soft flesh.

"You seem pretty worked up there, Mr. Montgomery." Butler smiled. "Just like the other night, when you assaulted Jackson at Wade's party. Wouldn't take much for anyone to believe that you attacked me, right here on your property. People know about that short temper of yours, don't they? A man's got to defend himself. Maybe," Butler said as he looked at the mallet and back at Dodge. "You weren't too happy that I came back here to get the rest of my things. Maybe you flew off the handle, started coming at me with my own tool, in fact," he said, staring down at his hand with a smile. "A man's got to do what a man's got to do to protect himself from some outsider with – what do they call it?" His tone was mocking. "Anger management issues."

"You see," Butler continued. "Your daddy always thought he was smarter than me." He took a step toward Dodge, just a few feet separating them. "Always thought he was better than me. More deserving than me. But just like you, he wasn't any of those things."

Dodge took a step backward as another bolt of lightning lit up the doorway behind Butler. He glanced sideways at the wall next to him, searching for a weapon but finding none.

Butler took another slow step forward. He continued to pound the heavy mallet against his palm, the odd smile never leaving his face. "Earl shouldn't have brought you here. Your granddaddy didn't want your daddy to come back here, and he certainly wouldn't have wanted you to come here either."

Dodge's knees bent slightly as the muscles in his calves tightened. He planted his feet firmly into the dirt floor of the barn, tucking the journal back into his pocket. If it was a fight to the death that Butler wanted, then that was what he would give him.

"Now, we get to finish this," Butler continued. "Just you and me. Just like it was with that snot-nosed daddy of yours."

Butler lowered his body and rushed head first at Dodge with a roar, the mallet swinging back behind his head. Dodge braced himself for Butler's advance, keeping his eye on the heavy weapon. Butler reached his left arm out toward Dodge, grabbing at his pelvis as his right arm brought the mallet down. Dodge shifted swiftly, and the mallet's head glanced off his left shoulder with a crack. Dodge cried out in pain, grabbing Butler's right arm with his own.

Butler pulled back, trying to rip his arm from Dodge's grasp. Dodge gritted his teeth and lifted his head back and then shifted his weight forward suddenly, his forehead crashing into Butler's nose with a sickening crunch. Butler staggered backwards, lifting his arms out at his sides to steady his balance. Dodge grasped his shoulder as Butler bent forward, droplets of blood falling into the dirt floor beneath him.

He raised his head to stare at Dodge. A thick, maroon trickle of blood dripped from his nose down into his snarling upturned mouth. He smiled as he reached up and wiped his mouth with the back of his hand. The mallet hung limply at his side, and he dropped it to the floor.

Dodge sighed, falling forward on his knees and gripping his aching shoulder. He did not think Butler would have given up this easily, and not before Dodge had even had a chance to disarm him. "Look, Butler," he said, breathing heavily. "We don't need to do this. We can just-"

He stopped in mid-sentence as he watched Butler lift up his pant leg to reveal a piece of black leather strapped to his calf. Dodge straightened, immediately recognizing the .22 caliber handgun he pulled from the holster. He heard the weapon click as Butler pulled back the slide.

Butler laughed. "What did you think was going to happen? You and I would have a little tussle and then we'd shake hands and be on our merry way?" He raised the gun, pointing it downward at Dodge's chest. The storm had all but passed over, and behind him he could hear a faint rumble of thunder in the distance as the rain slowed to a soft rhythm against the roof. Butler took a step forward and Dodge closed his eyes. He knew Butler would savor this moment, and Dodge would not give him the satisfaction of watching him do it.

And so it was that he had come here, just like his father had all of those years ago, to die. His father hadn't known it, and neither had he. He had come here believing he was going to get what he deserved, not realizing that someone here also believed that. A calmness came over him; even in his knowledge that he would die where his father had died before him, by the hand of the very same man.

He saw his mother's face smiling at him. He smiled, knowing he would see her again in just a few moments. *"I'm sorry, Mama,"* he thought, *"I'm sorry you didn't know he still loved you."*

When the gun went off, Dodge knew that by the time he heard the sound of the bullet leaving the chamber it would already be in his chest, moving through muscle and tissue, organs and blood. The crack echoed through the barn, and he drew in a deep breath, waiting for a sharp pain before the exhale. He opened his eyes.

223

Before him Butler lay face down on the floor. Over him stood Martin, a long two by four gripped in both hands and a shocked expression on his face.

Dodge doubled over and breathed out heavily. Both hands fell forward and he steadied himself against the barn floor. He looked up. "Martin?"

"I just, I just…" Martin stammered. He stared at Butler's crumpled body beneath him as he bent over to pick up the gun and withdraw its clip. "I was just coming by to see if I could catch you before you left. You weren't in the house and I heard yelling in here so I came down and saw him. I've never knocked anyone out before." He continued to stare at Butler's crumpled body as he shakily pulled out his cell phone to dial 9-1-1. He looked over at Dodge. "Say, do you still have that dog leash I lent you?"

———————————

"You know that everyone around here isn't like Butler, don't you?" Earl asked as they sat at the table in the kitchen watching the red and blue lights from the sheriff's cars bounce off the walls. The rain fell almost unnoticeably against the windows, the storm pushed onward. An ambulance had taken Butler away, alive and handcuffed to a metal gurney.

Dodge winced as he leaned back in his chair and looked at the bright white bandage wrapped around his shoulder and chest. He glanced up at Earl. "I do, Earl."

They could hear Martin out in the hall, regaling Anne and Miss May with his story once again. "It's all about physics, really. Angles. You take one object, and with the right angle and enough energy you can create enough force to really make a good whack." They heard a heavy thump. "Just like that, see? One good blow in the right spot on the skull is all you need. I don't know why more people don't know that."

Earl sighed. "Yep, there's always going to be those kinds of people in the world. People who've had bad lots in life and they take it out on others, for whatever reason. Color of their skin, religion, where they come from, it doesn't much matter to them what their hatred is for. It really doesn't. And it doesn't mean that everyone around them is like that, just sometimes people get confused, you know? They no longer know what's real, and what they just made up in their own minds. They just want it to be true so badly it takes over them, makes them do bad things to good people."

Dodge nodded his head.

"I guess I didn't realize Butler would have used any excuse he could have to get rid of your daddy. It was jealousy that made him do what he did. Listen to me, Dodge." He leaned over and looked him in the eyes. "Your granddaddy didn't want to be a Montgomery. And your father didn't want to be a Montgomery. Maybe," he said as he leaned forward, "Maybe it's time someone redefines what a Montgomery is."

Dodge stared at him from across the table. "I get it, Earl," he said warily with a thin smile. "I get it."

Earl nodded and they sat in silence for a few moments. "You almost died today, Dodge." Earl leaned back in his chair. "You almost died right in the very same spot your daddy did. What would that have meant to you?"

"Closure," Dodge replied.

Earl sat back in his chair and nodded his head. "Yep, I suppose so."

Dodge shook his head. "Not a closure I was looking for. I guess this has been a long time coming. Too long. Butler was willing to kill for this." He looked around at the room before him. "He was willing to kill to have something he thought he could never have. But you are right, Earl, this is mine. This was my father's, and his father's before him. Whatever that means, my family's blood is in me, and I suppose the only way someone can really take it away from me is by spilling that blood out of me. Just like Butler tried."

Earl nodded again. "The wrongs of the past don't always stay there, do they? Or maybe they do just until it's time to make them right again."

The screen door opened with a sharp wail and the sheriff entered, Clay following behind him. Martin, Anne, and Miss May came in from the other room. The sheriff nodded his head at Dodge and Martin. "You fellas are both alright, then?" They each nodded. "Good, good. Mr. Montgomery, I know you were getting ready to leave today, but I'm afraid I'm going to have to ask you to stay in town for just a little while longer, seeing as how we've got an attempted murder investigation, and a possible murder investigation." He looked down at the black leather journal he held in his hand.

Dodge nodded at him. "Actually, sheriff, there isn't really anywhere that I need to be, other than here." He looked at Earl, who gave him a small grin. They stood, and Dodge followed the group out to the front porch. Outside, the sky had finished falling, and beneath it the earth lay wet and warm. Dodge began to shut the front door and then paused, leaving it open so his neighbor would know he was home.

Epilogue

Dodge Montgomery slid his truck into its usual spot on Main Street. The brightly painted sign in the drug store window announced the impending arrival of Spring in swirls of pastel pinks and yellows with a reminder to stock up on garden supplies and sunscreen. He climbed slowly from the truck's cab, the twinge of pain in his joints alerting him that a storm was not far off. He sighed as he shut the door and absently reached down to caress his left knee. The pains came more frequently, but were not unbearable, the final betrayals of the body before the mind. They reminded him of the way a forgotten memory could dislodge unexpectedly from its safely hidden place and shoot forward without warning, leaving the recipient reeling with a fleeting recollection, and to wait achingly for the next.

He shuffled slowly to the door of the lawyer's office. Henry had been on him for months – or was it years – to get his affairs in order. "Listen Dodge, neither of us is getting any younger," he had said to him on their last hunting trip.

"Thanks, Henry," he had said through labored breaths as he watched him tote his shotgun easily over his own thick shoulder. "But I don't pay you to point out the obvious."

As he opened the door, he recalled the number of times he had stepped through this lobby since his first time meeting Henry. He found himself feeling the same distressing sadness he felt each time he entered a familiar place, knowing it could be the last time he ever did so. Henry's receptionist smiled at him and he nodded. They exchanged pleasantries as she picked up the phone and alerted Henry of his arrival. With a wave of her hand, he nodded and found Henry in the hall, his smile wide and an arm outstretched toward the open door of his office. He knew Dodge did not like him to meet him in the lobby. That he did not need to lead a frail old man down a short, familiar hall.

"Henry." Dodge nodded to him as he entered and sat down in one of the red leather chairs before Henry's enormous desk.

"Dodge, my old friend," Henry smiled. Dodge had always liked Henry, and for some reason trusted him above any of the other lawyers in

228

the firm, regardless of how many smiles and handshakes they awarded him. "What brings you by the office today?" Henry sat down in the chair behind his desk.

"It's time, Henry," Dodge started. He gripped the soft leather arm beneath him and shifted his body forward from the deep recesses of the chair. He had always hated these chairs.

"Finally time to draft your will, is that right?" Henry asked, rolling his own fat chair closer to his desk.

"Not exactly," Dodge replied. He knew Henry well enough by now, after countless social functions and hunting and fishing trips. But he knew that what he needed from him this time was something that would go beyond the bounds of their professional association, or even their social relationship. "I won't be drafting a will at all."

He watched Henry's eyes narrow. He guessed Henry had dealt with many older clients, some much farther from reality and closer to senility than Dodge.

"What's that, Dodge?" Henry clasped his hands tightly in front of him.

"I won't be drafting a will," Dodge repeated, "because it won't be necessary." He paused, studying Henry's face. "I am also going to ask that this conversation stay between you and me," Dodge stated. "What is it you lawyers call that?"

Henry cleared his throat. "Attorney-client privilege?"

Dodge nodded. "Yes, that's it. I want to be ensured that this conversation will stay between the two of us," he said, "even after my death."

Henry sat back in his chair. "Our attorney-client privileges extend as long as you are alive, after that…" his voice trailed off.

"After that it is just the honor among two old friends," Dodge said, staring at Henry.

Henry nodded. "I understand," he said. "Yes, Dodge, of course, you have my word. Now could you please tell me why on earth you are so adamant about not having a will?"

Dodge sat back in the leather chair, for once taking comfort in the leather that felt like it was swallowing him whole. He chose his words carefully as he always did. "I won't have a need for a will, Henry, as I have a living heir."

Henry's mouth dropped open slowly, his thick jowls curving up around it. Dodge could tell he was starting to reconsider his honorable promise a few moments before, and Dodge's own mental capacity.

Dodge put a hand in the air. "I know what you are thinking," he said. "It's a long story and I am in no position to remember or relay all of the details." This was a lie. He remembered all of it, along with the sadness, bitter regrets, and disappointment. He knew Henry would want all of the facts, the details, as if those were the things that mattered instead of the throbbing grief and the tender ache that came with all of them. "All you need to know is that James had a child. More specifically, he had a pregnant girlfriend when he-" Dodge stopped. He could not bring himself to say the last words, knowing what he now knew. *When he died, when he was pushed, when he was murdered...*

Dodge could see Henry trying to will his body to lift his jaw up from the position it had fallen into. "Listen," Dodge said, "Earl knows all about the child."

"Earl?" Henry asked incredulously. "Earl Mayfield?"

Dodge nodded. "He was James' best friend. He was the only person James told about his girlfriend in New York, the last time he was here." He did not elaborate on his son's last trip home. He knew Henry understood that he didn't have to.

"You let Earl come and tell you about James' child," Dodge said. He pulled two envelopes from his jacket pocket, one bulging and one thin. He slid them over the desk toward Henry. "That is ten thousand dollars, cash," he said as he nodded at the thick envelope. "You're to hire a private investigator," he paused and placed his hand over the envelope as Henry looked up at him. "A *discreet* private investigator. Someone up North. Have him find James' child, once I am gone and once Earl comes and tells you."

"What makes you think-"

Dodge waved his hand in the air. "He'll come. Earl will do the right thing. I know he will."

"And Butler?" Henry picked up the fatter envelope and peered inside. Dodge shook his head. "Nothing for Butler. There won't be a will, all of the money will go to James' child as my last living heir."

Henry looked up at him. "Dodge, we still need to get a will in place. I mean anyone could crawl out of anywhere and say that they're your heir."

Dodge shook his head. "There won't be any will, he can't know that I knew about him." The words slipped errantly from his mouth before he could stop them. Henry peered at him suspiciously, catching Dodge's slip up. "I'm just going to leave it at that Henry." He pointed at the second envelope. "In there are some of my hairs, for that D-N-A analysis." He recalled typing the letters into the computer at the library, after convincing the volunteer behind the desk that he had forgotten his ID and just needed to log on for a few minutes. "You're going to need to do that, and those are so there won't be any need to go exhuming my body."

"But, Dodge, don't you want to find your own-" He paused, catching himself on the word *grandson*. "...heir?"

Dodge stared silently at the desk before him. How could he explain to Henry – explain to anyone - that his own son, his very flesh and blood, had never wanted him to meet his child? That he would rather have lived a thousand miles away from him and have kept his whole family a secret rather than have them even know he was alive? That he understood exactly why he would want that, and that he agreed with him?

"No," Dodge shook his head. "I wasn't supposed to know about their conversation. James told Earl the night before he died, and he swore him to secrecy. Like I said, I know Earl Mayfield and he's a good man. If he kept it from me, well," Dodge's voice broke, another physical betrayal he found he could no longer negotiate with his mind. "Well, he was right, and I don't want him knowing that I knew."

His brain paused once again over the question that had looped through so many times over the passing years - what would Fiona think? But he

231

knew the answer. He had secrets of his own, like the one he had kept hidden from that day after her death. When he had watched the car float silently on top of the river before plunging head first to the bottom with the three bodies of the men inside. The men who knew how she had really died. He was a murderer just like his own father, Fiona must know that, as James knew it as well.

The memory shot forward, up from the dark place where it had lay, known but forgotten. Fiona's funeral, the whispers and the stares. He had caught voices, people speaking in hushed tones, when he had slipped behind the pastor's door to compose himself.

"She was just so young," the woman's voice floated from beyond the crack in the doorway. "To die at such a young age from a heart condition, it's just dreadful."

"I know, I know," said the other one. "I heard," she paused, lowering her voice, and he muffled his sob behind his handkerchief, "that it may not have just been a heart condition however."

"What?"

"The coroner, Dr. Wells? I heard that he told Dodge he could only ascertain that her heart had given out, due to her condition, but that it may not have been the primary cause of death. That he could have the body taken to Birmingham for a full autopsy and Dodge flat out refused."

"He must've been in shock after all," murmured the other woman.

"You know Lillette Sterling said Fiona was going into Birmingham on a regular basis, without telling Dodge or anyone else where or why she was going."

"You don't mean," said the other woman.

"Who knows? I mean she was so much younger than Dodge. Lillette said it wouldn't have surprised her to find that she had been visiting someone in the city. Small town living never truly suited Fiona, we all knew that."

"I don't believe it," the other woman said with a huff. "With one of the richest husbands in town and a young son that she just adored? Why, I

saw her at the last Garden Party and she just hung on Dodge like a
schoolgirl."

"If she was having some sort of clandestine affair she would of course
want it to look like she was madly in love with her husband."

"You don't really think that Dodge Montgomery could have..." Her
voice trailed off as a man's voice called from across the hall and the
women moved from the door.

Dodge leaned against the wall, shoving the handkerchief back into his
pocket. Lillette Sterling spreading lies about his wife did not shock him.
Her resentment and jealousy knew no bottom, just like the venom that
continually spewed from her pink rimmed mouth. Lillette had known
exactly where Fiona had been going in Birmingham, and she was the one
who had told the others. What better way to deflect from her own guilt and
the guilt of her husband than to intimate in her hushed tones that Dodge
may have had a part in her death rather than they themselves.

"Dodge?" Henry said, setting the envelope into a drawer in his desk.
Dodge looked up at him.

"What's that, Henry?"

"I asked, what's to happen to your estate if we can't find him?"

"Let it rot."

"Now, Dodge," Henry started.

"There will be no will, Henry. If you can't find James' child, then it's
just as well." He remembered years ago, secretly hoping it would be a
granddaughter. And when he found out through his own discreet
investigation all those years ago that it was a boy, he had been unfeeling.
He had never wanted a son, someone to continue on the tarnished legacy of
his family. He had wanted a daughter, just a little bit of Fiona maybe, but
never a son. He had always known that, just as James had always known it
too.

"James," he called softly as he rapped his knuckle against the door of
his room. It opened, James peering eye to eye with his father standing
before him in the hallway. He looks too much like me, Dodge thought to
himself, not enough like Fiona.

"What?" he answered, his insolence toward his father unchanged even after all the months they had been apart.

"Is there something you want to tell me?" It was an awkward spot to bring it up, here in the hallway just outside his door. But his son had not returned home for warm chats before the fireplace. He had come for his money, and he would be gone again as fast as he had re-appeared.

James shrugged. "Nope, nothing," he said, staring at his father with his usual blank look. That he had gotten from Dodge, the ability to display no emotion at all, when deep inside you burned with a rage that made the inside of your skin feel like it was on fire.

"Alright, then," Dodge had said, and turned from the door. "When are you returning to New York?

James shrugged. "Probably tomorrow. Henry said he could just wire the money up to me once I sign some papers."

"And will you be coming back?

"No," James replied quickly. But he had looked away when he said it, knowing Dodge would be able to recognize the slightest bit of hesitation, and for one brief moment Dodge felt a pang of relief.

Dodge nodded, looking over James' shoulder into the room beyond. "I'll keep your room waiting for you. Just in case."

He had moved quickly from the doorway to the top of the stairs, the door behind him shutting solidly. Their conversations were always short; any longer and they began to veer into those areas neither wanted to go – anger, resentment, hatred, love. He knew it might be the last time he spoke to his son on this visit home; he had not known it was the last time he would speak to him ever.

"Alright, Dodge," Henry broke into Dodge's memory with a heavy sigh. "I understand. Is there anything else I can do for you today?"

Dodge shook his head. "No, Henry, that will be all I think." He rose from the chair and extended a shaky hand across the desk.

"Will I see you on Saturday for the turkey hunt?" He followed Dodge slowly out of his office.

"I'm not sure about that," Dodge said, buttoning up his coat at the door. He looked out to see a low set of clouds fanning out over Main Street. "Perhaps," he said, with a wave as he shut the door.

He looked up at the darkening sky above him as he shuffled back to his truck. His bones did not need to tell him what his mind already knew. He did not have long, and would soon, blessedly, join Fiona and James, leaving behind what had meant so little to them and so much to him. And somewhere out there his grandson would finally learn of their existence, too late to ask him himself who they had been, why they had hated or had loved one another, or the secrets each had kept. He stopped, looking over the tops of the buildings before him.

"Please God, let him not be like me," he pleaded to the sky above him. *"Let him be like his father."*

Made in the USA
San Bernardino, CA
05 March 2017